Guardian

by

A.J. Messenger

First Print Edition August 2016

ISBN-13: 978-1536852226

ISBN-10: 1536852228

Cover images credit:

Atorn Buaksantiah | Dreamstime.com

Leigh Prather | Dreamstime.com

Books by A.J. Messenger

The Guardian Series

Guardian (book one)

Fallen (book two)

Revelation (book three)

Learn more about new releases and contact me

I welcome you to visit me and subscribe to my newsletter to be the first to know about upcoming releases.

 ajmessenger.com

 facebook.com/ajmessengerauthor

 @aj_messenger

Dedication

For my dad, who inspired me to become a writer.

Table of Contents

"There are more things in Heaven and Earth, Horatio, than are dreamt of in your philosophy."

– William Shakespeare, *Hamlet*

Preface

This can't be. It can't.

"Please don't go," I implore, choking back tears. "You can't die. You can't. Please, no."

If he hears my cries there's no sign.

It's my fault. My. Fault. The searing pain in my chest drives me to beg to be taken instead. Let it be me. Not him. Please, not him.

Was it really only months ago that I remained blind to the evil around us? The evil that did this? I can't bring myself to wish that I could go back. To the person I was. To the time before I met Alexander …

Only now I realize I'll never be safe.

Now I know I'm next.

Chapter One

I can't breathe.

I'm in the bathroom again grasping both sides of the sink and struggling to pull air into the crushing hollow where my lungs should be. Sweat forms rivulets along my brow, tickling past my ears and down my neck, disappearing into my cleavage. My heart hammers to the beat of a single thought: I need to lie down. Now.

Or I am going to die.

I know it's a panic attack, okay? Or an anxiety attack, or whatever my mom or the therapist she sends me to calls it. But none of that matters because my heart is pumping hard enough to punch a hole through my chest. Knowing it's all in my head only makes it worse.

I would give my kingdom for a bench to lie down on right now. The toilets in here don't even have lids to sit on. I hold out my hand, shaking, under the faucet and push down hard on the "water-saver" knob with the other, but nothing comes out. *Thanks, San Mar High—way to kick a girl when she's down.*

I try two more sinks until I find a working tap so I can splash my face. Oh thank God, the coolness helps. I rub water feverishly over my forehead and cheeks as I gulp in air and let it out raggedly several times. As my heart begins to calm, I slowly slide my hands down my face and peer out between my fingers into the broken mirror above the sink. Pale skin and stark blue eyes stare back. My light brown hair ("dirty blonde" as my mom always calls it—the least-attractive-sounding hair color ever) is now wet around my brow and in complete disarray. I drop my hands and continue to stare at my reflection.

Stop being such a wuss, Declan. You're officially an adult now, so pull up your big girl pants and get back to class.

Insulting myself somehow makes me laugh a little… or keeps me from crying at least. I take another deep breath and stretch off the black ponytail holder on my wrist so I can tie back the long, wet strands plastered to my cheeks. As I maneuver my hair into place, I can't help but sigh. I thought senior year would be different.

Actually, that's a lie.

I held a childish, secret *hope* that I had only 18-years-worth of anxiety in me and then it would stop. Just like that. It was magical thinking mixed with a giant dollop of desperation. My birthday today proves how idiotic it was. Why would this year be different than all the others? I'm still the same old malfunctioning freak as before. Nothing has changed.

Maybe it's good to be starting school again. The summer was long and unusually hot for the Northern California coast, making our whole town crankier than a beach community has any right to be. And although the crowds that descend on San Mar have always attracted a certain level of crime, we had far more trouble this year than usual. I think everybody was ready for the tourists to pack up and take the heat—and the criminals—with them. Mostly though, I'm looking forward to getting through senior year at San Mar High and moving on. Right now I'm a small fish in a small pond. I'm looking forward to having a larger ocean to hide in.

I turn to the full-length mirror on the wall and inhale deeply and let it out in a long, slow breath. My heart has descended back into my chest and is beating almost normally. I smooth my hands over my crisp, pale blue cotton top and discover wet spots down the front from the water I splashed wildly all over my face. *Great. Nice job, Declan.* I punch the large silver button on the ancient hand-dryer jutting out from the wall and bend down to stretch my shirt underneath the hot air. After a few cycles, my ears plead with me to stop so I straighten the fabric as best I can and turn back to the mirror to try to make myself presentable. My jeans are worn and supposedly lucky because prior to today I never had a panic attack in them (so much for *that* theory), but my shirt is new. I bought it during a rare mini shopping spree with money I made working at Jack's Burger Shack (Home of the Famous Hula Burger!) over the summer. It's nothing fancy—every dime goes to my college fund so H&M is pretty much the top of my budget—but it's a cute top with cap sleeves and white stitching along the edges and, most surprisingly, it's sized perfectly for my five foot, one inch frame. Finding decent petite clothes within my budget is usually impossible. I once bought a tank dress in the children's section out of desperation.

The clock on the wall says I can't avoid going back to class any longer. I bend down and adjust one of my sandal straps, let out a deep sigh, and push open the door to join the throngs of other students heading in all directions in the hallway.

I'm relieved to see Finn and Liz standing outside homeroom. Their heads are bowed over Liz's notebook and Finn's floppy brown hair is obscuring his boyish face. Liz and I already compared schedules so I know we have most of our classes together. As I walk closer, Finn looks up and waves when he sees me.

Finn and I have been best friends since the first day we met in pre-K. A cute little beagle puppy wandered onto the school playground with its head stuck in an old twelve-pack box and all the kids were laughing. Finn and I were the only ones who ran over and helped the poor little guy. When we released him, he didn't dart away like we expected. Instead he licked our faces appreciatively and rolled onto his back so we could rub his tummy. We made a pact right then and there that one of us would somehow adopt him. Finn's mom arrived first for pickup and he managed to convince her to take the puppy home. They posted signs everywhere to try to find his owner but no one came forward so Finn got to keep him. He named him "Zeno" after one of his favorite philosophers.

Even if we hadn't rescued Zeno that day, it would have been a curious meeting because I felt a level of ease around Finn that I've never experienced with anyone else. Years later, I realized it's because Finn is so honest. I always know where he stands, with no hidden motives. He has Asperger's and his thoughts drop out like gumballs. Lying doesn't make sense to him—even little white ones. I remember asking him in first grade what he thought of a drawing I did of my cat, Willow. Without hesitating, he said it looked more like a badger and I needed to work on my fine motor skills. I crumpled up the paper and threw it in his confused face before stomping off, but while I was sulking it occurred to me that he was the only one being straight with me. Teachers and parents always cooed "Great job!" or "It's beautiful!" no matter what my drawings looked like. If I wanted the unvarnished truth, I could ask Finn. Most people don't understand and they think he's rude, but I think he's pure. Life would be a lot easier to navigate, in my opinion, if everyone practiced gumball honesty.

"Hey Dec, Happy Birthday," says Finn as I join them.

"That's right," chimes in Liz. "Today it's official. Nicely done, by the way, making your birthday land on the first day of school."

"Yeah, you like that? I wanted to be sure to suck all the fun out of it."

Liz smiles. "Well eighteen is big. What are all the things you can do now that you couldn't do before?"

"What do you mean? Like vote?"

"Yeah, or gamble," she says.

Finn shakes his head. "It's 21 in Vegas. But you can be incarcerated now in an adult penitentiary."

I flash him a look that says "very funny."

Finn just smiles and shrugs. "I have two classes with you guys. In the morning," he says as he holds up Liz's schedule. He has a special deal where he leaves most afternoons to take classes at UCSM (the University of California, San Mar) because he passed every high school math and science requirement years ago.

"They may be the last two classes we'll ever have together," says Liz. "In exactly ten months we'll finally be saying goodbye to this place—and all the asshats in it—for good. Hard to believe." She's wearing skinny jeans and an Avett Brothers t-shirt from the concert we went to over the summer. Her dark hair is in two low pigtails with a hot pink streak across her bangs. Liz moved to San Mar in sixth grade and even though she probably could have fit in wherever she wanted, for some reason she chose to fit with Finn and me. I liked her even before I saw her stand up to Molly Bing on her first day at Mission Middle. Molly marched over and ordered Liz to move because she unknowingly sat at Molly's regular lunch table. Liz just calmly looked Molly up and down and said, "Ken's waiting for you at another table, Malibu."

The nickname "Malibu Barbie" was born and it stuck. People still use it interchangeably with Molly's original moniker, "Queen B." Finn and I joined Liz for lunch that day and the three of us have been inseparable ever since. She *gets* Finn, like I do.

Liz's expression changes when she notices my hair is damp. "Hey, you okay?" She reaches over to tidy a loose strand around my face.

"Yeah, just another one of my 'you-know-what's," I say, trying to make light of it. "I was in homeroom early and suddenly I had to get out. No idea why. First day back maybe."

Liz peeks around the doorjamb into the class and leans back out again. "Well I have an idea why: Queen B's in there. She'd make anyone want to bolt out of a room."

I smile half-heartedly. "If only it was that simple."

Finn reaches over and squeezes my hand. The first time he ever saw me having a panic attack we were just kids. He paced nervously back and forth, tapping his hand to his chest, because it upset him to see me hurting and he didn't know what to do. My mom suggested I tell him how he could help so I asked if he wouldn't mind holding my hand whenever it happened, to let me know it's going to be okay. He's been doing it for me ever since. I squeeze back and smile before we let go.

"You know, speaking from a strictly scientific standpoint, Molly should be a very happy, friendly person," says Finn. "Studies have shown that when your looks conform to universal beauty standards you gain advantages in every area of life."

"Yeah right, Finn," Liz says with a laugh. "Go tell her she should stop being such a royal be-otch because her face is symmetrical."

The final bell rings and the three of us file into homeroom and sit down in the only row with empty seats, up front.

Mr. Brody walks in after us but my eyes are drawn to the new student that follows behind him. Tall, with tousled, dark-chocolate colored hair, he radiates a bright intensity that hits me like a physical vibration. His hands are partly in his pockets, pushing his jeans low on his hips, and his t-shirt hugs his broad shoulders, revealing tan, muscular arms. Everything about him trumpets health and the outdoors. His deep green eyes scan the room with an open, easy confidence as he strides in my direction. I realize too late that I'm staring at him like a dumbstruck fool and I flush crimson as he sits down in the empty seat next to me. His eyes meet mine for an instant and a smile forms at the corners of his mouth before he turns to face forward. Oh God, he saw me gawking. I look down and try to melt into the floor and disappear.

I peek around and see that I'm not the only one taking notice. Everyone is focused intently on our new arrival. He must sense all those pairs of eyes boring into the back of his head. Strangely though, he doesn't seem at all affected. He's exuding a relaxed calm that flows over me in waves, spiriting away all remnants of my crippling anxiety from earlier. I know it's crazy to think the feeling is coming from him but whatever it is I don't want it to end—I've never felt anything so soothing. I'm probably just lightheaded. I was in my usual rush and missed breakfast this morning. I'll have to remember to eat the granola bar I stuffed in my backpack.

Mr. Brody welcomes everyone and opens with a joke about us finally becoming seniors when he's interrupted by a loud burst of static from our ancient P.A. system followed by a number of unintelligible announcements. When the broadcast finally stops, he takes roll and I pay close attention as he makes his way through the alphabetical list in his hand. When he calls out "Declan Jane," Liz has to kick my foot under the desk because I'm so focused on listening for the name of our new student. As he reaches the end of the list, Mr. Brody pauses and lifts a pink slip off his desk and copies something from it in pen at the bottom of the roster. Finally he looks up again and says, "Alexander Ronin?"

"Present," a deep, accented voice answers from beside me.

Chapter Two

"Oh my God, don't you just *love* his accent?" Molly's shrill voice echoes off the tile as she and her sidekicks enter the bathroom.

"Is he British?" asks her friend Suzie.

"He's *Australian*, you moron," says Molly.

"Well whatever he is, he's *hot*," replies Becca. They all giggle.

Lunch period just started and I'm in the last stall by the window. I contemplate waiting until they leave before coming out but I decide I'm being ridiculous. I want to meet up with Liz and Finn and I have a feeling Molly and her minions are going to be fawning over mystery man Alexander for a while. As I open the stall door and walk over to the sink, all talking ceases, accompanied by accusing stares as if I'm interrupting a private business meeting.

"Hi, Molly. Ladies," I say with a smile and a nod to each, trying to take the high road. I can't believe Finn and I used to be friends with this mean-girl poster child when we were kids. Molly musters a forced grin that almost makes me laugh out loud because it's accompanied by the stink eye that she usually reserves for me. An uncomfortable eternity passes as I wash my hands in silence. Before leaving, I force myself to casually apply my Dr. Pepper Lip Smacker lip gloss (a vestige from childhood, what can I say?). I don't want Molly to know she intimidates me. Finally, with a tickle of panic rising in my chest, I walk out with a giant sigh of relief and head to the quad.

"Sooo … what do you think of our new student?" asks Liz.

"Who do you mean?" I know she must be talking about Alexander but new students arrive in San Mar all the time because university professors often come and go with their families.

"C'mon, Declan." She isn't buying my coyness. "Alexander Ronin? Mr. Australia? The Aussie Adonis? Any of these jolt the Jane memory banks?"

I laugh. "He's pretty cute. Obviously."

"Judging by the fact that every girl in school is falling to pieces just mentioning his name, I'd say he's more than cute. And as soon as he opens his mouth that accent of his seals the deal. But I've never been intimidated by a pretty face so I talked to him."

"He talked to *us*," corrects Finn, "and you've never been intimidated by anything."

Liz smiles. "That's true. But I *would* have talked to him if he hadn't come over on his own. I wanted to meet him before Molly Bing could go all 'welcome wagon' crazy as class president and tell him all the wrong things about this place. Anyway, Declan, I found out he's not just hot, he's also nice. Like, surprisingly, *disarmingly* nice. And he asked about you."

"It must be hard moving to a new ... wait … what did you say?"

"He asked about you. His grandfather is a visiting professor at UCSM and they just moved here from Sydney. They're renting a house on your street actually—the one on the corner."

"On my street? What did he say about me?" *Please tell me it's not about me staring at him like an idiot.*

"Finn and I were telling him about how long we've all lived here and how we're all friends and when I said your name he asked if you were—and I quote— 'the girl with the sea-blue eyes that I sat next to in homeroom,' unquote."

"Oh my God. Really? I was staring at him like a crazy person. That must be why he asked."

"I don't know about that. He seemed interested."

"Yeah, right—interested in making sure I'm not a lunatic."

"No, interested as in 'that girl is cute.'"

"C'mon. He is waaaay out of my league. And he doesn't know me."

Liz shakes her head and sighs. "You are seriously deluded about what league you're in. And you're right he doesn't know you—*no* guys ever know you because you never let anyone in. But it looks like it doesn't matter anyway." She tilts her head to the right and my eyes follow to see Molly and her friends surrounding Alexander. "Molly's got her claws in him now. He'll be sucked into her orbit and we'll probably never hear from the poor guy again."

I nod. I'm sure Liz is right, but inside I surprise myself by hoping otherwise. There's something about him. Something different. He was in all three of my morning classes and the few times I dared to peek over he met my eyes from across the room and gave me a slow smile that made my heart pause mid-beat. I actually peered over my shoulder to see if he was looking at someone else. He must smile like that at everyone—he's new and trying to make friends. Liz is nuts to think he's interested.

I make my way through the rest of the day and discover that Alexander's afternoon schedule differs from mine. I decide it's a good thing because I can finally concentrate. My last period is English Lit with my favorite teacher, Miss Dunhill. She hands out the list of books we'll be reading and discusses expectations and assignments. Before the end of class, she walks over to my desk and leans down, speaking quietly, "I know you've probably read all of the books on the syllabus already. Here's a second list I put together just for you."

I smile at her and eagerly pore over the list. There's a handful I haven't read yet and I mentally sort through my schedule to figure out when I can get to the San Mar library. Our school library rarely has what I'm looking for. With all the budget cuts, I'm surprised we still have a part-time librarian.

When the final bell rings I rush out the door. I'm covering a shift at Jack's for Liz and I have just enough time to get there on my bike. I didn't bother to drive this morning because the weather was so beautiful. Most of the tourists don't realize it, but San Mar's best days are in September and October.

I cut through the parking lot on my cruiser to save time and wave to Liz and Finn as they get into her car. Liz is driving Finn to Stanford to meet with a professor about working in one of his research labs. A funny thing about Finn: he's a genius and I'm sure he'll end up inventing something revolutionary to change the world one day, but he doesn't drive because it involves "too much sensory processing all at once." Luckily for him, San Mar has an extensive bus system and he's an avid bicyclist. For longer trips, Liz usually drives him where he needs to go. Her parents gave her a cute little blue Fiat for her birthday and she enjoys the forty minute drive to Stanford. I offered to drive Finn around, too, but he refuses to ride in my 1972 VW Bug because apparently "it meets no current safety standards." I attempted to sell him on the fact that its canary-yellow paint job makes it highly visible on the road but he just looked at me with a dubiously raised eyebrow. The day after I plunked down nearly all of my savings to buy it, I discovered it must have been painted bright red in an earlier incarnation. Someone in the parking lot at Trader Joe's scraped the rear fender while I was getting groceries for my mom and the dented gash they left looks like a bloody scar. They didn't even leave a note. *Dirtbags.*

After the accident, I christened my car "Archie." I don't know why but I suddenly imagined him speaking with a cockney accent and feeling indignant about what happened:

"Wot koynd of yooman bee-in wood 'it me loyk that and take off?" he said, mirroring my thoughts exactly. If only he could remind me when the gas tank gets low. The gauge is stuck on empty and I've run out more than once. The problem is, my budget is basically "no money" and it's hard to estimate how many miles are left when I fill up a few bucks at a time. Liz won't even ride with me anymore because of the last time we got stranded. She bought me a gas can and wrote on the bottom with a sharpie, "Keep Archie full, you wanker!" I stow it under the hood.

When I get to Jack's, the line of customers is out the door but after it slows the gang surprises me by singing Happy Birthday and presenting me with a "cake" constructed of Krispy Kreme donuts (the only donuts worth eating, in my opinion) piled into a pyramid on a platter. I wasn't expecting anyone to remember, but Jack says he couldn't let a milestone like turning eighteen pass by without some fanfare. I'm touched, and I have a giant smile plastered on my face as I thank everyone and blow out the candles. We all inhale donuts and talk until the next rush of customers beckons.

When my mom picks me up at eight I catch a strong whiff of myself as a giant Hula Burger as I plop down onto the front seat of her car, exhausted. I can't wait to get home and take a shower.

"Happy Birthday, sweetie," my mom says as she leans over and kisses my cheek. "I can hardly believe you're eighteen today." She reaches out and squeezes my hand as she starts driving. I know what's coming next because she says pretty much the same thing every year but I enjoy hearing the story. I missed her this morning because she had a client meeting.

"When I woke up this morning I was thinking about the morning you were born," she says, starting in. "You came right on your due date and my contractions started the minute I woke up. Your dad used to say that even before you were born you were punctual but also kind enough to wait until we had a full night's sleep." She pauses with a slightly wistful smile before continuing. "By the time we made it to the hospital, the doctor barely had time to suit up. You popped out so fast it was as if you couldn't wait to join the world. At first, you didn't make a sound. You just looked around with those big blue eyes of yours as if you were thinking 'So *that's* what it looks like from out here.'" She glances over and smiles. "The moment I saw you it was as if a part of my heart that I didn't even know existed unfurled … I swear it's as if I blinked my eyes and all this time went by in an instant. Here you are, all grown up."

I smile and look over. Her eyes are watery. "Thanks mom," I say as I squeeze her hand back. "I can't believe I'm eighteen either." I don't mention the soul-crushing panic attack I had as a birthday present. "All I know is, it's been a long day and I'm totally beat. Thanks for picking me up."

"Of course. I can't believe you wanted to work today. How was your first day of senior year?"

I shrug. "Okay. Pretty much the same as every other year I guess."

"Have you eaten dinner? You look like you could blow away. "

"Yep, chicken salad and a banana shake." My mom is, inexplicably, always worried about me eating enough. Years ago, one of my therapists told me exercise might help with my panic attacks so I took up running with a feverish intensity. It didn't end up helping my anxiety any, but I became hooked on losing myself in a long run. It clears my head. Even better than yoga, which I also tried. Now I run every morning and my mom is determined to make sure I get enough nutrients and whatnot. She shouldn't worry, though. I'm slim, but healthy. I love food way too much to ever get crazy skinny.

"I also had some Krispy Kremes," I add. "Jack and the guys surprised me with a giant donut tower. I told him how you build one for me every year because I hate cake."

"They built you a tower? Like the one we had over the weekend? You must be on Krispy Kreme overload. If you had to work, though, I'm glad you got to celebrate a little."

"I *wanted* to work. More money for my college fund," I say as I smile and pat my purse, rattling the bulky pile of change inside. "The guys let me take the whole tip jar tonight."

"Oh honey, I wish I could help you out more so you didn't have to work so much. Houses just aren't selling the way they used to. Maybe once the economy picks up …"

My mom is smart and conscientious and good at what she does. The problem is, she's in a profession that doesn't always reward the nice guy and she's the nicest guy there is. She's drawn to those who most need her, not necessarily those who can bring in the biggest transaction. Her clients love her, but she'll never be the top salesperson in town. After my dad died she used the insurance money to pay off the house, but other than that we just get by. During lean months, I help out, but she's scrupulous about always paying me back when her commission checks come in.

"Don't worry about me, mom," I say to reassure her. "Dad always said it builds character to pay for things on your own anyway … and it sounds good on a college application to boot." She smiles but a wave of sadness passes over her eyes at the mention of my dad. I decide to change the subject. "How was work today?"

She perks up a little. "It was great, actually. Your birthday must have brought me luck. We got a walk-in. A couple came in looking to buy a vacation home and our good friend Fred Fillner couldn't steal them from me like he usually does. He was in the back stuffing one of those giant subs he loves into his mouth and pestering the interns."

I laugh. "I hope it turns into a huge commission for you."

"You and me both, sweetie. You and me both." She sounds weary but hopeful as we pull into our driveway.

The next morning in homeroom Alexander is sitting in the same seat as before but now Molly has claimed the spot next to him. He's so tied up in conversation with her I don't think he even notices as I walk by to an empty desk.

By the time third period Art History rolls around I've given up on ever actually speaking to him. He's constantly surrounded by admirers and I've convinced myself he's probably a lothario anyway. How can he *not* be when he looks like that and girls are practically throwing themselves at his feet?

Our teacher, Mrs. King, arrives uncharacteristically late to class looking frazzled. "I want to apologize to all of you for being late because you know how I value punctuality. All I can say is I have had one *heck* of a morning. First the power went out to my building, then as I was leaving my dog escaped, and to top it all off, I got a flat tire. At any rate, I'm glad I finally made it here in one piece, so let's get started." She plops down her purse and Starbucks coffee on her desk and as she grabs a folder the coffee cup starts to topple. In a flash, Alexander is out of his seat with his hand over the desk, miraculously catching the cup mid-tip and righting it firmly into place. The whole class bursts into applause.

I look around to see if I'm the only one who noticed. Everyone seems unaware, but I could swear Alexander put his hand out *before* her coffee cup tipped. My mind must be playing tricks on me.

"Thank you, Alexander!" says Mrs. King. "That's all I need now is to spill coffee everywhere. If I didn't know better I'd say the gods are against me today."

"It's never the gods, Mrs. King. It's just one of those days," replies Alexander.

Mrs. King dives into a presentation on famous art forgeries and leads us into a discussion: Should only the quality be considered or is it truly less of a work of art if it's deemed a fake? Most of the class weighs in and the majority feels that if a piece of art is virtually indistinguishable from the original, the fact that it's a forgery shouldn't matter a great deal because it's just as good, technically. Finn points out that many art pieces are of indeterminate origin—even experts can't agree on authenticity—but that doesn't make them less beautiful or worthy of admiration. Molly joins the majority in the "who cares" camp. She declares that if it takes an art expert to tell the difference, she may as well own a fake rather than pay millions for an original.

"What do you think, Declan?" asks Mrs. King. I'm peering off into the middle distance and I think she assumes I'm daydreaming but I'm just contemplating the question.

"I disagree," I answer.

"With what?"

"That it doesn't matter."

"Go on."

"I understand what everyone is saying about technical quality. But when I see an original piece of art, I look at it differently. I think about the artist and the period it was made and the subject they chose and I take my time to truly contemplate it. I wouldn't feel the same if I knew it was a forgery. Maybe the difference is in me, rather than the art itself."

Mrs. King nods and I detect a hint of a smile. I feel a small burst of pride that I may have said the right thing. She's a fair teacher but hard to please.

"Alexander? I don't think we've heard from you yet. What do you think?" she asks.

Alexander turns and looks at me as he answers. "I agree with Declan. I think the spirit of an artist is imbued in their work and if you're paying attention it affects you differently when you view an original."

A ridiculous thrill runs up my spine when he says my name. His eyes stay on mine as he speaks, as if he's taking my measure. God, he's good looking. But there's something more. He's somehow brighter than everyone else in the room. Almost as if he's incandescent and glowing from the inside. I feel certain that if I touched his skin it would be pleasantly warm …

The bell rings loudly, startling me out of my reverie, and I file into the hall with the others as we all head to the quad for lunch. I walk slower than usual, hoping that Alexander might catch up and talk to me now that we made a connection of sorts over our art opinions. Finn urges me to hurry, though, and when I turn around I see Alexander has disappeared, leaving me embarrassed at my imaginings.

"You want to go to the Boardwalk later? It's the last local's night of the year," asks Liz as we sit eating our lunch.

"Can't," I answer, "I'm babysitting Charlie Bing tonight."

"I'll never understand that setup. How does Molly get away with not having to watch her own little brother?"

I shrug. "Her mom doesn't make her. It's probably for the best. I wouldn't want to leave Charlie—or any other five year old, for that matter—alone with Molly."

"I still don't get it."

"Look at it this way. It's fifteen bucks an hour. Cash. And I like Charlie. So I'm glad Mrs. Bing is an enabler."

Liz shrugs in agreement. "Can't argue with that. How about you, Finn? You in? I'm buying."

"Maybe," says Finn, "as long as you don't make me ride the Cave Carts again."

"Awwww, really?" groans Liz. "But it's so *random*. How can you not like riding in rickety old carts through the dark while being assaulted with flashing lights and weird noises?"

"I'm with Finn on this," I say. "That ride is seriously deranged."

"Ex-*actly*," says Liz. "And whoever designed it must have been seriously high … that's what makes it so good! How can you not love those weird little pop-up cavemen and that terrible music? Doesn't the fact that it makes no sense make you like it? A *little*?"

"No," replies Finn. Case closed.

I laugh. Finn can be very rigid. He's never eaten a piece of fruit in his life, for example, and I doubt he ever will—I think it has something to do with the texture. But if he really cares about you, he can sometimes surprise you.

When he was five he had to have his blood drawn for an important medical test and he steadfastly refused, to the point of kicking and screaming when his parents tried to pick him up to bring him to the nurse. It was very unlike him and no amount of bribing with Legos or ice cream or anything else he loved made him budge. Finally, in desperation, his mom sat him down and pleaded, with tears in her eyes, telling him she needed him to have his blood taken. For her.

Finn looked at her, wide-eyed, his voice shaking, and said, "You really want me to do it?"

She nodded, and after a long pause, his eyes welling with tears, he stood up and walked haltingly over to the nurse. Without a word, he sat down, stuck out his arm, and slowly bowed his head.

The next day, his family came over to our house and I overheard his mom and dad relay the story to my parents in the next room.

"Did it hurt?" I asked Finn.

"A little," he said.

"Why didn't you want to do it? You could have gotten a new Lego set."

Finn stopped rolling his wooden car along the carpet and answered with his head down.

"I thought if they took my blood I would die."

His answer shredded me, even then. He thought they were going to take *all* of his blood and he loved his mom so deeply that he did it anyway. I still have an urge to hug Finn whenever I think of that story. He's so smart but so literal and his heart is so big. I won't be surprised if he ends up going on the Cave Carts with Liz after all, if she begs him.

When I arrive for babysitting, Mrs. Bing spouts instructions at me as she rushes out the door. As a beautiful divorcée she's constantly going out and it amuses me on some level that my college fund is being fueled in large part by her active dating life since I have no love life of my own. Molly's dad is a prominent CEO that left years ago—right before Charlie was born—and married his secretary. Total cliché. I feel sorry for Mrs. Bing because she's so pretty but insecure. I wonder if that's always been the case or if her husband leaving made her that way.

"Do I look okay?" she asks. She runs her hands down her dress to smooth it as she turns to me.

"You look beautiful," I answer. She truly is stunning and the dress shows off her Pilates-carved figure.

She smiles gratefully. "Molly's locked away in her room as usual but if you need something, bang on her door and she'll answer. Eventually. Charlie's in the family room watching TV. He had an early dinner. You can leave after you put him to bed at eight. Money's on the table. You have my cell number. Wish me luck!" She waves and is gone in a flurry.

I hear a little voice behind me as I kick off my shoes and set them by the door. "Declan!" Charlie runs into the foyer and hugs my legs.

I kneel down to his level so I can hug him back more easily. "Charlie! I'm so happy to see you, big guy."

"I hurt my toe today," he declares with a frown.

"Oh, no. Which toe?"

"The one that had roast beef." He points to his middle toe.

I laugh. His toe looks unharmed. "You're in luck because the roast beef toe heals the fastest." I kiss the tip of my index finger and touch it to his toe and he smiles wide.

"Come see my new castle!" He takes my hand and leads me to his room where we're immersed in fiery battles with knights and dragons until the prince finally saves the princess (although it turns out she was pretty tough and didn't really need saving) and it's time to get ready for bed. Three bedtime stories later he's fully asleep. I lean over and kiss the top of his head and step quietly out of his room, leaving the door open a crack. I walk down to the other end of the hallway and knock softly on Molly's door. She hasn't emerged from her room all evening and I want to make sure she knows I'm leaving.

"Molly?" I call out.

There's no answer.

"Um, Molly?" I repeat, louder this time, as I knock again.

I hear some shuffling and steps coming closer. The door whips open, startling me.

"What?" Molly barks.

"I just wanted you to know I'm leaving."

The expression on her face tells me she has no idea why I'm bothering her with this information.

"In case Charlie wakes up."

She stares at me blankly.

"So you know that there's no one else here to help him if he needs something," I explain as I hold her gaze. I feel a nervous-y panic creep up the back of my throat but I gulp it down. This is for Charlie.

"Got it," she says and shuts the door firmly in my face. I release the breath I was holding in as I stare at the wood grain of her door only inches from my nose. *I swear if I didn't love Charlie so much I would never come back here again.*

I head back down the hall and peek in on Charlie once more to ensure he's still asleep. Then I tiptoe down the stairs and quietly escape.

The next two days, I busy myself getting organized with my classes and working at Jack's after school. I push Alexander out of my mind. Every girl in school is pursuing him, including Malibu Barbie, and it's lunacy to imagine a universe where Declan Jane ends up with Mr. Australia anyway. First of all, he towers over me. Being small ("petite," as my mom insists) doesn't bother me most of the time, but I have to admit that every once in a while I'll catch my reflection in a window when I'm walking next to someone tall and stately like Molly Bing and I'll be startled—absolutely gobsmacked, I swear—because I barely reach her shoulders. It's like I *forget* that I'm short. In those moments I feel as if I'm seeing myself as others must see me and it's jarring. There's nothing wrong with being short, mind you, but let's be honest, it's not exactly a coveted feature by the world at large. Just look at the way the word "short" is used in everyday language: "I got shortchanged;" "He was short with me;" "She got the short end of the stick." All negative. Even so, I'd have to say height is close to the bottom of my list of defects and insecurities. Nearer to the top would be too bookworm-y, too pale, I talk way too much when I'm nervous, and I can't carry a tune even if you hand it to me in a sealed Ziploc bag. Finn literally used to *beg* me not to sing during circle time when we were kids. And let's not forget the giant elephant at the top of the list: I'm a freak who has panic attacks all the time.

Despite all my shortcomings (there's that word "short" again), somehow I've had my share of guys come knocking through the years, telling me I'm cute (the bane of most short girls, but I don't mind it), or funny, or even pretty. But none of them know the real me underneath—the girl who's frantically throwing water on her face in the bathroom and sobbing to her therapist because nothing ever works.

I've never been interested enough in anyone to want to risk revealing the true me. Until now …. Why can't I stop thinking about Alexander?

Ms. Tamen is marching up and down the aisles collecting papers. It's Friday and calculus homework is due. She pauses beside a desk a few rows behind mine and makes a loud announcement. "Class, Mr. Crandall did not see fit to do his homework." Pencils cease, mid-scratch, as everyone braces for what's surely coming next. I pivot slowly in my chair to see

David Crandall, a quiet boy I've known since kindergarten, looking worried.

He should be.

Finn, Liz, and I call Ms. Tamen "the Trunchbull," after the viciously cruel headmistress in *Matilda* by Roald Dahl.

"Perhaps that's why he scored only 48% on our quiz today," Ms. Tamen adds. Shaming is her trademark. She wields it like a weapon to supposedly motivate students, but David just looks humiliated.

She folds her arms and rests them on her thick belly as she continues the onslaught. "Mr. Crandall, I would like you to tell the class you're sorry. When you don't master the concepts, you can't contribute. And when you can't contribute, you're not pulling your weight. Please explain to your classmates what was more important than doing your homework last night. Then you can apologize: To me first, and then to the class."

David shifts uncomfortably in his seat. His face is telegraphing panic mixed with stinging embarrassment as his eyes slowly trail over our faces, searching for the least damning thing to say. As the seconds tick by and we wait for him to speak, the only sound is the low, steady buzz of the fluorescent lights above our heads. My heart pounds sympathetically in my chest.

"Well?" demands Ms. Tamen.

The electric hum of the lights grows excruciatingly loud.

"It's my fault!" I say finally. The words spill out before I even realize my mouth has opened.

The whole class turns as one and gapes at me. David's face flashes astonishment followed by intense relief. Ms. Tamen's eyes bore into mine and panic rises in my throat as I continue speaking.

"I'm sorry," I stammer. "I um, I borrowed David's book yesterday … because I couldn't find mine. He said he would lend it to me and then I forgot to return it … so he couldn't do his homework last night." As I'm speaking I notice David's book, open on his desk. "I, uh … I only gave it back right before class this morning. So it's my fault." My eyes meet David's. "Sorry, David."

David nods slowly, an expression of utter bewilderment on his face.

"Your book is on your desk, Miss Jane," Ms. Tamen replies, her words dripping acid.

"Yes … um, no. I mean yes. I did lose it, but then I found it … this morning … in my locker." I try desperately to maintain my breathing. What I *really* want is to lie down flat on the floor in corpse pose.

"That's fortunate. Because you'll need it to complete the problems on pages twenty to thirty-nine. Due Monday." She turns to the class abruptly. "Let this be a lesson to all of you to keep track of your belongings. Miss Jane is going to be a very busy girl this weekend. And Mr. Crandall, consider this your one and only 'get out of jail free' card. Have your homework on my desk first thing Monday morning. No errors."

The bell rings and I feel all eyes on me as we gather our books and pile out. As I walk through the door I spot David across the hall, waiting for me.

"Wow, Declan," he says. "I don't know what to say. I have no idea what came over you, but thanks. *A lot.* I was dying in there and you saved me."

"I can't stand it when the Trunchbull does that to people," I say.

"The trunch who?"

"It's just a nickname—a character from a book."

"Oh. Well, hey, I feel bad that you got assigned all that extra work because of me. Do you want help? The only thing is, I may make it worse for you. My parents made me take this class and I think I'm in way over my head." He looks down, embarrassed.

"That's okay, David. Don't sweat it."

"Seriously?" His shoulders go slack with relief. "Thanks again, Declan. I owe you. Big time." He smiles and touches my arm before he runs off to his next class.

"Why did you do that?"

The voice comes from behind me and I turn around, startled, to see Alexander.

"Do what?" I ask.

"Why did you say you borrowed David's book?"

"How do you know I *didn't* borrow David's book?"

He smiles. "Let's just say that acting may not be your strong suit." The glint in his eyes makes me smile back.

"I beg to differ. I was in the school play three years in a row in elementary school."

"Interesting … what parts did you play?"

"Um, lemme think … a tree … the dog in *Annie* … and 'jungle animal number four.'"

He pretends to look impressed and I laugh. "I stand corrected," he says. "You clearly have a great deal of acting experience under your belt." His eyes crinkle irresistibly as he smiles and I feel my legs turn into flimsy foam pool noodles beneath me.

"But that still doesn't answer my question," he continues. "Why did you do it? Is David your boyfriend?"

"What?! No," I say, startled out of my wobbliness. "He's just a friend. Sort of. I've known him since kindergarten. He used to throw tanbark at me during recess. He lives on the next street over from mine. But he doesn't anymore. Throw bark, I mean. He still lives near me." Oh God, I'm rambling.

"So you did it because he stopped throwing bark at you?"

I laugh. "No ... I guess that's just a bonus."

Alexander smiles but doesn't say anything. I can tell he's waiting for my real answer.

"I don't know why I did it," I say. "I guess because I couldn't stand to see the Trunchbull shame him like that. She's a bully. And I hate it when people with power use it for intimidation."

He stares at me for a long moment with an expression I can't pin down. His eyes slowly trace a path around my face before focusing on my eyes again. When he speaks, it's as if to himself. "The Trunchbull? That must make you Matilda."

As he holds my gaze I seize the opportunity to study him up close. His eyes are soulful, intelligent pools that I could lose myself in for a day. All of his features come together in classic harmony but I notice a slight imperfection—a jagged scar on his temple, near his left eye. Instead of marring his good looks, however, it only serves to make him more gorgeously human.

As we stand, silent, I feel the same soothing calm rippling over me that I sensed the first day in homeroom, only now it's combined with an undercurrent of electric intensity. Alexander's eyes hold mine but he doesn't speak a word. How can he make me feel so serene yet flustered at the same time? His expression is bewildering—a mixture of surprise, confusion, and something else that's turning my legs into pool noodles again. I don't know what to say or do so I mumble that I'd better get to class and I turn to walk away while my legs are still semi-operational. Immediately, I realize my mistake. Alexander's morning schedule is identical to mine and he's surely following directly behind me to our next class. I silently curse the wedge sandals I'm wearing to make me look taller. My right ankle wobbles slightly and I tip to the side before steadying myself as I walk self-consciously. *Please oh please let me make it to Chemistry without falling on my face.*

Chapter Three

"I heard what happened in the Trunchbull's class this morning. Brutal. I hope David Crandall knows how lucky he is that you have a ginormous heart and a complete disregard for your own self-interest." Liz is driving us to Jack's for our afternoon shift.

"It was awful. You would have done the same."

"I doubt that very seriously. But I'm glad I had a dentist appointment. How did that woman ever become a teacher anyway? I mean, c'mon, she must have considered career choices at some point. I wonder what was next on her list?"

"Prison warden?" I suggest, and we both laugh.

"Dominatrix?" says Liz. We laugh even harder.

"Why the hell anyone ever let her become a teacher, I'll never understand," Liz mutters as we pull into the parking lot.

We're both scheduled until closing but it slows after eight, so Jack asks if one of us wants to go home early. Liz jumps at the chance because she has a forensics competition to prepare for. She and Finn have won practically every debate award that exists in California. Last year their team even went to the nationals. I've attended a few events and it's actually fun to watch them skewer the competition with their well-constructed arguments and rebuttals.

"Oh wait, I was supposed to drive us home," Liz says as she's gathering her things, "I'll come back for you after closing."

"Nah. Don't worry about it. I'll call my mom."

"You sure?"

I nod. "Yes. Now go study. What are you guys arguing this time?"

"The United States government should substantially increase its exploration and/or development of space beyond the Earth's mesosphere," she says as she grabs her purse and heads out the door.

"Good luck with that!" I call out after her.

At nine thirty, Jack locks the doors and we start closing procedures. He plugs his iPod into the speaker dock and starts blasting some of his favorite '80s tunes—which I have to admit have now become some of my favorites, too—as we clean. Tonight's playlist is a bunch of one-hit-wonders. He sings "*Ah! Leah!*" by Donnie Iris dramatically into the pull-out faucet as he washes dishes and I sing backup as I dance in and out of the walk-in refrigerator, putting bins away. As I reach for the last tub of cheese slices from the prep area I see Jack's phone vibrating across the counter so I turn down the music and hand it to him. It's Jack's husband, Al, calling to say their dog threw up again all over the living room floor. I tell Jack to go on ahead and I'll finish the final mop and lock-up.

"You sure?" he asks. When I insist he says, "Let me check that night security is here." He goes outside and comes back a few minutes later. "Okay, Declan, security's here. It's Antonio tonight. I told him you're still inside. Is your mom picking you up?"

"Yep, I just need to call her. I'll be fine. I know you're worried about Coco. You should go home and make sure she doesn't need to go to the vet."

"Okay, thanks. You're really sure?"

I nod.

"All right. I'll leave my iPod so you can keep listening if you want. Al made the playlist. "*867-5309*" is up next I think. You don't want to miss out on Tommy Tutone."

"Thanks," I laugh. "Now go." He walks out the back door and I lock it behind him.

The '80s hits aren't the same without Jack's theatrics so I plug my phone into the speaker dock instead and sing along to the songs in my latest playlist. One upside of being alone is that I can belt them out as loud as I want—basically murdering each melody—and no one's around to complain. When I'm nearly finished mopping, I hear the chime of a text arriving. It's my mom, reminding me that she's at a realtor awards dinner downtown and won't be home until late. Shoot. I forgot about that. I shift to plan B and decide to take the San Mar Metro home. There's a bus stop across from Jack's and the next bus arrives in about twenty minutes.

Antonio waves to me as I emerge through the back door. He's doing his perimeter walk around the large parking lot that serves not only Jack's but also the Greek gyro place next to us and the falafel bar on the other side. A familiar figure is sitting on a bench in the eating area outside. "Hi, Jimmy," I say as I hand him a bag of food. This is our routine. Antonio knows Jimmy, too, and he always lets him wait here.

"Thanks, Declan," Jimmy says as he accepts the bag and peeks inside. "How you doin' tonight?"

"Pretty good, I guess. There are two cheeseburgers in there—the customer wanted no sauce so we had to make new ones—and a bunch of fries, too, from our last batch."

Jimmy nods in approval.

"You headed to the shelter later?" I always ask and he always gives the same answer: "Maybe. Maybe I will." Jimmy has his ways and he makes up his own mind about things.

"Well here's bus fare in case you want to catch a ride downtown." I hand him a few dollar bills from my share of the tip jar. I know he won't accept more than that.

"You're always good to me. Thanks, Declan," he says as he meets my eyes.

I smile back. I like Jimmy. He has his problems, but I sense his innate goodness. He's kind and gentle at his core. They say everybody has a story to tell and I've always felt in my heart that Jimmy has a particularly sad one.

With a mild climate and a welcoming city council, San Mar has a large homeless population. I volunteer at the shelter and I've read all the debate in the local paper and what I've come to understand is that the reasons for homelessness vary so widely that no "one" solution can solve it all. Some people try to paint the issue with a broad brush, but the only connective tissue, as I see it, is that every human being deserves to be recognized as an individual, not lumped into a category.

I say goodbye to Jimmy and exchange chitchat with Antonio before I walk across the street to the bus stop. After a few minutes, a couple in their twenties walks up. They've obviously been drinking and the woman is clearly seething as she sits down hard on the bench and folds her arms, turning away from the man. Each time he starts to speak, she whips back around and shouts over him, "You were kissing her, Daniel! Don't insult me by lying about it!"

Finally "Daniel" manages to get a word in, but he's not helping his case. "Aw, Cara. I don't know what you think you saw but that's not how it was. Look at you. How many drinks have you had?" His tone is condescending and he plants his palm unsteadily on the plexiglass wall of the bus stand in an attempt to stay upright.

"Not enough!" she yells in his face. Her tone has shifted to one of pain over anger and I feel it viscerally, like a punch to the gut. My heart goes out to this wronged girl.

Back and forth they go, over and over. They're so consumed by their arguing I'm not even sure they notice me. Daniel's explanations and excuses are feebler by the minute and Cara isn't buying it. *I'm* not buying it either. Somehow I know in my bones he's a liar and this isn't his first time. My heart rate begins to surge and I suddenly feel nauseous. As Daniel keeps up his barrage of excuses, I can see Cara's outmatched and starting to waver. She's going to take this jerk back. I stroke my throat nervously. It's starting to constrict. Oh God, not now. Not here.

I check my watch. Five minutes until the bus is scheduled to arrive. Even then, I'll be trapped in a moving vehicle with these two and their tragic soap opera. I consider calling Liz but I know she's studying and it would take too long for her to get here anyway. I look across the street and notice Jimmy waiting for a break in traffic to cross. He must have decided to take the bus downtown after all. I wonder if it might help to have him here with me but panic is crawling up my throat fast and I can't wait. I stand abruptly and start walking, and then running, toward home. Before too long I have to bend over and grasp my knees to try to suck air into my lungs. Over and over I run a few yards and have to stop. My heart is bursting and I want more than anything to just lie down, spread-eagled on the sidewalk. I'm bent over again, struggling to breathe, when I hear someone call my name.

"Declan?"

With hands still firmly on my knees, I turn my head to see an old, classic white Jeep Wagoneer with wood siding pull to the curb. The passenger-side window is down and Alexander leans over from the driver's seat, peering out, puzzled. "Are you okay?" he asks.

I briefly consider lying but realize I can't possibly pull it off in the state I'm in, so I go with the truth instead. "Um … no. I'm very unwell, actually." I manage to huff out the words as I alternate between looking at him and staring back down at the sidewalk, trying to breathe.

"Stay right there," he says as he parks and hops out.

Before I know it he's at my side, resting his hand on my back. "You're going to be okay, sweetheart," he reassures, and with his Australian accent his words don't sound at all ridiculous as he guides me gently to his car.

At first I'm relieved to have him beside me but then a new wave of panic swells. What am I going to say when he asks what's wrong? What if he wants to take me to the hospital? Oh God, I can't tell him it's all in my head. Somehow I need to convince him that I'm okay.

As the thought takes hold, I suddenly realize that I *am* okay—*more* than okay. The peaceful calm I've felt in Alexander's presence is back and it's more intense than I remember. It floods over me in wave after wave, washing away my anxiety. I feel supremely relaxed and as I melt into the sensation I slowly become aware of the electric touch of his hand on my back. Like a pulse building to a powerful charge, it fills the air around us. I look up at him, startled.

Alexander takes a step back and quickly stuffs his hands in the pockets of his jeans. "You look like you're feeling better now?"

"Yes, much better ... thank you. I don't know what was wrong with me." I wave my hand in the air, trying to convey that I'm as bewildered as he is about why I was a crazy wreck only a few minutes ago. It's not a total lie—I *am* better. Other than the fact that my skin is still tingling where he touched me, I feel so calm he may as well have interrupted me doing downward dog instead of having a street-side panic attack. I just pray he won't ask questions. What explanation can I give? I can't even think straight with him standing in front of me in all his gorgeous perfection waiting for me to say something more.

I look up and meet his eyes and repeat with a slightly embarrassed shrug, "Thanks again for your help. I'm good now."

"Well I don't know how they do things in America, but I'm not about to leave a damsel in distress on the sidewalk. Can I give you a ride home? My house is on Miramar, too."

The fact that he knows where I live is not lost on me and a smile spreads across my face. "Um, sure. That would be great."

He opens the passenger door wide and holds his arms at his sides as I step in.

When he slides into the driver's seat and closes the door, the electric energy that surrounded us on the sidewalk begins to build within the confined space of the car. I swallow nervously and try to think of something to say.

"Just get off work?" he asks as we pull away from the curb.

"Yes, how did you know?" I'm so thankful he isn't asking why I was bent over on the sidewalk trying to breathe that I exhale audibly with relief.

He glances over, amused. "Your shirt was my first clue."

My face flushes to match the bright red "Jack's Burger Shack" t-shirt I'm wearing. *Of course.* Not only am I in uniform, but I'm probably stinking up his car with the smell of Hula Burgers for Pete's sake.

"How long have you worked there?"

"Almost two years. My friend Liz worked there first and then she recommended me and we're both there now. I work after school most days. Jack, the owner, is a nice guy."

"In that case I'll have to try it out sometime after school."

I nod. *Wait, does he mean he wants to try it out because Jack is nice? Or because I'll be working?* The thought of the latter both thrills me and sends my nerves into overdrive. I start babbling like an idiot. "Jack's is known for Hula Burgers, so I recommend you get one of those. And a side of fries. You can't have a burger without fries, right? The sweet potato fries are the best. And the milkshakes, too. Most places make them with fake syrup but we use all real ingredients. My favorite is banana. Do you have burgers in Australia? I mean, I guess you must have them. That was a stupid question." *Oh God, Declan. Please. Stop. Talking.*

Blessedly, Alexander appears unfazed by my inane rambling. "Sure, we have burgers and chips. The lot of toppings are different though."

With his accent, everything he says sounds alluring, even burger toppings. I force myself to bulldoze those thoughts to the side of my brain so I can focus on making coherent conversation. I somehow manage to recount a few funny stories about work and Alexander laughs—a deep, genuine, throw-your-head-back laugh that invites me to join in—and it puts me at ease. Soon we're talking effortlessly and I don't want the ride to end.

"How do you like living in San Mar?" I ask as we're in the final stretch home.

"It's growing on me," he says with a glance in my direction.

"It must be hard coming to a new school senior year."

"It's not so bad. We move around a lot."

"Do you miss Australia?"

"Aye. A little." He pauses. "But my grandfather always says it's the people around you that matter, not where you are." The way he looks at me as he says the words makes me wish we had a thousand miles left to go.

We turn onto Miramar Lane and I start to direct him to my house.

"I know which one is yours," he says with a smile.

"You do?"

"I've seen you leave in the morning to go running. I get up early to surf." He gestures to his surfboard in the back of the car. "I'm across the street, two down on the corner," he says as he pulls into my driveway.

"I don't think I've seen you surfing. I run a loop down to the beach and back."

"I go to a few different places. We all look the same out there in our wetsuits, anyway. Like a bunch of seals."

I laugh and he smiles. I softly press the button to release my seatbelt and as it recoils into the doorframe there's a stretch of silence. I turn to say thanks for the ride but my voice croaks as our eyes meet. Alexander holds my gaze and leans almost imperceptibly closer but then abruptly halts and his demeanor changes. "I'll wait here until you go inside," he states plainly, turning to face forward.

"Oh. Okay." I feel embarrassed that he must have been waiting for me to leave. *Way to read a situation, Declan.* I mutter thanks as I open the door quickly and step out. Before I let go of the handle, though, Alexander calls to me.

"Declan?"

I lean down and he meets my eyes with an intensity that makes my breath hitch in my throat.

"I'm glad I ran into you tonight." His voice is low and filled with promise and anticipation. When I try to respond I find it almost impossible to operate my lips and limbs as needed to say goodnight and close the door. I manage to walk to the front of the house where I dig around in my purse under the glare of the porch light for far too long trying to locate my keys. *Aw, for the love of ... why do I keep so much junk piled in here?* I finally manage to extract them and unlock the door. I peer over my shoulder and give Alexander a short wave as I step across the threshold. He waves in return and starts backing out of the driveway.

Safely inside, excitement and confusion wash over me as I press my back against the door and try to process what just happened. I tell myself I'm crazy to allow even a scintilla of a thought that Alexander might be interested.

But I can't stop myself from smiling wide at the idea.

Chapter Four

Over the weekend I make two transparent attempts—one Saturday morning and again on Sunday—to "bump" into Alexander as I run by his house on my usual loop to the beach and back, but he's nowhere in sight. Something is going on at his house Sunday morning, however. The town librarian and a few people I don't recognize are going inside as I run past. I wave to Mr. Remy, the owner of the San Mar Book Café, as he walks up the driveway. I wonder if the gathering has something to do with Alexander's grandfather—maybe a book club? The rest of the weekend I'm holed up working through the extra calculus problems the Trunchbull assigned me. More than once I curse myself for speaking up in class.

At school on Monday Alexander doesn't approach me. In fact, unless I'm imagining it, he's actively *avoiding* me because every time I get anywhere near him he moves away. His attitude is more cordial than outright rude, but it's still weird. I guess I let my silly notions turn a friendly car ride into something more and now he's doing his best to discourage me. How humiliating.

Oddly though, I swear he's watching me from afar. But that makes no sense whatsoever. Eventually I stop stealing looks at him because it just sends my mind wandering to ridiculous places that can never be. *I mean, c'mon Declan, did you really think he would be interested in a girl he saw freaking out on the side of the road?* I don't mention anything to Liz or Finn because I'm embarrassed and I honestly don't know what to say anyway.

After school Finn and I go to the first journalism meeting of the year. I considered being a journalist at one point, but a job with constant deadlines and breaking news probably isn't the best pursuit for someone who may bust out with a panic attack at any moment. I've contented myself with writing articles for the school newspaper since middle school and I'm hoping I can steer my writing skills to good use in some other way as a career. Molly Bing is the editor of the student newspaper and she revels in it. Not because she loves journalism, per se, but because she loves being in charge and telling people what to do. As we walk in the door, she's handing out assignments and I'm surprised to see Alexander with her. She must have invited him to join. As I absorb the snapshot before me of Malibu Barbie standing next to Mr. Australia my stomach sinks. They're made for each other— both gorgeously perfect human specimens.

Immediately I stop myself. *What am I doing?* I've never been a whiner … and besides, who wants some guy who's trying to avoid me, anyway? I'm better than that. *"Yes you are, Jane!"* my inner drill sergeant concurs in one of her much-needed pep talks. I smile a little.

"Declan!" Hearing my first name, spoken by an actual person, snaps me back to reality. Molly is giving me an assignment.

"Did you hear about the increase in crime over the summer?" She continues without waiting for a reply. "It's still a problem. I, for one, just had my iPad stolen from the front seat of my car and Suzie's bike is missing." She looks at Suzie (one of her minions, as Liz would say) and Suzie nods back, appropriately indignant and supportive. "Don't you know someone at the police department? Why don't you find out what's going on and how we're supposed to protect ourselves."

"You can start by not leaving your iPad on the front seat of your car," Finn mumbles next to me.

I laugh and nudge Finn with my elbow as Molly glares at us. "Got it, Molly. I'm on it. And Finn wants to help." Finn groans under his breath but I know he likes working together on stories.

Molly hands out the rest of the assignments and then turns to Alexander. "You can work with me on the story on Mrs. Preston. She's retiring and we need to write a retrospective on her contributions to the district for the last twenty years."

Alexander nods. There's no way Molly needs help with a simple puff piece on our principal but the snarky side of me tells me journalistic collaboration isn't what she's after.

After the meeting, Finn and I walk to our bikes and discuss next steps for our story. As we're talking, I scan the parking lot to see if Liz has left yet. I want to ask her if she wants to study later for our calculus test. Her Fiat is gone, but I notice a tall, immaculate blonde leaning against Alexander's Jeep, waiting for him as he walks up. He greets her warmly with a hug and they both get in and drive away. *His girlfriend?* The idea leaves me with a lump in the pit of my stomach that has no right being there.

"So do you want to head to the police station now?" Finn's words distract me from my silent rumination.

"What? Oh, right. Sure, Finn." He wants to see if we can interview Chief Stephens. I know if the chief is available he'll make the time to talk. He helped us before and I think he enjoys Finn's affinity for spouting crime data. I also have a strong suspicion he has a thing for my mom because he always inquires about her. His wife died of cancer a few years ago and it was terribly sad—she was well known and well liked throughout town. Their two sons, Jake and Zach, are both in college now.

I ask for the chief at the front desk and after a few minutes he walks up and waves us in to follow him to the back.

"How are you guys? And how's your mom doing, Declan?" he asks as we sit down in his office.

"We're good. And my mom's doing well, thanks for asking," I answer with a smile.

Finn silently endures several minutes of our chitchat social niceties. He'll join in if he has to, but the truth is, he doesn't see the point. Until I explained it to him years ago, he thought people only made small talk because they had nothing else interesting to say. As soon as he senses we're wrapping up, he jumps in. "We're doing a story for the San Mar High newspaper about the increase in crime lately."

The chief nods. "There was an uptick this summer and it hasn't gone down as it usually does. It looks like a new group came into town over the last few months and they've joined some of the informal homeless encampments. We've been breaking them up but they keep moving around and growing larger. We're hoping they push on. They're more of an opportunistic, violent type than we've had here before."

"Violent?" I ask, surprised. "I haven't read anything about that in the Sentinel." The San Mar Sentinel is our local newspaper.

"Violent crimes were down nine percent last month," adds Finn.

"So far it's been confined to fights within the homeless camps and it hasn't attracted news attention. We've boosted patrols to get it under control. You'll see an increase in next month's data, unfortunately," he says with a nod to Finn.

"And you think they're responsible for the increase in property crimes, too?" I ask.

"We aren't sure yet but it's looking like this latest influx includes a well-organized ring of thieves. There's also drug involvement. So far most of the trouble has been concentrated in the beach flats and, like I said, despite our budget constraints, we've managed to increase patrols and we've made some arrests. They won't last long in San Mar."

"Do you have any tips for people in the meantime, to protect themselves?" I ask.

"Common sense, mostly: don't leave valuables in your car, lock your doors and windows, and be sure to lock up your bikes," he answers. "We have a safety page on our website with a long list of tips that would be good to include with your story."

I finish my notes and we thank the chief for his time.

"Be sure to tell your mom I say hello," he calls out to me as we head for the door.

"Will do," I reply with a smile.

The sun emerges from behind a cloud and warms our backs as Finn and I traverse the lawn in front of the police station. "What the chief said about violence kind of worries me," I admit as we reach our bikes.

"That should be the *least* of your concerns," replies Finn.

"What do you mean?"

"I keep an alphabetical listing of everything possible to worry about in my head."

I pause as I unwind my lock and peer up at Finn, one eyebrow raised.

He smiles and shrugs. "What? You're not the only one with anxiety."

I nod. "Fair enough. So why, exactly, should I not be worried? I'm almost afraid to ask."

"I also track the statistical likelihood of any one of those things happening. 96% of the worries on my list are mathematically more likely to happen to you than crime violence. San Mar is a fairly safe town and you lead a low-risk lifestyle."

I stare at Finn quizzically. I am definitely not reassured. "Promise me you'll never tell me the list of things that are *more* likely to happen."

He shrugs his shoulders. "Suit yourself," he says as if I'm taking my life in my hands. I punch him in the arm and he laughs.

He swings his leg over his bike so he can go home to host his online book club. Normally I'd be in any book club that Finn started but this one is focused around an incredibly long and involved sci-fi book series that I never got into. Once a month, he connects live with fellow series lovers from around the world to discuss their shared fanaticism.

"Have fun," I call out as he rides away. I feel a little melancholy as he waves and disappears around a corner. I'm so at ease when I'm with Finn, as if I have a solid foundation to stand on. But he obviously has more anxiety under the surface than he lets on. I hope I provide him with the same feeling of support he gives me.

I check my phone for messages and then toss my purse into the basket on the front of my cruiser and head in the opposite direction from Finn. I've decided to go to the homeless shelter to see if I can gather more information.

To my surprise, Jimmy is inside the shelter having a meal. I wave to Sarah, the director, as I walk over to Jimmy's table. "Hey, Declan," he says with a smile and a wave of his fork as he continues eating.

"Hi, Jimmy," I say as I sit down across from him. "It's good to see you here. Hey, can I ask you a question?"

He nods while he's chewing and I press on. "Have you noticed some new people in San Mar recently who are causing trouble? In the beach flats?"

He stops mid-bite as he's raising another forkful of chili to his mouth and his face darkens. "I wouldn't know anything about that."

"C'mon, Jimmy, it's me. I'm just trying to write an article for my high school newspaper—it's harmless. What's been going on? Is it a gang?"

"It's not harmless. People I know got hurt. You need to stay out of it," he scolds.

"Why?"

He puts his fork down and looks me in the eyes. "Because you're a nice kid. That's why. You don't need to get wrapped up in that. Stay away from there, you hear me?"

The urgency in his voice surprises me. Jimmy isn't one to get riled up easily but whatever's going on has him seriously rattled. "Okay, Jimmy. I hear you," I say as I stand up. "I have to go talk to Sarah. I work at Jack's on Saturday, though, so I guess I'll see you then?"

He gives me a firm nod and continues eating.

I confirm with Sarah that it isn't any of the "regulars" that are causing trouble, and she tells me that the new group—whoever they are—hasn't been to the shelter. Her sense is that it's more of a roving ring of thieves passing through and hiding amongst the homeless. She says the police have spoken with her and increased their presence to discourage any problems. She's cautious but she feels that it's being handled well and eventually the trouble will move on.

The sun is still out when I leave and I decide to ride along the cliffs on my way home. It's a little out of the way, but the trail along the ocean is wide and paved so I don't have to worry about cars or traffic lights and I can enjoy the view. I may even take a look at the beach flats to see if anything stands out for my story—but only from a distance. Jimmy's warning and the chief's mention of violence resonated with me.

As I pedal along Seacliff Drive, a strong breeze off the ocean whips my hair across my eyes so I stop for a second to corral it into a ponytail. I also dig out a cardigan from my backpack and put it on over my tank top. I pause to take in the view of the water and the boats in the harbor in the distance. I love living by the ocean. I love the endless blue immensity of it, the soft, repeating crash of the waves, and the rough scrunch of sand under my bare feet. What I would gladly live *without*, however, is the fog that creeps in most nights and leaves a gray shroud over the town until it burns away the next day—sometimes not until noon. But over the years I've made peace with it by appreciating the slow and quiet quality the mist ushers in as it gradually swallows everything in its path.

I ignore the turnoff to my house and keep going all the way to the San Mar Beach Boardwalk. The Big Dipper rollercoaster looms large in the sky as I approach. The seaside park looks promising but also slightly spooky with deserted rides and wisps of fog beginning to circle. At this time of year it's open only on limited days.

I look toward the beach flats in the distance as I turn around and cross over the railroad tracks. All summer long, the tracks bring hordes of tourists in open-air train cars to the boardwalk from Redwood Park in the mountains on the "Trees to the Seas" run. My tire wedges into the groove of one of the tracks when I'm not paying attention and I nearly crash as it sticks. I jerk the handlebars to try to wrench it out of the narrow rut and I manage to recover but the bike lurches to the side and my purse flops out of the basket and onto the ground. I stop and bend over to retrieve it and that's when the hairs on the back of my neck stand up.

I slowly raise my head to see three men towering over me. The oldest, clearly the leader, looks about my age. His voice is slow and precise, like a spider creeping up my spine.

"What have we here?"

I take in his laser-cut features and nearly black pools for eyes. His hair is dark and he's dressed all in black, making his white teeth stand out with striking singularity. His impeccable grooming stands in direct opposition to the neglect shown by his two associates. They're garbed in grubby jeans and long-sleeved flannels over stained t-shirts and I get the impression the grime on their bodies is in layers.

"You want some *help*?" says the sweaty one on the left. The other one laughs.

"I'm good, thanks," I say loudly. I attempt to sound confident but I don't think I'm pulling it off.

"Nice basket," says the leader as he nudges my basket with the tip of his boot. The other two laugh. "You're not in a hurry are you?"

I slide my hand into my purse, feeling for my phone so I can try to dial 911. My mind is racing. I know the police are patrolling the area regularly according to the chief. Maybe I can buy some time until they drive through.

"I was just leaving," I say as I place my foot on the pedal of my bike. "I have plans and my friends will be here any minute." I stare at the leader with what I hope is don't-mess-with-me grit. As our eyes meet, however, he appears jolted with surprise. *That's weird.* Does he think he knows me? I'm certain I don't know him—I could never forget those black eyes.

Whatever the cause of his reaction, it makes him more determined. He places his boot firmly against my bike tire. "How about delaying those plans? Just so we can talk awhile." Then, without moving his eyes from mine, he adds, "Gentlemen, why don't you relieve this young lady of her bike so she can walk with me ... unencumbered."

Before I can react, a car horn honks urgently and we all turn toward the sound. A familiar wood-paneled Jeep Wagoneer speeds in our direction and comes to a hard stop beside us on the road. Alexander steps out—practically while the car is still in motion—and walks over to me briskly. My eyes are wide with a mixture of intense relief but mostly disbelief. He's my knight in shining armor, *again*? Where did he come from?

"Ready to go, Declan?" Alexander asks. "I'll take that," he says as he grasps the handlebars of my bike away from one of the sidekicks. He puts his other arm around me, protectively. "Why don't you go get in the car and I'll be there in a tick."

Before I can move, the leader nods at him and says, "Alexander."

Alexander acknowledges him soberly, "Avestan."

My mouth drops open. They *know* each other?

"I should have known she'd be with you," Avestan says.

"She's not *with* me," replies Alexander. "You know better than that."

Is he insulting me?

"It's interesting that you feel the need to emphasize that point," says Avestan.

Alexander ignores his remark. "There's nothing for you here," he says.

"I most disrespectfully disagree," replies Avestan. "San Mar has been very welcoming. Look around. I'm sure you've seen what's happening. Go ahead and leave with … *Declan*." He rolls my name around on his tongue as if it's a delicacy he hasn't bitten down on yet. "But I'm sure I'll be seeing you again. Both of you."

With his right arm around my waist and his left arm holding my bike aloft by the frame, Alexander walks me to the

Jeep. He opens the passenger door and waits for me to be seated before he walks around to the back and throws my bike and backpack in. I feel Avestan staring at us the entire time with an intensity that makes me shake. Or maybe it's just the adrenaline. Being near Alexander usually calms me, but I'm feeling unmoored because when he gets in the car he looks angry as he steps on the gas and pulls out onto the road.

We gain some distance before I say a word. I'm so bewildered that I blurt out the first thing that comes to mind. "You know that guy?"

"Yes," Alexander answers, his mouth set in a firm line.

"How?"

He doesn't answer.

I try a different approach. "How did you know where I was?"

There's a long stretch of silence and then, instead of answering, he turns to me in a sudden outburst. "What were you doing down there, Declan? Are you crazy or just a fool? Because those are the only two explanations for riding around the beach flats on a bike, by yourself, at dusk."

I'm taken aback. He's *yelling* at me? I'm the one who was almost robbed or God knows what. Shouldn't he be comforting me right now? My legs are shaking visibly and I see Alexander look over and notice for the first time.

"Oh Declan, I'm sorry. What am I doing?" He reaches over to put his hand on my arm as he slows the car and turns at the next light into a small strip mall. "Are you okay?"

"I think so," I say softly as he parks and shuts off the ignition.

He pivots in his seat to face me and takes my hands in both of his. I'm still shaking uncontrollably. "Breathe slowly," he says and a flood of soothing stillness washes over me. I look into Alexander's eyes and I feel completely safe as the remaining adrenaline slowly drains away. In its place is that familiar electricity where his hands are touching mine.

"Better?" he asks after a few minutes.

I nod and he gently pulls his hands away.

"How do you do that?"

"Do what?" he asks.

"You always make me feel so calm."

He shakes his head. "It's not me. You're doing it yourself by focusing on your breathing."

I search his eyes for a long beat. I don't believe him but I'll let it go for now. "I'm not crazy by the way. Or a fool," I say softly. "The sun was out and I rode to the boardwalk and my tire got stuck in the train tracks. I wasn't 'riding around the beach flats.' I was over a mile away ... I'm not dumb."

Alexander sighs before he answers. "One thing I would never call you is dumb."

I look up to meet his eyes. "As happy as I was to see you, I want you to know that I think I could have taken care of myself if you hadn't shown up. My mom and I took a self-defense class, and I'm a fast runner."

Alexander's expression is a mixture of surprise and profound skepticism. He chooses to comment, however, only on the first part of my statement. "You were happy to see me?"

The look in his eyes makes me laugh. "I was *relieved* to see you."

"You said happy. No take-backs."

The way his eyes light up as I laugh makes me almost forget what we were arguing about. It's so confusing being around him. One moment he's ignoring me at school and now he's joking with me after coming to my rescue. As I try to sort it all out in my mind, his expression shifts again.

"Listen," he says, "I don't think I need to tell you that those guys back there—the ones you're saying 'you could have handled on your own'—are dangerous. You, especially, need to be careful."

"Why me especially?"

He shakes his head. "Just promise me you won't go back and you'll stay away from Avestan."

"How do you know him?"

"It doesn't matter. Please just trust me on how dangerous he is to be around ..." he looks down as if he's wrestling with how much more to say, "... and how dangerous I am to be around, too. You should stay away from both of us."

Us? He's lumping himself in with Avestan?

"Why would I need to stay away from *you*? That makes no sense."

He stares at me solemnly but doesn't answer.

"Are you joking?"

He shakes his head. "No."

"But you helped me. Why would you be dangerous?"

"I shouldn't be here with you."

I search his eyes for a long time, contemplating what he could possibly mean. Only one thing comes to mind. "Are you a stalker?"

His response is wide eyes and bewilderment. A multitude of expressions pass over his face so quickly it looks as if every muscle is twitching in turn before he bursts out laughing.

"What? It's not that crazy of a thought, you know." I try to sound offended but his laugh is infectious.

"I promise you I am *not* a stalker," he says, sounding relieved that I broke the tension between us.

"Well how else would you know where I was and that I needed help ... *twice*?" I feel foolish, but it's true. How come he keeps turning up at the right time?

"It's a small town. We travel the same routes. I swear to you I'm not stalking you. Stalking is serious ... and disturbed."

"Well then why are you dangerous? That's a frightening word to throw around."

His expression changes and he backpedals, but only slightly. "Look, I would never harm you purposefully. I can't explain why but it's better if you stay away from me."

"But I don't want to stay away from you," I blurt out without thinking, without filtering.

There's a long moment of silence and the air between us is charged with anticipation as I wait, nervously, for his response. His eyes meet mine but then he looks away and his face hardens. "I should take you home now."

I turn to stare out the passenger window so he can't see the stinging hurt on my face. "I can ride my bike from here," I say as I lean down to reach for my purse on the floor. I mistakenly grab it near the bottom and as I lift it onto my lap the contents spill everywhere. *Great. Can anything else possibly go wrong?* All I want is to get out of this stupid car so I can continue feeling mortified in private.

Alexander leans over to help retrieve the items and as I bend forward to do the same he lifts his head suddenly and my nose smashes into the back of his skull. Hard.

"Ow!" I cry. The pain is blinding.

"Are you okay?" he says, full of concern.

"I don't know," I mumble. My eyes are watering and I'm holding my nose. "Are you?"

His expression changes to horror as I pull my hand away. "Cripes, Declan, you're bleeding like crazy. I gave you a bloody nose. I'm so sorry."

I feel the blood flowing and I tilt my head back instinctively and pinch my nose. "I'm the one who smashed into you," I try to say but the blood starts to run into my mouth so I stop and clamp it shut.

Alexander is frantically searching the car for something to help stem the flow but he comes up empty. "Use my shirt," he says finally as he reaches behind his neck and pulls it off over his head.

The ridiculousness of the situation strikes me suddenly: all I wanted was to get away and nurse my humiliation in private and now I'm stuck here in his car, bleeding down my face, with Alexander sitting next to me half naked. A laugh erupts from my chest. It begins as a slight giggle and builds into convulsions that shake my body the more I try to repress it. I can't stop and it's not helping the bleeding any.

"What?" Alexander is holding his shirt out but as I lower my eyes to look at him he can't help but laugh in return. "*What?*"

"I don't know," I say, still laughing. "Look at me." I wave my free hand to point to my face. Tears of laughter are running down my cheeks and my nose is still bleeding like a hose. "I can't use your shirt for this. I'll ruin it."

"Are you kidding? Who cares about my shirt? You need it. Trust me. You look like Redbeard the Pirate."

I laugh harder and feign offense but finally concede and grab the shirt out of his hand. I ball it up and hold it against my nose. Alexander smiles as I peer over at him, my head tilted back. After a few minutes the bleeding slows and the next time I pull the shirt away to check, it blessedly seems to have stopped.

"Does it look better?" I ask.

"Uh, yes … if by better you mean that it isn't actively gushing blood anymore."

"I guess you *are* dangerous," I say.

"I tried to warn you," he replies with his lopsided smile.

I'm suddenly acutely aware of the space between us in the car again. I rub his shirt under my nose and across my chin to wipe the blood away and I run my fingers under my eyes to remove any remaining trails of tears from my laughing fit. I hope I'm presentable.

"How do I look now?"

He tries to suppress his laughter.

"Is it really that bad?

"Well, your face is still covered in blood from the nose down, and now you've smeared blood under your eyes as well. If a copper came by right now, you'd be rushed to hospital and I'd be arrested."

I smile and we both burst out laughing.

"Guess I'll have some explaining to do to my mom when I get home."

"Oh no you don't … are you crazy? I can't drop you off at home like this." He looks around the strip mall. "I'll get something to clean you up properly."

"You're not wearing a shirt," I remind him.

"Oh, right," he says, looking down. "I might have a jacket in back."

He leans over close as he reaches into the back seat to feel around for his jacket. He smells so good, like a mixture of fresh soap and the outdoors. I close my eyes and inhale, trying not to notice his bare skin so close to mine. Too soon, he finds what he's looking for and leans back with a gray hoodie. "I'll be back in a tick," he says as he puts it on.

We're parked in front of Rico's, my favorite Taqueria. He goes in and emerges a few minutes later holding a paper cup with water in it and a stack of napkins. He opens my door and sets down the cup on the ground. Then he kneels in the doorframe, dips the corner of a napkin in the water, and holds it in the air. "Okay, turn towards me and let's see what we can do here."

He begins to gently wipe away the blood on my face and I'm sure I must look like an extra from a horror movie. Nice way to punctuate my earlier mortification. In comparison to the museum-quality specimen kneeling before me, the state I'm in is so comical I almost have to laugh to keep from crying.

Alexander uses every napkin and then finishes by dipping his thumbs in the water and wiping gently underneath my eyes, across my cheeks, and along my chin. His thumb grazes my lips, parting them slightly, and he pauses. In that moment, as our eyes lock, I'm consumed with one thought: *please kiss me. Now.* I never realized it was possible to feel so powerfully attracted to someone—as if every molecule in my body is straining toward his. Everything else falls away as I will him to lean forward and close the distance between us.

I move closer and Alexander stands abruptly, dropping his hands. "I think I got it all off."

Embarrassed, I turn in my seat and mumble "thanks," and quickly gather the remaining spilled items from my purse.

He tosses out the cup and napkins in a recycling bin a few doors down from Rico's. As he walks back to the driver's side to get in, I decide to follow through with my original intention before the bloody nose debacle.

"Where are you going?" he asks as I step out of the car.

"I can ride my bike from here."

"What? That's crazy. It's getting dark. Let me drive you. We're both going to the same place."

He's right. What excuse can I give other than that I want to be alone? That I want to be away from him and all his mixed signals that leave me confused and embarrassed?

My grumbling stomach gives me an idea. "I'm going to grab something to eat first. Just leave me my bike, I'll be fine."

"What are you talking about? Declan, you've just been through a traumatic experience. I'm not going to leave you to ride home in the dark by yourself."

"I'll have my mom pick me up."

He stares at me, bewildered.

I try another tack. "Listen. I'm starving and this is one of my favorite restaurants. If I go home now I'll be dreaming of their warm chips and salsa all night."

He continues to stare as if he's conversing with an alien.

"If you insist on staying then you can come in and eat with me." I extend the invitation knowing it's probably the last thing he wants to do.

Surprise plays over his face at my offer and now I'm surprised, too, because I sense indecision. Eventually he shakes his head. "It's dangerous. I shouldn't be around you. I'll wait out here for you to get your food and then I'll drive you home."

His eyes lock on mine and I search them for a long beat before I reply.

"Look, can I be honest? You're scaring me with all this 'dangerous' business. But unless you're going to tell me why,

I don't buy it. I don't sense any danger from you. Just the opposite in fact. I don't understand why we have to avoid each other—and I think it's wildly unfair that you won't explain it—but I can't make you, so I'll just have to accept it. Right now, though, I'm hungry. I've had a trying day and I'd like to sit down and eat at this restaurant. I'll feel rushed if I know you're out here waiting for me. So how about if we go inside and get some food? It's out in public, crowded with people—that doesn't seem dangerous to me. You can go back to keeping your distance tomorrow. In the meantime we'll just be two mates having dinner as your Australian brethren would say."

He smiles. "Is that how my brethren would say it?"

I smile back and shrug.

He stares at me, thinking. "Well I *am* hungry … and it'll give me a chance to hear about those self-defense moves you learned in your mum and me class."

"Very funny. It was a good class. If you try anything dangerous I may be forced to demonstrate on you."

"I think I might like that," he says with a smile.

My heart does a little flip at his words. Why does he do that? Half the time he's avoiding me and the other half he's giving me that smile that makes my knees weak. I decide to ignore his capriciousness for now and just enjoy myself. We walk into the restaurant and over homemade chips and salsa and spicy enchiladas, we end up talking and laughing for hours. I feel so at ease I can't believe we met only a week ago. He tells me stories about growing up in Australia and about his grandfather. His parents died when he was young and I share that my dad died, too, when I was ten. It still hurts to talk about. Alexander starts to say that he'd like me to meet his grandfather when he stops himself.

"Why can't we just be friends?" I ask. "Why is that so dangerous?"

He lets out a deep sigh and leans over the table, his eyes holding mine. "Declan, if it was possible for me to be around you and just be your mate, I would." He peers down at his folded hands. "But it's not." When he looks back up, his eyes are dark pools. "Not by a long shot."

The heat from his gaze makes my throat go dry. *Did he really just say that?*

Without another word, he lifts the check off the table and walks to the register to pay. I sit dazed as he comes back and lays down some cash for a generous tip. I'm still speechless as we walk out.

It's a short drive home and when I get out of the car I wait as he lifts my bike out of the back and parks it by the garage.

He walks me up the steps to the front porch and pauses before the door, setting my backpack down. For a long moment he just stares into my eyes. Regret colors his voice as he says "Bye, Declan."

"Why?" I say quietly. "Why does it have to be this way?"

He shakes his head. "It's the only way it can be. You have to trust me."

"I hardly know you."

"Then trust your heart," he says softly. He holds my gaze for a moment longer and then turns and walks away.

Trust my heart? My heart wants me to run after him and demand answers. But he's determined to stay away, and that's the bottom line. I feel utterly confused and forlorn because I don't understand anything that has happened and it's clear he isn't going to enlighten me.

My mom is waiting in the foyer when I walk in. She's obviously been peering through the blinds, watching us. "Who was that, sweetie? He looks like a Greek god for heaven's sakes," she says with girlish delight.

My mom is a romantic. She and dad met in college and he was the love of her life. She says he literally sparkled when she first saw him. I remember being embarrassed as a kid when I would catch them kissing all the time but inside I cherished the security of knowing they were in love and enjoyed each other's company so genuinely. I know she wants me to find that same kind of happiness with someone someday, but in this case she's barking up the wrong tree. Now that I finally like a guy—a lot—he apparently can't be around me for some reason that involves mysterious danger he won't explain. It all sounds so crazy when I think about it clearly. Maybe Alexander *is* dangerous—dangerously insane.

"He's just a friend from school, mom. He gave me a ride home."

"So that's who you were having dinner with when you called?"

I called her from the restaurant to let her know where I was so she wouldn't worry.

"Yeah, but seriously, mom, it's no big deal. We ran into each other and we were both hungry so we got some chips and salsa. We're just friends." Not *even* friends, actually. How much further away from friends can you get—let alone boyfriend and girlfriend—than avoiding each other completely?

"Well, I admit I was peeking a little," she says sheepishly, "and the way he was looking at you, sweetie, it didn't look like just friends to me—for either one of you."

Chapter Five

The next few weeks pass by more slowly than any length of time I have endured in my entire life. It's maddening to go to school every day and see Alexander keeping his distance from me while he's friendly with everyone else. Why isn't it dangerous to be around *them*? Part of me wonders if it was all a line and I'm a total chump. But the way he looks at me sometimes from across the room …*Trust your heart,* he said. I don't even know what that means. All I know is you can't make someone want to be with you if they don't want to—whatever the reason. As the weeks go by, our night at the restaurant seems distant and surreal. I'm beginning to think it never happened. What was I thinking anyway? Wanting to add a boyfriend to my life? Between school, work, babysitting, and volunteering at the shelter—not to mention dealing with my panic attacks—the last thing I need is more complications. Especially with "Mr. Dangerous."

I bury myself in keeping up my GPA, going on long runs, and serving up burgers at Jack's. Molly publishes the crime story Finn and I worked on for the school paper and we get a lot of great online comments. The story opens with a dramatic purse-snatching and rescue incident that I interweaved throughout to build suspense. I included other stories of campus victims of theft and I provided the latest information on the ring of thieves responsible along with a detailed list of crime-prevention tips. Finn took some great photos and he made a chart that illustrates how a person's vulnerability to crime decreases as they enact each safety measure. We also created a trend line that shows the recent spike in crime on campus and in San Mar as a whole. Liz told me she thinks it's one of the best pieces Finn and I have ever done together.

Speaking of Liz and Finn, they don't know what to make of me. I'm not my typical cheery self and I can't offer an explanation. I don't usually keep things from them but what would I say? "Alexander likes me but he says he has to avoid me because he's dangerous?" When you say it out loud it sounds like either he, or I, or both, are crazy. For that reason alone I should keep my mouth shut, but what if there truly *is* danger? Wouldn't it be better if Liz and Finn aren't involved?

I overhear them talking one day and they chalk up my melancholy to the long stretch of gray weather we've been having and a bad case of senioritis. Their explanation is better than any excuse I can come up with so I don't contradict it. And truth be told, it isn't all an excuse. I truly *am* sad this will be our last year together. Finn will probably be off to Stanford (or whatever school he wants, frankly), and Liz is a good bet for Stanford, too. Both of her parents went there and she's incredibly brilliant and accomplished. Our school's college counselor said that with my grades and test scores I have a chance at some top schools, too, but I don't see how we could afford it, even with financial aid. And if I'm being totally honest, my panic attacks weigh heavily, too. What if they get worse under the pressure of being at a four-year college far from home? I hope to go to UCSM but I may end up going to Cabrina, the local community college, and transferring later to save money. No matter what happens, I know Liz, Finn, and I will always be friends, but things will never be the same again and I'm going to miss them. That is a deep and honest truth.

We're at Surf Pizza having lunch and discussing the upcoming Winter Wonderland dance.

"So, are we going to go?" asks Liz. "Should we start looking for dates?"

I don't mention that I'm harboring a ridiculous fantasy that Alexander will be overcome with his feelings and ask me to the dance in spite of himself.

"Maybe we should all just go as a group," I suggest, "like we did last year."

"Okay, but Liz steps on my feet, so I'm dancing with you, Declan," Finn states with his usual bluntness.

"Is that so? Well you're too short for me anyway, Finn," retorts Liz, pretending to be offended.

Finn just shrugs and smiles. Liz is a smidgen taller than Finn and it's her go-to taunt whenever he says something insulting. Finn couldn't care less.

"I'll bet Scott Griffin is going to ask you again," I say in a singsong-y lilt to Liz.

"And I'll bet Ryan Dell is going to ask you-oo," she sings back. She smiles and sticks her tongue out at me. Scott and Ryan are boys that have liked us for years. They're both cute and nice enough but neither of us is really interested.

"I thought you were thinking about asking Serena," I say to Finn.

"Wait, is Serena the girl that you said you didn't know?" Liz asks Finn.

"That was *Selena*," I answer. Selena is a cute girl who approached Finn to say hello when we were walking downtown one day. He stared at her blankly so she reminded him they had taken a summer film class together. No matter how much additional information she provided, Finn insisted he did *not* remember her. I smoothed it over as best I could and after we walked away I explained what might have been a nicer way to handle it, but Finn said he didn't want to lie or pretend because he didn't even know she *existed* until she walked up and spoke to us.

Liz still looks confused.

"Have you suffered a blow to the head?" I say. "I'm talking about *Serena*—Finn's old girlfriend."

"*That* Serena? The girl he gave a twenty dollar bill to for Valentine's Day? Judging by her reaction, Finn, I don't think she'd be willing to give it another go after that."

"I still don't understand what was wrong with it," Finn argues. "I like to get money as a gift. The problem is with you NTs."

NT is short for neurotypical and it's the way Finn refers to people who don't have Asperger's or similar brain wiring (or what he calls NDs, for neurodiverse people). The world is full of NTs and NDs according to Finn, and neither group truly understands the other. The highest compliment I think he ever gave me was when he told me in elementary school that I was the best NT he'd ever met.

I throw my arm around his shoulders. "Oh Finn, you know we love you. But if we have to explain again why she was mad, I don't think it will ever make sense. I, however, as one representative of the female population, would like to say that I would be fine with a twenty dollar bill as a gift. I could put it toward my college fund.

"That's the funniest thing about the whole story. I would love to get money from a boyfriend. Then you can buy whatever you want," chimes in Liz, ever practical.

"Exactly," says Finn, feeling vindicated.

"You know, you two would actually be perfect for each other," I say jokingly to Liz. "Maybe you and Finn should go to the dance together as a couple."

I expect Liz to laugh but instead she blushes and then catches herself and coughs out a fake chuckle. Liz. Blushing. The two don't go together. Has she developed romantic feelings for Finn? After all these years as best friends I wonder if it's possible. It makes sense, though—they're like two opposite puzzle pieces that surprise you when they fit together seamlessly.

Finn, meanwhile, is oblivious and already on to the next topic, asking if we're ready for our upcoming chemistry test. He has no idea anything has changed between him and Liz. He isn't great at reading people. I'll have to talk with him later when we're alone.

Mrs. Bing calls early Saturday morning to ask if I can watch Charlie at noon. I have schoolwork to do and I was looking forward to a day off work, but she's desperate so I tell her of course I'll help. She thanks me profusely before hanging up.

I go for a long run, take a shower and I'm downstairs and ready to go at 11:45. My mom has already left for an open house showing.

I drive Archie over to the Bing's and as I pull up to the curb, Charlie is waiting for me outside.

"Declan!" he yells as he runs towards me. I get out and greet him with a giant bear hug.

"Hey little man," I say with a smile as I release him, "do you know you have a Cheerio stuck to your cheek?"

Charlie probes around his face with his chubby fingers until he feels the Cheerio. He plucks it off and pops it in his mouth with a satisfied grin.

"Declan," I turn to see Mrs. Bing striding toward me on the front lawn with her keys and a large tote bag in her hand. She's looks as if she's dressed to go sailing. "Thank you so much for coming on short notice."

"Mommy, can I go to the park?" Charlie asks.

"Sure, honey," she answers. "You can take him to the park for as long as you like," she says, turning toward me. "I'll be back this evening. Not sure what time. Can I text you?"

Charlie takes my hand and pulls in the direction of the park down the street. "C'mon Declan, let's goooo!"

I laugh and turn to Mrs. Bing as I'm being yanked away. "Texting is fine. Stay as late as you want. Have a nice time!"

I hope it will be a late night. I count my savings in thousand dollar increments to keep me motivated and I only need $132 more to make the next thousand. If Mrs. Bing's date goes well it could push me over the edge. That'll make up for having to cram all my homework in tomorrow after my shift at Jack's.

At the park, Charlie is having a great time running around the jungle gym and going down the slides. He makes friends with a little boy named Marky and they pretend to be dinosaurs, running around and hiding behind the many trees in the park and jumping out, trying to scare one another. Marky's mom and I chat on one of the benches as we watch them. Eventually, Marky has to go home and Charlie takes a break to tell me he's thirsty. We walk over to the water fountain and I notice he has something in his hand.

"What's that?" I ask.

"A toy." He holds it out to me. It's a small snow globe of a stark, black and white winter scene. A broken fence runs behind one leafless tree in the middle of powdery snow with a gray sky. Charlie shakes it and the snow disperses and then drifts down to settle on the ground again.

"Where'd you get it?"

"That man over there. He said he was your friend." He points and as I follow where his finger leads I feel as though I exit my body. Avestan is sitting on a bench on the other side of the park, watching us. He smiles and waves. I grasp the edge of the water fountain to steady myself as my heart pounds.

I take a deep breath and gently remove the snow globe from Charlie's hands, doing my best not to scare him. "I'm sorry, sweetie, but you know that we don't talk to strangers and we definitely don't accept gifts from them. We can't keep this. Please promise me you'll never talk to that man again— or any other stranger—without checking with me first. He's not my friend."

I brace myself for Charlie's reaction but he must sense my apprehension because he just nods quietly and says he's sorry.

I lock eyes with Avestan as I drop the snow globe into the garbage can next to us. "Okay, sweetie," I say to Charlie, "go ahead and get your drink and then stay right here. I'll be back in less than a minute."

Many people are milling around the park, giving me the confidence to do what I'm about to. Even so, I take my phone out of my pocket and hold it in my hand in case I need it. To call the police? Alexander? I'm not sure. I don't even have Alexander's number. I wait for panic to start tickling my throat but for some reason it doesn't come.

I stride over to where Avestan is sitting and stand before him.

"Declan, it was merely a peace offering. I think we got off on the wro—"

I cut him off before he can finish. "If you ever come within a mile of Charlie again, I'll have you arrested," I say with a fierceness I didn't know I had in me.

I spin around before he can answer and walk briskly back to where Charlie is waiting. He takes my hand and I challenge him to a race so we can leave quickly.

When we get to the sidewalk I congratulate Charlie for winning and I turn to look over my shoulder. The bench is empty and Avestan has disappeared. Above us, storm clouds are rolling in, blocking out the sun. An icy shiver runs through me and I squeeze Charlie's hand tight. We run the rest of the way home.

Chapter Six

On Monday after school, Finn and I are biking home together and I seize the opportunity to talk to him about Liz and the dance. It's a little over three weeks away.

"Finn, can we walk our bikes for a second? I want to ask you something."

He looks at me questioningly and stops. "What is it?"

"Have you ever thought about Liz as a girlfriend?" I figure I may as well dive straight to the heart of it like he always does.

"Liz Warner?"

I nod. As far as I'm aware it's the only Liz we know, but leave it to Finn to want to confirm exactly whom I'm referring to.

He stops walking. I can almost hear his brain synapses firing as he mulls over the idea, attempting to calculate a complete answer.

After a minute or so he starts ticking off pros and cons. "I like the way she thinks. She's intelligent and she usually has an interesting viewpoint. She's also pretty in an unconventional way."

He pauses and continues. "We have a lot of the same interests and I enjoy being around her, even when she hassles me. And she usually laughs at my jokes … she's pretty funny, too. And that's unusual because I don't always get NT humor."

His list of pros is growing and I'm smiling because I haven't heard any cons yet.

"She gives me a hard time sometimes but she never treats me different from anyone else. I like that. She's taller than me," he pauses, "but I don't really care. She gets pretty grumpy when she's hungry, but I guess I can deal with that, too."

I laugh.

He sums up his assessment. "I guess I would have considered it except that we're friends. I wouldn't ever want to ruin that."

I'm touched by the thoughtfulness of his answer. "What if I told you that Liz wanted you to ask her to the dance?"

"I thought we were already going to the dance together."

"We are. As a group. But what if you asked Liz to go with you as your *date*, and I just tagged along as a friend, like always?"

He turns that over in his mind. "Does she *want* me to ask her out on a date?"

"Yes, I'm pretty sure she does."

"Then why hasn't she said anything? I talk to her every day."

"Maybe she's worried you don't feel the same."

He digests that idea. Finally, he says matter-of-factly, "Thanks, Declan. I'll think about it. Is that all you wanted to talk about?"

I nod, bewildered. He hops back on his bike and pedals ahead.

What the—? I feel bad now that I even said anything. If Finn was thrilled then it would have been okay that I told him that Liz liked him. But now I'm not sure if he returns her feelings and I wonder if I betrayed Liz's private thoughts by saying something. Geez, I was expecting a happy ending, why doesn't it ever work out that way in real life?

The rest of the week passes excruciatingly slowly and then it's Thanksgiving break. We spend Thanksgiving with Finn and his family, as usual. I look forward every year to Mrs. Cooper's cornbread stuffing and my mom's sweet potatoes. After dinner Mr. and Mrs. Cooper pull out old photo albums of Finn and I through the years and we have some good laughs going through them. In one picture we're naked preschoolers in his backyard blow-up pool. So embarrassing. But we can't stop laughing because our moms remember Finn asked me that day what happened to my penis. Apparently I told him my dad was using it.

Liz is skiing with her family in Tahoe and I'm covering her weekend shifts at Jack's but I don't have to work on Friday so my mom and I spend the day watching movies and recovering from all the carbs we ate the day before. We briefly consider doing some Black Friday shopping but our inertia keeps us on the couch.

I run past Alexander's house before work Saturday morning on my regular loop to the beach and notice a gathering at his house again. My heart sinks as the exquisitely beautiful blonde I saw waiting for Alexander in the school parking lot emerges from a sleek, black Mercedes. *Blondie's in the book club, too?* I wave to Mrs. Frye, the librarian, as she walks to the front door. Alexander's car is in the driveway but I don't see him. By the time I finish my loop and run back, all the cars are gone except for Alexander's and Blondie's. Ugh.

The week after break, the town holds its annual fundraiser. This year the proceeds are earmarked for the library. The hope is to raise enough funds to refurbish the building and extend the hours the library is open. It's currently closed on Sundays and Mondays due to budget cuts. My mom's realty firm is sponsoring the fundraiser and there's a dinner and a silent auction as well as karaoke. The theme is the '80s (partly my mom's influence, I'm sure) and her firm is pledging to donate one hundred dollars for everyone who sings on stage.

Seats are assigned and Liz, Finn, and I are at a table with some other kids from school. It seems like the whole town has turned out. After dinner there are a few brief speeches and then the karaoke starts. Mrs. Frye, the head librarian, is the first to take the stage. She sings "Everybody" by Madonna and she's fantastic. Who knew she was a closet pop star? Each time she sings "Everybody come and dance and sing" she waves her arms to get people up from their seats. By the time the song is over the whole dance floor is full. It's turning out to be a lot of fun. My mom gets up on stage next with a bunch of realtors from her office and they sing "Celebration" by Kool and the Gang. It's actually pretty funny. I have to hand it to my mom for getting up there. She sings only marginally better than I do, but the whole group is singing together so I guess she figures who cares. She's had a few glasses of wine, too.

One by one, people get up on stage and some of them really surprise me. Chief Stephens has a deep baritone and he makes everyone laugh as he does his best Barry White. I've always known Jack can sing, but he and Al do a duet and they're great. Soon, kids from school are getting up on stage, too. Molly sings "Vogue" by Madonna and of course she's good—Malibu Barbie can do anything. After she comes off stage there's a break while they announce raffle winners. Molly walks over and taps me on the shoulder. "You're up next."

"Um, what?" I say. We're all sitting at our table talking.

"Your mom put you down next on the list," she says.

That can't possibly be true—even my mom sees (or rather hears) beyond the veil of motherly love and knows I'm practically tone deaf.

"Doesn't everyone want to hear Declan sing?" Molly announces loudly to the table.

Finn says "No," and everyone laughs.

I demur, strongly, but Molly won't let it go. "It's for charity. You can't say no. It's your mom's firm." She widens her appeal to the other tables around us. "Declan won't sing," she calls out. "C'mon everybody, tell her to get up there and make some money for the library!"

Soon she has the tables chanting my name. *Why is she doing this to me?* Does she realize I can't sing? She keeps encouraging everyone to get louder until I have no choice but to give in to make it stop.

I turn to Liz with terror in my eyes. She shrugs and gives me a quick hug around the shoulders. "Maybe it won't be so bad. Half the adults in here are drunk anyway."

"Will you do it with me?"

"Noooo way, señorita," she laughs. "Sorry, but I draw the line at karaoke. I think my voice is worse than yours … if that's even possible."

"Great. Thanks for the pep talk."

Molly tugs on my arm and the people around us cheer as I get up and walk towards my own personal Defcon-one-level nightmare. I've never sung karaoke in my life—I don't even know how this works. Will I get to choose the song?

As I make my way to the front I see Alexander watching from a table nearby. He flashes what I think is a supportive smile but I honestly can't tell if his expression signals amusement or sympathy.

Chief Stephens is announcing the last raffle winner as I approach the stage. Molly remains behind me to prevent me from bolting, which is exactly what I have in mind. Before I can act, though, the chief turns and beckons to me with an outstretched arm. "And now it looks like Declan Jane is going to lead the second round of karaoke," he proclaims as he waves me up the steps.

Oh dear God, this is worse than I thought. He hands me the microphone and it screeches for a second and then I'm left in silence as he leaves me alone on the stage. I feel all eyes on me as we wait for the music to start. My eyes dart to the video screen and my panic abates somewhat when I see that at least, thank God, I know the song: "Stop Draggin' My Heart Around" by Stevie Nicks.

The music starts and I must have a pained expression on my face because I already sense worry from the audience. As I begin singing the first verse, I see people averting their eyes from the train wreck unfolding before their ears. I attempt a weak apologetic smile but by the time I hit the second verse I'm certain everyone is begging for it to end as much as I am. There's a commotion at the back of the stage and I pray someone has taken pity on me and is unplugging the amplifier. I'm shocked, however, to see Alexander step up beside me with a microphone in his hand. He sings the next two lines that Tom Petty sang in the original duet.

We sing the chorus together. He's hamming it up and the audience starts cheering. He gives me a little shrug and a smile of solidarity. Suddenly I don't care that he's been avoiding me. I want to hug him I'm so grateful. We finish out the song to thunderous applause. I catch a glimpse of Molly as we laugh and bow and she doesn't look pleased.

As Alexander helps me off the stage, his hand touches mine and I feel that familiar charge between us. The second I'm safely down, however, he pulls his hand away and steps back.

I look up at him. "I don't know how to thank you. That could have gone down as a recurring nightmare for the rest of my life."

"Big Stevie Nicks and Tom Petty fan," he explains, pointing to himself with his thumbs.

I smile. "Oh, so you were saving the song rather than me? Does that mean you're still avoiding me?"

"Trying to … wait a minute, was that awful performance just a ruse to get me up there with you? Now I feel used," he teases.

I push his arm. "Thanks a lot. So I was really that bad? I hoped I was just being hard on myself."

"You *are* way too hard on yourself. But in this instance, let's just say that now we can safely cross off both acting *and* singing from your list of career possibilities."

I laugh and his green eyes crinkle with that smile that spreads over me like a warm sun.

"But, Declan," he continues, "you have so many other qualities to recommend that it hardly matters."

The sincerity in his voice and the way he looks into my eyes makes me forget we're standing in a room full of people. He's been avoiding me so long that I began to think I had imagined the stillness, the peacefulness, I always feel emanating from him, mixed with that familiar electric charge ... I hold his gaze to prolong the moment but we're interrupted far too soon.

"Alexander! Come over to our table. Suzie has something funny to show you," shouts Molly. As she takes his arm and leads him away, she calls out, "Nice job on the duet" to me over her shoulder. The words are kind but an undercurrent of malice stabs through every syllable.

"Thanks," I say. Then, impulsively, I add, "It was fun!" just to tick her off. Alexander waves apologetically as she drags him away.

Safely alone, I take a deep breath and slowly blow it out as I walk back to my table. How I made it through that whole ordeal without having a panic attack is a medical mystery. My inner drill sergeant whispers *"Nicely done, Jane,"* and gives me a rare soft pat on the back.

The day before the Winter Wonderland dance, Liz, Finn, and I are in the quad having lunch as usual. Everyone around us is discussing who's taking whom to the dance. With only 24 hours to go, I realize that my fantasy of Alexander asking me at the last minute is becoming less and less likely. I must have a seriously bummed look on my face because even Finn notices.

"You okay, Declan?" he asks.

"What? Oh, I'm fine. I'm just rethinking that microwave burrito I just ate," I say, playing it off.

"I warned you guys never to eat the food here," Finn replies, but he sounds distracted.

He opens his backpack and looks up at me with a strange expression on his face—a nervous expression. Curiously, he says, "Wish me luck," and reaches into his pack and pulls out a bright pink rose.

He walks over to Liz and gets down on one knee in front of her. He holds out the rose, clears his throat and begins to speak earnestly: "Liz, I know we're friends and I don't want to ruin that … but I think you're beautiful and smart and you make me laugh and we have a lot in common and I feel good when I'm around you. I don't know if you'd ever want to be with a guy like me, but I'm taking the chance. Do you want to go to the dance? As my date?"

Liz is standing with her mouth agape as if she can't process what's happening in front of her. I see behind her astonishment, though, and it's obvious what her answer will be. Finn can't see it yet and he quickly blurts out in a jumble,

"And if you're not interested, let's go back to being friends and please forget this ever happened."

Liz takes Finn's hand and pulls him up and kisses him before he can say another word. It's like a fairytale and people start clapping all around us. When they stop kissing and smile at each other, I can see that Liz's eyes are watery. An emotional Liz is a sight to see. I'm teary myself.

Finn, slightly oblivious as always, has to confirm, "So that's a yes?"

"Yes, Finn. Clueless, adorable Finn ... that's a yes," says Liz with a laugh before she grabs his face and kisses him again.

As I smile at them both I can't help but think how I love Finn for surprising us all like this—I didn't know he had it in him. He must have been planning it and memorizing his speech since he and I spoke weeks ago and he never let on. He has singlehandedly renewed my faith in happy endings.

The bell rings to signal lunch period is over and as we're gathering our things to head to class I overhear some girls chattering behind us about the dance. I'm listening vaguely—not fully tuned in—until I hear Alexander's name and my ears perk up. The rest of what they say feels like a sucker punch to the gut that thrusts all the air from my lungs.

"Did you hear that Alexander Ronin is going with Molly Bing?"

Chapter Seven

My crazy, hopeful balloon of a fantasy—that Alexander will ask me to the dance—has been popped unceremoniously and is now spinning on the ground, pitifully, as it loses all air. The idea of seeing him with Molly, of all people, is too much. I veer off from Liz and Finn as we walk, with the excuse that I have to go the bathroom. I truly think I'm going to be sick.

I've been had. There's no other explanation. How could he be dangerous to me but not to Molly? Why couldn't he just tell me he wasn't interested? Did he want to make a fool of me? *Well, mission accomplished jerkoff.*

How can I go to the dance now? I feel a slight pang of regret that I turned down Ryan Dell's invitation, but I remind myself it wouldn't have been right to lead him on. He deserves to go with a girl who returns his feelings and, although I like Ryan as a friend, I'm not that girl. Maybe I'll just stay home. Why torture myself when I don't have to? Liz and Finn would be disappointed, though … and it will be nice to see them together as a couple for the first time. Why should I let Queen B and Mr. "I'm dangerous" Australia ruin the dance for me? I told Liz and Finn I would go and I need to stick to our plans and have fun anyway. *"You can do this,"* concurs my inner drill sergeant. I push open the bathroom door with renewed determination and head to class.

Liz and Finn invite me to dinner with them before the dance but I beg off. I want to give them some time alone. It also gives me more time to decide what to wear. They plan to pick me up after dinner so we can drive to the dance together.

I'm laying out dresses on my bed when my mom walks up and stands in the doorway. "I always loved dances when I was in school," she says wistfully.

"Will you help me decide on a dress?"

"Of course, sweetie, you know how I love to help," she gushes.

"Okay, I've narrowed it down between these two." I hold up a simple silver sheath I wore as a bridesmaid in my cousin's wedding and a light blue chiffon cocktail dress with a fitted waist and fluttery cap sleeves. It's an expensive designer number that Liz's mom bought for her. Liz gave it to me because she said it didn't fit her right and she thought it would look good on me. She never even took the tags off.

"Try them both on for me, but I'm leaning toward the blue one, to match your eyes," says my mom.

I know she's going to tell me I look beautiful in both. My mom sees me through the fuzzy lens of mom eyes. I wonder if I should ask Liz and Finn for their opinions, too, when they arrive. On the other hand, what does it matter what I wear? Alexander is going to be there with Malibu Barbie and I'd have to show up naked to compete with that star wattage.

I try on the silver one first and spin around and we both think it looks nice. When I put on the blue one, even I have to admit I agree with my mom when she says emphatically, "That's the one, honey. It reminds me of Julie Andrews' dress in *The Sound of Music*."

I smile as I look at my reflection in the full-length mirror on my closet door. The dress fits me perfectly and the color brings out the natural honey highlights in my hair. I'm wearing my hair loose and wavy on my shoulders and I have to admit I feel very pretty in a casual, not-trying-too-hard way. That's exactly how I want to look tonight—carefree, without a hint to anyone that my heart is crushed inside.

My mom helps me pick out some shoes and I brush on a little blush, mascara, and lip gloss. I'm ready to go by the time Liz and Finn ring the doorbell.

Liz has on a silk, knee-length kimono dress. It's fuchsia-colored mixed with deep shades of blood orange, and it has clusters of tiny white and light pink flowers in a delicate pattern. A few butterflies are printed partially in front and partially behind the flowers to make it look as though they're flitting in and out. It's beautiful. She has her dark hair in an up-do with two porcelain chopsticks holding it in place. The hot pink stripe across her bangs matches perfectly. Finn looks very cute, as usual. He's wearing flat-front khakis that hang low on his hips with a dark belt buckled slightly off center and a long-sleeved, white dress shirt, open at the collar. His brown hair is mussed in his typical way. I wonder if Liz helped him get dressed. They look very cute together.

We all exchange compliments and my mom snaps a zillion pictures—she loves Finn and Liz as much as I do. She stands in the doorway as we walk to the car and yells out "Have fun!" as we pull away from the curb.

The festivities are well underway when we arrive. It's dark in the gymnasium and a large, glittery, disco ball (required by law, I suspect, at every high school dance) is spinning as it hangs from the ceiling. A D.J. is on a platform at the front of the room and music is blaring. Hundreds—maybe thousands— of reflective snowflakes are strung from the ceiling and down the walls. I have to admit, grudgingly, that Molly and her team have done a nice job with the decorations. To our left there's a winter scene photo backdrop with an old-fashioned sleigh to sit in for pictures. Liz and Finn have some photos taken together and then we all ham it up and have group pictures taken. Liz and I sit in the back seat of the sleigh looking terrified while Finn pretends to drive. We stumble out of the sleigh laughing when I notice Alexander standing near the refreshment table, watching us. He's alone. He smiles and raises his hand in a wave but I look away quickly.

My eyes scan the room for Molly. It's dark and there's a large crowd on the dance floor making it hard to see. He must be getting her a drink. I'm careful not to look in his direction again.

Liz and Finn ask if I want to dance and I tell them to go ahead and I'll join them later. They're holding hands and I can't help but smile as I watch them walk to the dance floor. I feel like getting something to drink but I don't want to run into Alexander, so I stay put and try to act casual as I scan the room again for Molly.

"You look beautiful," says a voice with a familiar accent. Alexander has sidled up beside me, startling me out of my feigned nonchalance.

"Thank you," I answer tersely. He has no business telling me I look beautiful when he's here at the dance with someone else. I face straight ahead as I answer, but out of the corner of my eye I sneak a more thorough look at him. He's wearing a slate gray suit and a crisp, white dress shirt, open at the neck. The suit fits his tall, athletic frame perfectly. With his dark, unruly hair and deep green eyes, he looks like he stepped out of a Gucci ad, for Pete's sake. He has no right to stand beside me looking like that. A familiar electric charge begins to build between us and I force myself to ignore it.

After an interminably long stretch of silence, he speaks again. "Are you mad at me, Declan?"

Am I *mad* at him? The nerve of this guy—I don't even know if mad is a strong enough word. I start running through a list in my mind of what I've been feeling: hurt, confused, disappointed, heartbroken. And, yes, *mad*: mad that he's been avoiding me for months; mad that he won't explain this mysterious danger that he probably made up anyway; and I'm *furious* that he's here with Molly … *Molly!* It's obviously safe for him to be around *other* people—just not me. And I'm really, *really* mad that he's standing here now, asking me if I'm mad, as if he has no clue how much he's toyed with my emotions.

All the frustration I've been feeling for weeks builds up until I'm seething inside, but I take a deep breath and I don't reveal a word of my inner thoughts. Why should I give him insight into what I'm thinking, when he won't give me any answers of his own?

Instead, I say tightly, "Where's Molly?"

"Molly?"

"Molly Bing. Your *date*? Shouldn't you be keeping tabs on her?"

"What are you talking about? I didn't come here with a date."

The news is welcome but confusing. "I thought I heard that you and Molly were coming together."

"She did ask me, but I told her I was going with a group of friends. I came with my Art History study group."

"So you're not together?"

"With Molly? No, Declan, she isn't my type."

He gazes at me directly and I search his eyes for the truth. "What is your type?"

"I think you know the answer to that." His voice is low and the look in his eyes makes my knees weak. He parts his lips as if to say something more and then hesitates. A slow ballad is playing and I can tell he's struggling with a decision. Finally, he holds out his hand. "Would you like to dance?"

We walk hand in hand to the dance floor as if in a dream and he puts his arms around me. As we slowly sway together, every nerve in my body is electric, in a heightened state of awareness. He pulls me against his chest, softly, and the magnetic charge between us holds me there. I never want this to end.

We dance to two more slow songs and when the D.J. switches back to faster fare we stay out on the floor. Finn and Liz join in, too, and we all start taking turns making up stupid-looking dance moves that everyone else has to copy. Soon it spreads and the whole floor is dancing ridiculously. My stomach hurts from laughing so hard. After another few songs we're ready for a break. Liz and I excuse ourselves to go the bathroom while the guys get our drinks.

"Okay, what is going on with you and Alexander? I'm detecting some serious vibes there," Liz says, conspiratorially, as soon as we're out of earshot.

"I don't know. I thought he was here with Molly but he's not. There's a bunch of stuff I haven't told you about, but I really like him. I've never felt this way about anybody before."

"Wait a minute ... Declan Jane finally fell for someone and you've been holding out on me? We are waaaay overdue for some serious girl talk, sister, and I expect you to spill *all* the beans. I have some things to share about Finn, too," she laughs. "Have I told you what a good kisser that little genius is? Who knew?"

"I'm so happy for you guys, Liz. I honestly get teary every time I think about it. You're perfect together."

"Oh, I luvs my sappy friend who cries at everything—even Hallmark commercials," Liz says teasingly as she throws her arm around my shoulder. "By the way, Finn told me what part you had to play in all this matchmaking business. I have to admit I was a little pissed off at first. But I know Finn would never have gotten it in a thousand years if you hadn't spelled it out for him, so I guess I'm grateful. How did you even know I liked him?"

"That day, when I said you two should go to the dance as a couple—you blushed. You never do that and I know you like a book my friend. It wasn't hard to put it together."

She smiles wide and kisses my cheek with a loud, overly-dramatic smack. "Thanks for being such a hopeless romantic and always looking out for me. I guess I'll have to forgive you for also being a complete buttinsky."

"I prefer 'matchmaker.' I just thank God it all worked out. When did you start liking him? Romantically, I mean."

"I don't know exactly. Sometime over the summer I just started seeing him in a different way. He's so smart and preppy and earnest and cute with that mussed hair and the way he talks, and that messenger bag he always has strapped across his chest." She smiles with a faraway look in her eyes. "And we have so much fun together. I started thinking, 'Why not?' But I honestly thought it was a crazy idea and I don't think I ever would have said anything. I figured the feeling would pass. But then it didn't." She looks up at me with surprise, her smile widening.

"I still can't believe you didn't tell me," I scold as we make it to the front of the line finally and she heads into an open stall.

When we get back to the table, Finn is standing alone with two drinks in his hands. "Where's Alexander?" I ask.

"He's dancing with Molly so he gave me your drink to hold."

Finn has no idea how devastating this news is to me and I try not to show it. I thank him for my drink and accept it with a shaky hand. I'm no longer thirsty.

Liz's eyes are sympathetic. "He's probably just dancing with her to be nice … right Finn?" She nudges him in the ribs but Finn just shifts to the right because he thinks she's elbowing for more room.

"All I know is, I was pouring you a drink and I turned around and they were holding hands and Molly was leading him to the dance floor. That's when he handed me Declan's cup."

I scan the floor until I find them. They're in the middle of the crowd but I can see Molly smiling up at Alexander as they dance to Maroon 5. She lifts her arms and twirls around suggestively in front of him. Alexander doesn't appear eager to be out there but he doesn't seem to be in agony either. He's smiling and dancing along with her. After a few more turns Molly moves in closer and entwines her fingers in Alexander's hair at the nape of his neck. Before I can fully register what I'm seeing, she leans in and they kiss. My heart stops mid-beat and freefalls through my body. I feel dizzy and turn away before I can see any more.

"I'm going outside for some air," I tell Liz quickly, my eyes stinging from holding back tears.

"I'll go with you," she says.

"No, I'm okay. I just want to be alone for a minute. It's stuffy in here."

"You sure?"

I nod. Liz didn't see the kiss. She and Finn were facing in the other direction, but I don't want to tell her because I know if I talk about it tears will start flowing and I won't be able to stop.

"Okay, but come find me if you want to go. Finn and I don't mind."

"What? That's crazy. I would never make you guys leave early." I try my best to sound lighthearted. Liz is already being so kind because Alexander is dancing with Molly. I couldn't bear to see the pity in her eyes if I told her the full extent of it.

I slip out one of the side doors and the blast of cold air that hits my face is just what I need. I take a deep breath, lean against the wall, and look up at the moon shining between the clouds. The vastness of the stars makes my problems with Alexander feel small and insignificant.

I look to my left and see a group of kids at the far corner under the streetlight. They're smoking so I slide further down the wall to make sure I stay upwind. I settle into a shadow where I can't be seen easily. I want to nurse my hurting heart in private.

I take a deep breath, close my eyes, and try to shut out the image of Alexander and Molly kissing when I hear an unwelcome voice.

"Would you like some answers?"

My eyes snap open to see Avestan step out of the shadows in front of me. Instinctively, I step into the light by the door and grab the handle.

"I'm not going to hurt you, Declan. I'm trying to help you," he says, enunciating each word slowly.

I look over my shoulder. The kids are still smoking at the corner but I keep my hand on the door nonetheless as I meet Avestan's eyes. He's immaculate, dressed all in black, as before, and I realize as I survey his face that he would be darkly handsome if he wasn't so menacing.

"Has Alexander told you *anything* about us?" he asks.

I don't answer. It's unsettling to hear him refer to Alexander and himself as "us."

"I'll take that as a 'no,'" Avestan says, reading the expression on my face. "But you must be curious?"

"I don't want any information from you," I hiss.

"Answers are answers, Declan, no matter who they come from." His voice is mellifluous, hypnotizing. "Don't you wonder how he knew my name? How he knew you were at the boardwalk that day? I've known Alexander a long time and I can tell you everything you wish to know. You only have to follow me."

"Follow you?"

"Follow me to somewhere quiet where we can talk."

Alarm bells are clanging in one part of my brain—the sane part I'm sure—but at the same time, I feel *lulled* somehow. I'm so curious. Alexander isn't telling me anything, so why not listen to someone who will?

I shake my head to clear it. "Why can't you just tell me now? Here?"

"This is going to be a long conversation, Declan. I'm sure you have many questions. It's noisy inside at the dance and out here it's cold. We can go somewhere public. The San Mar Diner is just down the street. Come with me and we'll go inside, get some warm tea, and I'll tell you everything you wish to know."

His offer of tea seems so civilized and harmless. And it's only a short walk to the diner …

"You start walking first and I'll think about following behind you." I'm shocked at myself for considering his offer, but I'm so utterly, *maddeningly* curious.

Impulsively, I hold up my phone and snap a picture of Avestan. I email it to myself with a subject line that says, "I went with Avestan to San Mar Diner." I figure it can act as insurance against Avestan trying anything and if worst comes to worst it will provide a timestamp and clue to the police. I send a quick text to Liz and Finn so they won't worry. I tell them I decided to go home and I didn't want to make them leave early so I had my mom pick me up. It's a white lie, but essentially true—I *will* call my mom and ask her to pick me up. Only it will be *later*, at the diner.

I fudge the truth a little to Avestan as well. "I just sent a picture of you along with your name and where we're going to my friends, so don't even think about hurting me."

"Declan, we obviously got off on the wrong foot. You'll see that I can be a friend. I can answer all your questions. You just have to be willing."

"Willing to what?"

"Willing to listen. Willing to come with me despite how Alexander may have misinformed you. You just have to be willing to come … *willingly*," he says as he starts walking down the hill. I follow a few steps behind. When he reaches the sidewalk, he turns and extends his hand to take mine.

"Are you willing to join me?" he asks.

I surprise myself by reaching out to take his hand.

"Declan, no!" The shout reverberates down the hill and startles me out of my trance. Alexander speeds toward us in a blur. "Stop!" He's beside me in an instant and he pushes Avestan away. "I don't know what game you're playing, Avestan, but it ends here. This is between you and me. It has nothing to do with Declan," he growls.

"It has more to do with her than you think I realize, doesn't it?" taunts Avestan. "Look at her! Declan wants answers, Alexander, and it seems I'm the only one prepared to give them to her. She came with me willingly."

"Is that true?" he asks me with horror in his eyes.

"Maybe … I don't know … I couldn't help myself. You won't give me answers to anything, and he said he would, and you told me you were dangerous. I honestly don't know what to believe, Alexander, and frankly I don't understand why you care anyway!" The image of him kissing Molly sears into my brain.

Alexander stares silently with a confused and pained look in his eyes.

"I still don't hear him offering to explain anything to you, Declan," says Avestan. "Why not come with me and find out the truth?" He extends his hand to me again.

Alexander's fist connects with Avestan's jaw before I even see his arm move. There's a loud crack and a bright white flash of light at the point of contact. Avestan flies several feet and lands on his back on the sidewalk. He's up in an instant. He grabs his jaw, which is jutting oddly to the side, and slides it back into place. *Am I dreaming?* He walks purposefully toward Alexander with an evil intensity that makes me shudder. He strikes Alexander's chest and I hear a sickeningly loud, fleshy crack and, again, I see a flash of light, darker this time, at the point of contact. Alexander is propelled at least a hundred yards through the air but he rolls onto his feet instantly and he's back on Avestan in seconds. I can't believe what I'm seeing. They trade punches back and forth at a frenetic pace and the sound of cracking bones grows louder with each new assault. The flashes of light are now nearly continuous. They're both getting seriously hurt and I'm terrified and starting to panic. We're far enough down the hill from the school that no one can see or hear us.

"Stop!" I cry, tears of anguish streaming down my face. "Alexander, I don't want any answers. I don't care! I just don't want you to get hurt! Please just stop. I won't go with Avestan. Ever. I promise. Please just STOP!"

Alexander and Avestan freeze mid-strike and stare at me, their eyes wide. They're looking above my head and I instinctively look up but don't see anything. When I look down I catch a flash of shimmery white light around my hands but it's gone before I can be sure. *Is this what it means to see stars?* I expect to awaken in a hospital bed at any moment.

Alexander runs to my side and puts his arm around me, hugging me close. His face and body are battered and misshapen but, as I watch, everything swollen shrinks back and settles into place the way it should be, like time-lapse photography of a healing wound. The same thing is happening to Avestan as he stands up and brushes off his coat.

That's it. I'm dreaming.

"This isn't over," Avestan says with deadly determination. Silent fingers of fog swirl slowly around his feet as he turns and walks away.

Alexander looks into my eyes for a long beat. "We need to talk."

I stare at him in a daze, still expecting to wake up at any moment.

"Are you okay?" he asks.

I nod.

"Can I take you home?"

I nod again and he takes off his jacket and puts it around me as we walk to his car. He's silent, deep in thought, during the drive.

I assumed he was taking me to *my* home, but he pulls into his driveway on the corner and comes around to open my door.

"This okay?" he asks.

I nod. I'm equal parts confused, curious, and convinced I'm actually still passed out on the sidewalk at school. As we go inside and close the door, a distinguished-looking older gentleman steps into the hallway from the kitchen and calls out, "How did the dance go?" He startles when he notices Alexander isn't alone.

Alexander quickly introduces us. "Edwin, this is Declan. Declan, this is my grandfather, Edwin." Surprise (*or alarm?*) flashes in Edwin's eyes when Alexander says my name.

I hold out my hand, "It's nice to meet you, Mr. Ronin."

He quickly regains his composure and answers with a reassuringly tight squeeze. "It's a pleasure. Please call me Edwin."

He raises an eyebrow in Alexander's direction, and Alexander quickly ushers me down the hall. "Declan, let me show you to my room while I talk with Edwin for a minute."

Why is he calling his grandfather by his first name? Is it an Australian custom? When we reach his room, Alexander asks if he can get me anything. I assure him I'm fine and he says he'll only be a few minutes. The door remains open a crack when he leaves, enabling me to hear bits and pieces of their conversation in the kitchen down the hall.

"Why did you bring her here?"

"Edwin, I have to tell her."

"What? Why?"

There's a long, muffled reply that I can't understand.

"This is highly dangerous ... I don't ... you've gotten yourself into, Alexander. Unprecedented."

"You saw her, Edwin. Everything about it ... it's all unprecedented."

"Avestan saw it, too?"

"Yes... he's threatening to tell her about us ... he'll twist the truth ... convince her ... and follow him. She'll be ... forever."

"Are you sure about this? Can she be trusted with the truth?"

"I think so …. Yes, I *know* so."

There's a long stretch of silence.

"So you agree?"

"… don't see what choice we have. But I saw the way you looked at her … putting yourselves … grave danger, Alexander. You cannot … your …vow."

I can't make out the rest and a minute later I hear footsteps coming down the hall so I run over and sit down on the edge of the bed.

Alexander opens the door slowly and closes it behind him before he walks over and sits down beside me. We turn to face each other and he takes my hands in his and looks into my eyes for a very long time.

Finally, with a heavy sigh, he says softly, "I'm ready to tell you everything."

Chapter Eight

"I don't need you to tell me. I won't listen to Avestan," I say as I look into his worried eyes. As much as I desperately crave answers, I don't want him to tell me until he's ready—not forced—to share it. I'm also concerned, and a little frightened, about what I overheard. I don't want to put anyone in danger, myself included.

"I want to tell you. You deserve answers. And with everything you've seen now, it's more dangerous for you not to know what's at stake," he says softly.

After a long pause he looks down, nervously. "I don't know quite where to start."

Whatever it is that he's about to say, his nervousness is making *me* more nervous by the second. "Maybe you could tell me how you know Avestan?" I suggest.

"Okay. How shall I put this." He takes a deep breath and meets my eyes. My stomach flutters anxiously.

"We're guardians," he says, finally. "Well, Avestan is more like the opposite of a guardian, but Edwin and I are guardians."

"Guardians?"

"Guardian spirits would be a more accurate way of putting it," he elaborates reluctantly.

"Spirits? You mean as in ghosts?" I'm starting to wonder if Alexander and his grandfather are both a little nuts.

"No. More like spirits as in energy … *angels*," he says, searching my eyes to read my reaction.

"You're saying you're my guardian angel?"

"Yes. But we're guardians to all. Not just one person. We go where we're most needed."

I nod slowly, my eyes wide. It all sounds perfectly insane and I consider thanking Alexander very much for the information and then carefully and politely leaving because he's obviously a lunatic.

But then I remember what I saw earlier … he and Avestan healed themselves before my eyes and the power behind their punches was frightening. And what were those flashes of light? I decide to keep asking questions. "If you're a guardian, what is Avestan?"

"He's a dark guardian." He pauses. "This is hard to explain."

He thinks *this* part is hard to explain? How about every other crazy thing he's said so far?

"There's a balance of energy in the world," he continues. "Good and evil have always been inextricably bound. Avestan has embraced darkness and he and others like him are trying to tip the balance."

"So he's a *dark* angel?"

"Yes, you could call it that."

"And you and Edwin are good angels?"

"Yes," he smiles, looking relieved.

"And there are more good angels like you?"

"Yes, many more." He smiles again. "The balance has always favored the good."

"Are they all Australian?"

He looks at me wide-eyed and then bursts out laughing. I feel like an idiot, but how I love his laugh. When he collects himself, literally wiping tears from his eyes, he answers. "No, we come in all kinds—but I love that you asked. I needed that. I didn't realize how nervous I was to tell you all of this."

"Guess you'll have a good one to share at the next angel meeting," I say dryly.

He nods with a smile.

"You actually *have* meetings?"

"Yes," he laughs, "once a fortnight."

I nod, silent, taking it all in. *This guy is definitely cray-cray.*

"I know how all this must sound to you."

I nod again, slowly. He doesn't know the half of it.

After a pause he asks, "Do you have any more questions?"

Do I have any more questions? Is he serious? He thinks he can just tell me he's an angel and we're done? My mind is reeling and I'm still trying to decide if he's insane. On the off chance he isn't, I continue probing for more information.

"How old are you?"

"Nineteen in this body. But I've existed far longer."

"How much longer?"

"I've lived many lifetimes."

"Are you saying you're dead?"

He shakes his head. "Energy never dies."

"So after we die, we become angels?"

"Sometimes. All energy lives on in some form."

"How do you become an angel, then?"

"Those who are ready—usually after many lifetimes—have gained the wisdom to be realized as guardians."

"So everyone becomes an angel, eventually?"

"Not everyone, no."

"Where do dark angels come from?"

"Some are fallen guardians. But most, like Avestan, choose their path rather than continuing the cycle of mortal lifetimes."

"Why?"

"Dark energy is a powerful force and some can't resist."

"If you're a good angel, then why did you say it was dangerous for me to be around you?"

"If Avestan knew I cared for you, it would draw him to you. He and I ... have a complicated history. I didn't want him to focus on you because I didn't want him to see."

"See what?"

"Your special qualities."

Okay, now I know he's out of his mind.

"You're an empath, for one," he states matter-of-factly.

"A what?"

"You know those anxiety attacks you have?"

Oh my God, he knows about those?

"They're not what you think," he explains. "Empaths are sensitive to energy fields—they absorb the energy of those around them. It's indiscriminate, but I can teach you to control it. You feel panic when you're surrounded by strong negative energy from someone nearby ... especially when there isn't enough offsetting positive energy from others to temper it. It's like being assaulted. It's a natural reaction for you to run away to fend it off and recover."

I'm reeling from what he just said. It sounds so simple. Can it be true? It *does* feel like being assaulted. I think back to some of my recent panic attacks ... I felt that girl's deep despair at the bus stop and I knew in my gut that her boyfriend was lying. The first day of school when I was alone in homeroom and Molly sat behind me I felt like I was drowning in black ink. *Why does she hate me so much?* As I mentally run through every panic attack I can remember, I realize Alexander may be right. My mom always said that I have an uncanny ability to pick up on people's moods. I just didn't realize I was literally picking them up.

"Okay, let's say I believe you. But how does being an empath count as a special quality? It doesn't sound like a good thing."

"Well, I know it doesn't always feel good. And I can help you with that—to manage it so you're not at the mercy of negativity around you. But it means you can sense *good* energy, too, and it makes you who you are, Declan. You're sensitive and able to see the beauty in others that most people miss. Look at your friendship with Finn—you feel his true heart and not the blunt comments and missed social cues that most people tend to get hung up on. You're kind and you're able to see through people's shells, into their souls. That's a rare and beautiful gift."

I'm touched by his words. It's like my whole world has stopped and pivoted as I consider for the first time in my life that maybe I'm not broken.

"But that's not your only special quality."

"There's more?"

"You have no idea," he says, smiling. "I could go on for days."

The utter sincerity in his voice takes me by surprise.

"You have one quality, in particular, that I didn't want Avestan to see. You have a pure aura."

My eyebrow lifts questioningly.

"Everyone has one. You can't see them, but guardians can. I've never seen an aura like yours before on a mortal."

"What do you mean? What do they look like?"

"It depends. They reflect the energy of each person. Your power as an empath allows you to sense auras without seeing them."

"Are you saying you can just look around and tell good people from bad people by looking at their auras?"

"Not exactly. It's rare that anyone is all good or all bad. Most people are still learning what's essential. Also, auras fluctuate. From a distance they reflect superficial mood changes and reactions to circumstances. You don't see the true richness of an aura until you've made a connection with the person. I saw your true aura the first time we talked. When you told me why you stood up to the Trunchbull and then you nearly slipped in your sandals as you walked away." He looks into my eyes and smiles at the memory.

I blush, embarrassed.

"Declan, you were so beautiful when you spoke to me that day, I felt like I'd been hit by a thunderbolt. You opened my heart again to how purely good mortals can be. You looked like a magical pixie come to life out of a storybook."

"Because I'm small?"

"No, because you're beautiful—inside and out. And *otherworldly*. Your aura was so bright I wondered how everyone around us couldn't see it."

I search the sincerity in his eyes, at a loss for words.

"Declan, you're so beautiful … and you have no idea. You wear your heart on your sleeve and you feel things so deeply. It's what makes you tear up even when you don't want to."

"I hate that I do that. How do you know that about me?"

"Declan, I *see* you."

Something about the way he says the words makes my eyes well up. As if he's peering straight into my soul and I feel understood and accepted, and *known*.

"Can you see it right now?" I ask softly.

He nods and smiles. "It's a bright white-blue light emanating out all around your body. It's vivid and it's beautiful."

He sounds awed and his expression is sweetly sincere. I smile, not knowing what to say. He sees me so differently than I see myself.

"So your aura is your soul?"

"And your body is your shell," he says, completing my thought. "It's just a picture for the world—nothing more. Your picture is just like your aura, by the way. It's beautiful, too."

The way he makes me feel when he looks at me that way ... can he really be an angel? "What does your aura look like?" I ask.

"Guardians' auras are bright white and immaculately pure. In our essential form, we're only energy. Our aura *is* us."

I nod, taking it all in. No wonder I always feel so good around him. I can tell by the way he's choosing his words that there must be far more to it probably—beyond understanding. Human understanding, anyway.

"Why did you shout 'no' tonight when you saw me talking to Avestan?"

"Let me ask you something, did you feel a pull? Like you were going along with Avestan's suggestions and you weren't sure why?"

"Sort of ... I remember thinking that everything he said sounded reasonable."

"His energy was drawing you in. If he could convince you to ignore your misgivings and take his hand, *willingly*, it would have been an acceptance. He could have destroyed all the good inside you, Declan. Some dark angels turn easily-influenced people one by one, but others, like Avestan, take their time. They look for those with the strongest, brightest energy and either turn them or extinguish them. For dark energy to triumph, the balance has to shift, person by person and town by town. Eliminating even one person—if it's the right one—can start a ripple effect. With an aura like yours, you must be close to being realized, and that's a very powerful thing."

"Being realized?"

"Yes, becoming a guardian."

"So if I went with him I would have become dark, like Avestan?"

"Worse. You would have been left in an empty place for eternity, forbidden to guardians and out of my reach. Your essence would be gone … it's not something I want to think about."

"I don't understand why he wants me—how *I* could make a difference."

"Everyone makes a difference. The balance is always close. Dark energy has risen and fallen through millennia and good and evil have always struggled for supremacy. It's happening now, all over the world. Many places have already tipped. Our job is to fight against it and make sure it doesn't spread."

"So you were sent to protect me?"

"We were sent to protect San Mar. To bolster and defend our majority here. We go where we're needed. Other guardians do the same. I gravitated towards your energy quickly."

"And Avestan was sent to destroy me?"

"Yes. Or he followed me here, but I suspect he would have found you anyway."

"Why?"

"Your energy. Avestan and the others like him seek to destroy the brightest lights and spread darkness among the rest. They turn people, inciting them to look out for themselves at the expense of others and focus on greed and power, intolerance and differences. The truth is, we're all the same, we're all connected, and we're all energy. There are no divisions. When mortals establish hierarchies that raise one group over another based on beliefs, gender, race, or anything else, they're missing the essential perfection of the universe. Dark energy can twist positive teachings and make people do hateful, evil things in the name of what they convince themselves is good."

"How?"

"To paraphrase Hemingway, 'Gradually, then suddenly.' A dark angel's influence starts small and eventually takes over."

"It sounds bleak."

"It can feel that way, but when mortals look to their better angels, as they say, there's always one around. Even small positive actions can spur virtuous circles that help maintain the balance."

I nod slowly. I have so many more questions but I feel exhausted. What I want to ask next seems silly in comparison to the weighty issues we've been discussing but I have to know.

"Are you in love with Molly?"

The surprise on his face is genuine. "What? No. Why would you ask that?"

I look down and answer quietly, "I saw you kissing her. That's why I left the dance."

He gently places his finger under my chin to tilt my head up. "I want to make sure you see my eyes when I tell you I was *not* kissing her," he says sincerely. "I agreed to dance with her to be nice and before I knew what was happening she leaned in and kissed me. I stopped it immediately. If you had stayed you would have seen that part."

I search his eyes and can see he's telling the truth. "She's so beautiful, though."

"Maybe, but her aura reveals her true self. You must feel that when she's around."

"I thought it was just me. She hates me for some reason."

"I've been trying to help her."

"Help her how?"

"Change her heart. See what's really important. Sometimes people get caught up in themselves and they're hurting and they end up being destructive. To themselves and others. But everyone has the potential to change … and learn. When you're around her, you *feel* her aura rather than seeing it. Next time we're out you can practice guessing auras. I think you'll be surprised by how much you pick up."

I smile at his words. Not only did he confirm he doesn't love Molly, but he also said "next time we're out," which implies he won't be avoiding me any longer. Before I can stop myself, another question spills out.

"How come you haven't kissed me?" *Oh God, did I really just say that out loud?*

A surprised expression plays over his face and I immediately flush scarlet. He smiles and tilts his head to the side before answering. "It isn't because I haven't *wanted* to, if that's what you're thinking." His voice is low and the look in his eyes is very convincing. "It's because I can't. *We* can't. Relationships between guardians and mortals are strictly forbidden."

"But you kissed Molly."

"*She* kissed *me*. But either way it doesn't matter because it didn't mean anything. I don't care for her. But with you, it *would* mean something." He pauses before continuing as if he's not sure how much he wants to reveal. Finally, he repositions his hold on my hands and looks into my eyes. "I can't kiss you, Declan ... because I think I'm falling in love with you."

I stop breathing. This can't be real.

"You ... love ... me?" My voice croaks and disappears into a whisper as I try to form the words.

"Declan, what I feel for you is more powerful than anything I've felt over all my lifetimes," he says with simple, heartfelt sincerity. "Your soul speaks to mine."

As I gaze into his eyes it's as if a small string of light flows from his heart to my own. I realize in this moment that it's been there all along and I don't think I could bear it if the connection was ever severed. "I don't understand ... then why have you been avoiding me?"

"When I first saw your aura that day, I told Edwin. He could tell by the way I spoke of you, and continued to speak of you, that something was different and I was in danger of getting involved. He assigned someone else to protect you but I insisted I could do it. I know best how to protect against Avestan. Edwin relented as long as I promised to stay detached. I agreed, but it was more difficult than expected. I was drawn to you—I *am* drawn to you. After our night at the restaurant I resolved to stay away completely but I couldn't help myself at the fundraiser ... or keep from dancing with you tonight."

I'm floored by his admission. He's an angel? And he's been avoiding me because he's falling in love with me? I feel as though I'm Alice, down the rabbit hole, and down is up and up as I knew it no longer exists. As he searches my eyes for a response, I stand up, overwhelmed, and pace to the other side of the room. When I turn around, my back to the wall, Alexander walks over and gently takes my hands in his.

"What would happen if we kiss?" I ask, looking up into his eyes.

"If a guardian and a mortal fall in love and act on it, the guardian loses immortality and becomes a fallen angel." He pauses before continuing. "And the mortal loses their life."

"All because of a kiss?"

"It's not the kiss, it's what it represents."

"What does it represent?"

"A return to earthly desires and connections, a mixture of energy states …"

"How often does it happen?"

"It doesn't. No guardian has fallen for a mortal before."

I gaze into his eyes, disbelieving.

"Even if it wasn't forbidden, it would be dangerous. Guardians are far stronger than mortals. If I ever … if *we* ever …" His voice trails off and I feel that familiar charge forming in the air around us. All I can think about is doing the one thing he just told me we must not do.

"We can never kiss?" I ask, my voice almost a whisper.

He shakes his head slowly, his mouth silently forming the word, "no."

As I lose myself in his gaze, the electricity between us builds, tangible. After a long beat, he tilts his head to the side and a sly glint forms in his eyes. "But if we *could* kiss, this is what I would do."

His voice is low as he starts off slowly. "I'm holding your face in my hands as I gently kiss your forehead."

I smile, besotted, and he continues.

"I trail light kisses down the side of your face to your cheek. I keep moving down, slowly, but I avoid your mouth—I'm coming back to that later—and I kiss your neck and gradually move over to your ear, tugging softly. You feel the heat of my breath on your skin and your lips part—just like they are now—as you let out a soft sigh. I like that, and I desperately want to kiss your lips, but I wait."

I swallow nervously and return his heated gaze as he continues.

"I lift you up against the wall and lean in as you wrap your legs around me. I kiss your mouth, hungrily, and you hold me to you, your fingers entwined in my hair. I feel your tongue, exploring, and you taste even better than I imagined."

Oh my *God*. I lean against the wall to stay standing because the bones in my legs have melted away. His lips are so close we're almost touching and the electricity between us is indescribable. Forget the consequences—I've never wanted to kiss anyone so desperately in my life. I don't think I can take much more but I don't want him to stop.

"Alexander?" A loud knock at the door brings us back to reality.

Alexander releases a deep breath and reluctantly drops my hands. He walks over to his bedroom door, opens it a crack and says, "Yes?"

I blow out a jagged breath of my own, still recovering. My God, if he can do that without even touching me then maybe he's right—we shouldn't ever kiss.

Edwin ignores Alexander's tone and gently pushes the door open. "It's getting late and you and I still need to talk some more. You should walk Declan home soon."

I look at my phone and see that it's after midnight. I realize how utterly exhausted I am. My mom expected me to stay late at the dance but I check my messages to make sure she isn't worried. Good—she hasn't called. Alexander starts to protest to Edwin but I walk over and gently put my hand on his arm to stop him. "It's okay," I say. "It's later than I realized and I should get home before my mom worries." I look up at Edwin. I'm so tired I don't even bother to study him with fresh eyes now that I know he's an angel. "Thank you for having me over, Edwin. It was very nice meeting you and I hope to see you again."

Alexander walks me to the door. He grabs one of his jackets on the way out and wraps it around my shoulders. With his arm around me, he holds me close as we walk down the street to my house. When we get to my door, we stand and face one another. My head is still reeling from everything he told me and I don't know what to say, so I go with what's in my heart.

"Your soul speaks to mine, too," I say softly, my voice cracking a little.

He hugs me close, resting his chin on the top of my head. After a while he bends down and I feel the heat of his breath in my ear as he whispers, "To be continued."

Chapter Nine

A light is on in my mom's room and I know she's probably waiting up for me so I knock softly on her door.

"Mom?" I peek in.

She has a book on her chest, but her eyes are closed and she's breathing softly and evenly. I walked over and gently pull the book from under her hands and place it on the nightstand with a bookmark to hold her place. She stirs and asks sleepily, "Did you have a good time at the dance, hon?"

"Yes, mom," I say as I lean down to kiss her on the cheek. She smiles and mumbles, "That's good, 'night sweetie." I turn off the light on her nightstand and tiptoe out of the room.

I brush my teeth and get undressed. I'm overwhelmed. I don't think I'll be able to sleep with all the thoughts swirling in my brain but I must be out when I hit the pillow because the next thing I know sunlight is peering through the cracks in my blinds and my alarm clock shows 9:17 a.m. I haven't slept this late in years. As I wrestle with what day it is and what time I have to be at work, I wonder if last night was all a dream. Guardians, dark angels, Alexander in love with me … it all seems perfectly ridiculous in the light of day. But I saw those flashes of light when Avestan and Alexander were fighting. And they both healed within seconds. I forgot to ask Alexander about that. I have so many questions and his answers last night just created more.

I'm an empath. That memory makes me smile. If it's true, I finally have an explanation for the anxiety that has plagued me my whole life. The relief I feel is a revelation. My thoughts hop and skip from one recollection to the next and I'm overwhelmed as I try to take it all in and reconcile it with the world I assumed I knew. I look at the clock again. I have to be to work at eleven but I want to go for a run to clear my head. If I leave quickly I can run for at least an hour, take a fast shower, and still get to work on time.

I hop out of bed, brush my teeth, and throw on my running clothes. It feels good to have a plan.

My mom has already left for work. There's a note on the kitchen counter with a big smiley face and a bunch of question marks that says "Can't wait to talk!" Hmmm. I'm out the door and take my usual route—a loop through the neighborhood and to the cliffs along the water. Focusing on my pace and being in the outside air is already helping to clear my head. When I get to the ocean I decide to take my shoes and socks off and get my feet wet. I love running barefoot on the sand. As I make my way along the water's edge I revel in the uneven roughness and the way the water squeezes out in circles as the sand yields to my footfalls. After a while I stop to face the water and let the frothy cold lap up and bite my toes. That's one thing about San Mar—the water isn't very warm, even in the summertime. When it's really hot out, escaping into the icy surf is bearable, even refreshing. But I can never stay in for too long. Kids don't care, of course. Whether it's 90 degrees in the shade or a cool day, they hurtle in without a thought, their skin bright red from the cold as they bounce up and down in the waves. Brave (or maybe crazy) adults do also, but the serious surfers always wear wetsuits. Finn and Liz swear by just going for it and diving into a wave, but I subscribe to the belief that the key is to go in gradually, getting each body part accustomed to the cold before you dip in another. My feet are almost numb and I move forward a little more to let the water lap up higher around my ankles. It feels good and I close my eyes and turn to face the sun peeking through the clouds.

A few minutes into my silent meditation I hear the unmistakable sound of feet pounding on wet sand and I look up to see a figure running toward me at an incredible pace in the distance. To my surprise, the blur becomes Alexander and he's at my side faster than seems possible.

"What are you doing here?" he asks accusingly.

Part of me wants to tell him it's none of his business because of the way he's asking, but the other part of me is so distracted by his appearance, I'm not sure if I can form words. He's wearing a pair of board shorts and nothing else. His sculpted shoulders and muscular arms and chest are tan and smooth and his swim trunks hang low on his hips, revealing the toned "v" beneath his abs. His dark hair is tousled and wet, and his skin is glistening as if he's been for a swim. He's staring at me with those deep green eyes of his waiting for an answer.

"I'm just going for a run," I manage to squeak out.

"Don't you remember what we talked about last night? Avestan is dangerous, Declan, and you're his target."

"You said I had to go with him willingly and I would never do that now."

"It's not that simple. He has ways to get around your defenses that mortals find hard to resist."

"I think I could resist," I say dryly.

Alexander stares, unamused. "This isn't a joke, Declan."

"What am I supposed to do then? Never leave the house because a dark angel is after me? I have to go to school and work, and I like to run by the ocean, and do a million other things that are part of living my life."

"I'm not saying you can't live your life," he says, softening, "but you need to be more cautious and let me protect you for a while—especially now that we're going to be spending so much time together."

"Protect me how? Wait … what? We are?"

"Yes," he says with a smile, "if you want to … but being with me only makes you more of a target for Avestan so we have to come up with a plan and some ground rules."

"I do want to, but I'm not sure I understand. I thought we couldn't?"

"The thing is, I've tried staying away from you and it doesn't work. So I want to try something new … if you want to. We can't kiss—that won't change—but I'd like to stop all this agony of trying to avoid you." He lets out a sigh of surrender and continues, "I just want to *be* with you, Declan. Always. I know it's not perfect, but it's the best I can offer."

"Are you saying you want me to be your girlfriend?" I say the words mostly just to hear them aloud.

"More than you can imagine."

I smile so wide my cheeks are in danger of splitting.

"Is that a yes?"

I nod, still smiling. *Can this be real?* So much has happened in the last 24 hours it's hard to take it all in. Alexander grins back, his green eyes crinkling in that irresistible way, and as my mind starts to drift dreamily, thoughts of work somehow break through the haze. "Oh! Shoot," I say with alarm as I check my watch, "I need to be to Jack's at eleven."

"My car is here. We'll have heaps of time if I drive you home. I can drive you to work, too, if you want. We can talk about ground rules in the car."

As we start walking along the shore, a thought occurs to me. "If you're so worried about protecting me, what are you doing down here at the beach?"

"I went by your house this morning and your mum said you were still sleeping so I thought I'd get a swim in."

I stop in my tracks. "You went by my house and talked to my mom?" That explains the note on the counter with the giant smiley face and question marks.

He nods. "She was very nice."

"What did you tell her?" I need to know what I'm in for when she asks me later about the Aussie god who came by looking for me.

"I introduced myself and told her I was at the dance with you last night and I was wondering if you were available for breakfast."

Oh my God. She's going to be peppering me with questions for hours. "Did you go looking like you do now?"

He looks down at himself. "I had my boardies on, if that's what you mean. But I had a t-shirt and thongs on, too—I'm not a barbarian."

"Thongs?"

"I think you call them flip flops," he answers with a grin.

I give up. I'll have to contend with my mom later. I notice he's still dripping wet. "Aren't you cold? The water's freezing."

"Aye, but it feels good. Reminds me what it means to be mortal."

I wrap my arms around myself and shiver. "Too cold for this mortal," I say and immediately regret it.

With a gleam in his eye he reaches down and scoops me up. "You sure about that?"

He runs into the ocean with me in his arms, splashing in up to his waist. I scream and protest as he pretends to hurl me in. My arms are around his neck and I nuzzle my face into his chest as he kicks up water to splash me. My lips graze against him and I taste the salt on his skin. Finally he relents, carrying me to shore and setting me down. I grab my shoes and socks that I left behind and balance on one foot, trying to brush off the sand caked on my feet.

"No time for that," he says, and he bends down to scoop me up again, this time over his shoulder. He runs across the beach as I hold on, bouncing against his wet back, laughing. When we make it to his car, he slowly slides me down the front of him until my feet touch the ground. His body is warm with his arms around me and as our laughter drifts off we stand silent for a moment.

"You can't keep doing this to me," I say softly.

"What?"

"You know what. I'm going to forget, or lose myself in your eyes, or just give in and kiss you one of these days if you keep it up."

He smiles. "Lose yourself in my eyes?"

I grin and slap his arm. "Seriously, I think you have more self-control than I do."

He shakes his head and his tone turns serious. "It's only that I would do anything to protect you." He searches my eyes for a long moment as if he's seeking an answer I can't provide. Then he quietly turns and opens the passenger door for me to get in. "We'd better go."

As I wait for him to walk to the driver's side, I feel a dark cold wash over me. I look out the passenger window and in the far distance I see Avestan standing with a group of men, staring in my direction. Are they all dark angels? Or just mortals he's grooming to follow in his path? I shiver with an awful sense of dread.

"What is it?" Alexander asks as he slides into his seat and closes the door. He can tell my demeanor has changed.

I don't answer right away. I peer out the window again and see that Avestan and the others have disappeared. *Did I imagine it?*

He mistakes my silence for frustration at our predicament. "If you only knew how much I want to kiss you, Declan." Then he pauses and looks at me as he adds, "I know this isn't ideal and if at any time you want out, I'll understand. I shouldn't even be asking this of you. It's selfish, but I can't help myself."

The look in my eyes reveals that I'm as hopelessly connected to him as he is to me. "The way I feel when I'm around you, Alexander, I'll never want out." He reaches over and holds my hand.

When we get to my house, Alexander waits for me downstairs while I get ready. I race through my shower, blow dry my hair as best I can and then give up and throw it into a ponytail. I slide on my red Jack's Burger Shack t-shirt and a pair of jeans and I'm back downstairs with nearly ten minutes to spare.

"That was fast," says Alexander, duly impressed. "Now we can cover some ground rules."

"Okay, let's talk in the car because I don't want to be late." I grab a peanut butter Larabar and he nods in agreement as we walk to the car.

"First rule," Alexander says as he's driving, "don't go anywhere alone."

He looks at me and I nod. I suppose that's reasonable. "Wait. What about when I go running?"

"I'll go with you. Or if I can't I'll make sure someone else is watching."

"Who?"

He shakes his head. "You're not supposed to know we exist. Edwin doesn't want me to reveal anyone to you, but just know that we're around."

"Okay … I guess."

"Second rule: Share your schedule with me so I know where you are at all times. I can drive you wherever you need to go. And I'm sorry to ask this, but you'll have to stop volunteering at the shelter for now."

"Why?"

"There's been some trouble. We're taking care of it, but I don't want you near it."

I think about what he's asking and then I shake my head. "I don't mind sharing my schedule with you but I'm not going to stop working at the shelter. I usually go on Tuesdays and Thursdays. I talked with Sarah, the director, and she said there hasn't been any trouble downtown."

"You can't be persuaded?"

"No, not on this point."

"Okay, then we'll figure something out." I nod and he continues. "This last one probably goes without saying. Don't go near Avestan or communicate with him in any way."

I nod. "That's an easy one."

"I'd also like to request that you not share what I told you last night with anyone."

I look at him, surprised. "Of course I won't. I thought that went without saying. Frankly, even if I did try to tell someone they'd probably have me committed."

He laughs but I'm only half joking.

We arrive at Jack's and Alexander insists on walking me in. When he introduces himself to Jack as my boyfriend, Jack's jaw nearly drops to the floor because he knows I've never been interested in anyone before. We make small talk for a few minutes and then Alexander hugs me and leaves.

As I walk to the front counter, Jack turns to me with a smile and a raised eyebrow. "We've got a lunch rush coming in any moment, darlin', but when it's over, I want to hear all the details about that new boyfriend of yours that just sauntered in here from the Land Down Under."

I smile back as I punch in my number to sign on to the register.

Chapter Ten

The rest of winter break flies by. I follow the rules Alexander and I have agreed on and they seem to be working. I haven't seen Avestan and his band of not-so-merry fellows again, and I'm starting to hope that maybe he's given up and is on the hunt for 'pure souls' to annihilate in some other part of the world. I have to joke about it because otherwise I'd be curled up in a corner somewhere under a blanket. Alexander explained that it's unlikely that Avestan will give up and look elsewhere because apparently I'm a "rare and valuable find." *Just my luck to have the kind of special qualities that attract homicidal dark angels.*

I remember the picture I snapped of Avestan the night of the dance and the thought makes me shudder. I search my phone to delete it but when I find the photo, I'm shaken to discover that it's turned completely black. For some reason that leaves me more unsettled than anything Alexander has told me so far.

As the days go by, I feel as though I'm living in a parallel universe: One where I not only have dark angels after me, but also one where I have a boyfriend for the first time in my life, and a completely new view of my anxiety. Alexander and I spend all our free time together and his calming energy keeps my panic attacks at bay. We've been quizzing one another about everything from cherished books to fondest memories. Alexander's recollections extend through so many lifetimes, it's fascinating. He's playful, witty, and thoughtful, (all things I knew), but I discover even more of his intelligence and kindness. I feel more connected to him every day.

"Favorite food?" I ask as we walk among the shops one afternoon in downtown San Mar.

"Jaffle," Alexander answers.

"Waffle?

"No. Jaffle. Grilled cheese. I love 'em."

"Jaffle … I like it. I'm going to start calling them jaffles. I make great grilled cheese, by the way. With tomatoes."

He smiles. "I love them with tomatoes. Favorite song?" he asks.

"Hmm. I don't really have one. It changes. But I love duets and I like songs with whistling."

"Whistling?"

"Yes, but I hate it when people whistle in real life. Outside of songs. It's weird."

He laughs. "Your answers are always so … unexpected."

"*Odd*, in other words," I say.

"Yes, but in a good way. I like being surprised."

A woman approaches with two kids in tow and asks me a question in a language I don't recognize. I try my best to understand as she gestures wildly, but I'm at a loss. Alexander jumps in, speaking in her native tongue, and she beams with relief. "Yes, yes," she says in English, nodding, "Thank you. Thank you." She smiles at both of us and heads in the direction Alexander pointed.

I look at Alexander, amazed.

He shrugs. "She wanted to know where she could get a jaffle."

"You're making that up."

"Okay," he laughs, "I'm making that part up. But she did want a restaurant that was vegetarian."

"What language were you speaking?"

"Farsi."

"How many languages can you speak?"

"All of them."

I absorb this new information. "Now *you're* the one who's unexpected … and very handy to have around."

He smiles and puts his arm around me as we walk into the San Mar Surf Shop. I slip my arm around him in return and rest my hand comfortably in the back pocket of his jeans. God, I love this. Where have you been all my life, Alexander? We head toward the sale racks. He wants to go surfing together and I need a new wetsuit.

After the break, there are a lot of surprised looks the first time we walk down the hallway at school holding hands. I'm sure people are wondering what the heck Aussie supermodel Alexander Ronin is doing with little Declan Jane but I don't care. I don't feel broken anymore. I'm not a freak. For the first time in my life I feel just as worthy of an Aussie god's affections as the next girl. And, just as importantly, I know he's worthy of mine.

Liz is thrilled for me. During many conversations involving our guys I've shared as many details as I can to satiate her curiosity, but I haven't revealed anything about the angel business, of course. Liz and Finn like Alexander a lot and he returns the favor. Things are going so well I can't help but wonder when the other shoe might drop, but then I chastise myself for such negative thoughts. Alexander is a force for good—we all are—so why can't it just stay this way? Didn't he say good always wins out?

"Okay," Alexander says, "let's start with Miss Dunhill over there."

We're sitting in the quad at lunch and it's just the two of us. Liz and Finn left for a space sciences lecture Edwin is giving at UCSM. Alexander asks if I want to try some aura guessing so he can teach me to trust my feelings about people. Miss Dunhill is sitting with some other teachers at the picnic table outside the teacher's lounge.

"Alright, hopefully this will be an easy one. I like Miss Dunhill." I concentrate on the energy I feel from her for a few minutes and try to attach a color to it. "I picture her aura as sunny yellow. Very cheery. But I also feel some light pink tinged with melancholy. Is that weird?"

"You're right on all counts. And no, the melancholy isn't weird, because she's pining after Mr. Brody and he's sitting across from her right now."

"Seriously?" I'm a little excited for Miss Dunhill. Mr. Brody is pretty funny and I suppose he's handsome, too, for an older guy. Miss Dunhill has been to our homeroom class a few times borrowing this or that and now I realize she was probably just making up reasons to talk to him. The thought of Miss Dunhill being crafty makes me smile. I study her expression as Mr. Brody talks to her across the table and then I see it, or rather feel it. "Oh," I say, "I think I feel that now. But does he feel the same way?"

"Focus on him and see what you think."

I concentrate but I can't get a clear read of Mr. Brody. He looks a little self-conscious as he's talking to Miss Dunhill, though, so I take a guess. "Yes?"

Alexander nods. "But he's afraid to ask her out."

I raise my eyebrows. "We'll have to see what we can do about that." I'm already concocting sitcom-like schemes in my mind to get them together. This is fun.

"Do you want to try Liz and Finn?"

"But they're not here."

"You know them well enough that I'm sure you can just think about them and picture their auras in your mind."

"Really? Okay, I'll start with Finn. I always feel so comfortable around him—he keeps me centered." As I try to conjure up what his aura looks like, it's clear to me why. "His energy feels honest … and also fiercely loyal … and kind. I picture a seamless cerulean blue. But I sense his anxiety about not always fitting in with the world, and that feels like darker shadows here and there."

"Good description," replies Alexander. "He has a solid, steadfast aura."

"Okay, now Liz." I can't help but smile as I focus on how I feel around Liz. One color is really calling to me, but it's so obvious I think it must be wrong. "Is it pink? I picture bright, shiny shades of pink radiating from her like sunbeams."

Alexander laughs. "Yep, that's about right. I liked Liz the first time I saw her aura. Finn, too. I can see why you're all friends. Okay, let's do another one. Someone you aren't as close with." He surveys the quad area. "How about Kelly Murphy?" He gestures with a nod to where she's sitting under a tree with a bunch of people.

Kelly is one of the nicest girls at school. She's friends with every group, accepts everyone, and no matter what you're doing, she makes it fun. I've often thought she would be a perfect cruise director. I can tell Alexander is choosing all cheery people on purpose.

"Okay, I'll try." I focus on her intently and do my best to pick up on exactly how her energy feels so I can assign a color to it. "I'm not sure … I picture it as a kaleidoscope or party sprinkles—it's all different colors."

He smiles. "You're good at this."

The bell rings signaling the end of lunch before we can go on. "Can we try more later?"

"Aye. It's good practice. Identifying the energy around you is the first step to being able to control what you let in."

I think about what he said as we walk to class. One person who can't seem to wrap her head around the fact that Alexander and I are together is Molly Bing. The venom she's been directing at me is poisonous and although Alexander has tried to teach me a little about how to protect myself from negative energy, I still have panic attacks when he's not around.

After school Alexander notices the hair around my face is wet again.

"You okay?" he asks.

I nod. "Remind me again why being an empath is a good thing?"

He pulls me in close and as I rest my head on his shoulder he whispers, "It is, Declan. Once you're able to control it, you'll see."

I lift my head and notice Molly walking to her BMW across the parking lot. She doesn't see me so I think it might be a good time to try to read her. "I want to guess what Molly's aura looks like."

"You sure? We haven't practiced with negative energy yet."

"I know, but you said the first step to controlling it is being able to identify it. I want to know what I'm dealing with. I can't rely on you to protect me all the time. I need to learn how to do this myself."

He nods and I concentrate hard on imagining what surrounds her. She's leaning against the car talking to her friend Suzie and I pick up a strong feeling of disdain. For some reason that makes me profoundly sad. "I don't think she likes Suzie very much."

Alexander nods.

I focus some more. "Gray ... I picture a mottled gray cloud all around her. And puce. I see gray and puce." It's depressing but I sense this is going to help me—putting a picture to what I feel from her is already making Molly seem less formidable.

"Very accurate. I'm not sure what the heck puce is, but the rest of what you said sounded right," he teases.

I laugh and he pulls me into his arms again. "We need to practice some more. I think you're ready. I talked with Edwin last night and I have some new ideas."

"If you say so." My voice is less than confident.

"Great—I do say so. Class starts at 7 p.m. In your room. After dinner with your mom," he adds with a smile.

I smile back, but inside I'm thinking how desperately I hope it works this time.

We're in the kitchen and pots and pans are everywhere. Alexander is cooking dinner—some Aussie food, he says—to thank my mom for all the meals she's been making for us. I've been enlisted to help. Edwin was invited also, but he had other business to attend to. Alexander didn't go into details but I wonder if it has to do with Avestan and dark angels.

The menu is meat pies and lamingtons, which Alexander tells me are little sponge cakes dipped in chocolate and rolled in coconut. I told him I was on board as soon as he said chocolate. My mom sits at the kitchen island and talks with us as Alexander and I chop onions and ready the small pie tins, lining them with pie crust. While Alexander browns the ground beef and simmers the sauce ingredients, we take turns plugging in our iPods and choosing songs to listen to as we talk. Alexander jokingly suggests "Stop Draggin' My Heart Around" so we can reprise our duet from the fundraiser. Yeah, right.

When everything is ready we fill the tins with the meat mixture and cover the tops with pie crusts. We slide them into the oven on a baking sheet and while the meat pies are cooking, we pull out the sponge cakes we made earlier and carefully coat them with chocolate icing and roll them in coconut. Then we make a giant salad and we're just finishing up as the timer for the meat pies goes off.

"Mmm, delicious," my mom says, sounding a little surprised after her first bite.

"Thanks, Mrs. Jane. I was hoping you'd like them. You'll have to come to our house next time and Edwin and I can barbecue. He makes great kabobs."

"That would be wonderful, and please, Alexander, you know you can call me Judy."

"Judy Jane ... I don't know if I ever told you but I really like your name. It has great alliteration."

"Thank you," she smiles. "I've always liked it, too. Stop me if I've told you this story before—I know Declan has heard it a hundred times. When I met her father I knew immediately he was the one but when he told me his name was Frank Jane that might have clinched it if I hadn't already fallen for him. I've always loved the name Jane. It's solid. You know you can count on a Jane. Plus, Jane Austen is one of my favorite authors and Jane Eyre is one of my favorite literary characters. Declan's first name probably would have been Jane if we didn't already have it as our last. But I love the name Declan—it means 'full of goodness' and I knew it was right for her the moment she was born."

"I agree," says Alexander, looking at me and smiling. He turns back to my mom, "Which Jane Austen book is your favorite?"

"Oh, that's easy—*Pride and Prejudice*. I mean, honestly, she had me at Mr. Darcy."

I'm wondering if my mom is a little tipsy from the two glasses of wine she had while we were making dinner.

"I think I've watched the BBC version of *Pride and Prejudice* with Colin Firth as Mr. Darcy at least ten times," my mom continues. "But I love all her books. Declan does, too. I've read them and re-read them so often. Jane Austen was a genius observer of human nature."

Alexander nods. "And what is it you like about Jane Eyre?"

"She's a strong female character. She has an iron core and knows her worth. Whatever life throws at her, she picks herself up and keeps going. She's also generous and she loves deeply and with such integrity. She reminds me of Declan."

I blush as my mom continues. "I just saw the latest film adaptation of *Jane Eyre* with Michael Fassbender as Mr. Rochester—*whew*," she says with a laugh as she picks up her napkin and fans herself comically. "It was *very* good."

Okay, now I know she must be tipsy. It's nice to see her laughing and enjoying herself though. I'm starting to realize how subdued she's been ever since my dad died. She hasn't dated once in eight years. Not once. And I know Chief Stephens likes her. I wish she'd consider it. She says she'll never find anyone like my dad so why even try? Maybe seeing me so happy with Alexander will make her consider giving life a chance again. She tells me all the time what a nice young man she thinks he is. Once she even told Alexander he was "an angel" for helping her load the car with a bunch of heavy real estate signs. I almost choked on the water I was drinking.

After dinner we clear the table and load the dishwasher and I tell my mom we're going to my room to do homework. It's time for our "Energy Control" class, as Alexander calls it. I'm feeling hopeful. Maybe this will work.

I close the door to my room and almost immediately that familiar charge starts building between us. It hasn't gotten any easier being alone with Alexander but so far I've managed to stay mindful of the consequences.

We start by sitting on the floor, legs crossed, facing one another. Alexander takes my hands in his and tells me to close my eyes.

"Okay, first let's just relax. Breathe in deep and let it out slowly and just focus on your breathing, nothing else," he says soothingly. Our knees are touching and an electric current flows between us as our hands make contact, but I focus on my breathing and soon the bubble of cool, calm comfort that I always feel in Alexander's presence washes over me and everything else dissolves into the background.

"Your aura is so beautiful right now," Alexander says with awe.

I smile and my heart does tiny flips at his words. "Hey, I'm supposed to be concentrating on my breathing right now. Stop distracting me," I say jokingly, eyes still closed.

"Right you are, Miss Jane. Always focused—one of the many reasons you're my favorite student." Then he adds sincerely, "It just feels so good to be around you."

I smile again and murmur, "Ditto."

"Okay, I know we've practiced breathing and concentration before, but I talked with Edwin and he said guided practice is the only way to gain enough control to be able to use your power consistently when you need it."

I nod and he continues, "That means I'm going to have to direct some dark energy at you so you can practice fending it off. It's not going to be easy, but it's the only way."

I gulp slightly.

"I'll be right here," he reassures, "and if at any moment it becomes too much, all you have to do is say 'stop' and I'll stop immediately. In the meantime, just concentrate on my words as I walk you through what to do. Sound good?"

I open my eyes for a moment to see him looking at me with concern. I nod and he squeezes my hands. "Remember, I'm right here. Everything will be okay."

I close my eyes again as he begins.

"Focus again on your breathing. Just relax. Breathe in slowly and deeply, filling your core, and exhale out fully." He pauses as I relax into my breathing for a minute or two. "Do you remember the night of the dance when Avestan and I were fighting? You shouted 'stop' and I think you caught a glimpse of what we saw."

My eyes flip open. "You mean the white light? You saw that? I thought I imagined it."

"It was real. You have more power within you than you realize—greater than any mortal I've seen. When you learn to control it, I promise you'll be able to defend against negative energy. And once you know you can protect yourself, you'll never feel uncontrollable panic again."

I nod slowly. He's giving me hope for a future without anxiety attacks. The thought is hard to fathom.

"Close your eyes again. Picture your power in the depth of your belly. You can see it as a bright white ball of burning light that radiates goodness. It's always there and it's always at your command."

I picture it vividly in my mind and I can almost feel it, radiating heat outward through my limbs.

It's as if he's reading my mind as he continues. "You can feel its warmth and it brings a sense of complete contentment that washes over you. Whenever you want, you can extend the warmth throughout your body and even release some of the energy through your fingertips. Imagine white light shimmering around you as it flows through your skin. You don't have to worry about depleting it because it's infinite, and as you release it to extend it out to the world it grows larger inside you and continually fills you with a sense of peace."

His descriptions are so serene. I melt into them. As he continues and I concentrate all my focus, the energy vibrates throughout my body until it grows so powerful I feel as though I'm levitating above the floor.

"I'm going to direct some dark energy toward you now. I'll start slowly with very little so you can become accustomed and not be afraid. When you start to feel it, I want you to focus on your power. Harness that burning white light in your belly and pull it to the surface to create a protective shield all around you. Imagine the shimmering light vibrating out in a circle, impenetrable."

I nod with trepidation.

"I'm starting now. Hold my hands tight when you feel it, and remember you can tell me to stop at any moment."

My heart is racing. I don't know if it's just nerves or if I'm already feeling the energy he's directing towards me. Suddenly I feel a jolt that is unmistakable. A sense of thick despair falls over me like a cloak and I have to choke back a sob. I start to sweat and my breathing becomes fast and shallow. I'm gripping Alexander so tightly my hands hurt.

I try hard to focus on his voice, "Remember to concentrate on your power. It's a bright ball of white hot energy ready at your command. Picture it, feel its warmth, and draw it out through your body to create a defensive barrier all around you."

It's hard to focus on anything through my panic but as I listen to his voice I picture the energy at my core and slowly, slowly it becomes vivid again. I feel radiating heat and concentrate on rolling it through my body, moving it wherever

I want it to go. It's a burning white ball expanding outward to create an impervious shield. I'm in control and it feels fantastic. I illuminate it more fully in my mind and imagine it as a weapon I can use against dark forces. Suddenly I'm a character in a movie in my mind, fighting dark angels bent on destruction. I picture the light shooting out my fingertips, zapping their dark energy into puffs of smoke.

"Ow!"

Alexander's startled shout makes me drop his hands and open my eyes.

"What did you just do?"

"I was picturing lasers shooting out of my fingers," I say sheepishly. "Did I hurt you?"

"No, just shocked the hell out of me." He looks at me curiously as if he's not sure what to make of it. After a pause, he decides. "Good on ya, for doing that. That was great, actually. I didn't know that was possible for a mortal. You continue to amaze, Miss Jane."

I smile back, "Thanks to you, Professor Ronin."

"Edwin was definitely onto something when he suggested this."

"Should we try again?"

"That depends. Are you going to keep your weapons holstered this time?"

I smile and we start the process over. Alexander increases the strength of the energy he directs at me each time and ups the level of enmity. It's difficult and draining. It's obvious now that he went easy on me the first time to build my confidence. By the last time, I have to shout 'stop!' and I fold into tears in his arms, choking on the blackness.

"I'm sorry, so sorry, babe," he murmurs as he holds me and caresses my hair, smoothing it and pulling me close, "It's over now."

He floods me with his energy—I can feel it melting over me in waves, calming me. Ever so slowly, the feeling shifts from tranquility to heightened awareness at our proximity. The vibration in the air becomes palpable and it's clear he feels it, too.

"Could we kiss as long as it's not on the lips? Maybe I could kiss you here?" I ask as I trail my finger softly along the side of his neck.

He lets out a low, wary sigh. "Declan, if we start kissing .... Maintaining things as we are is already hard enough. I don't think I can take much more."

The heartache in his voice mirrors my own. There has to be some way around our cruel circumstances.

"When I asked what would happen if we kiss, you said it had never happened before, so how can you know it's true?

"Edwin confirmed what the legends say."

"But Edwin was just telling you what he heard?"

"Yes, but Declan, all guardians know the consequences. I could never risk your life." His eyes are dark as he gazes into mine.

"You would lose your immortality?"

"Yes, I would be a fallen guardian. But you're all that matters. I don't know why we're even having this conversation."

"Would you become a dark angel like Avestan?"

"No. Avestan is immortal. He chose darkness. I would be mortal again, starting over. I wouldn't care if it didn't also mean losing you."

The anguish in his voice stops me from pushing the issue further. I attempt to lighten the mood. "Okay, I give up. I'm just trying to find some loophole for us. A girl can try, right?"

He seems relieved. "Yes, a girl can try," he repeats with a sigh. "And a guy can, too. Believe me, if there was a loophole to be found, I would have driven through it at light speed a long time ago. There's no way around it, Declan. Not in this lifetime."

Chapter Eleven

The next morning at school I'm actually looking forward to practicing my "energy shield" powers.

"Where's Molly?" I ask Finn. She was absent in homeroom and chemistry.

"You're searching for the girl who sends you spiraling into anxiety attacks?"

Finn sees the expression on my face and although he isn't great at picking up on things he can tell I'm hurt. "Sorry, Dec. I shouldn't have said that."

"It's okay. You're right—I do feel rotten around her. I don't know why she upsets me sometimes and I have no idea why she hates me so much."

"That's easy. I know why."

"You do?"

He nods. "Your latest transgression is dating Alexander, but it started long before that. She's been mad at you since that day in fourth grade."

Huh? "Finn, what are you talking about? What day?"

"The day she told you I was weird."

I shake my head. "Still lost. Can you please start at the beginning?"

"Okay. Do you remember when my mom told your mom I had Asperger's? It was near the end of third grade."

"I thought you said this happened in fourth grade?"

"You said to start at the beginning. Just go with it. My mom talked to your mom because you and I were best friends and she wanted your mom to understand my bluntness and stuff."

"How do you know this?"

"I overheard my mom talking to my aunt on the phone about it, but that's not important. Do you know what your mom said?"

"I remember her talking with me back then. She said something like we're all wired differently with unique strengths and challenges and she told me some of the things that were difficult for you so I would understand. I don't think she mentioned Asperger's. In fact, you were the one to first tell me about Asperger's later."

Finn nods. "My mom was nervous to tell your mom. She wasn't sure if it was the best thing to do because she didn't want to label me. She didn't even tell *me* until almost a year later—which still ticks me off because it was a huge relief. Before that I just thought there was something wrong with me and I was afraid to ask."

"Oh, Finn," I say sympathetically, hugging him around the shoulders as we sit beside each other.

"The way your mom responded made my mom cry … in a good way. She was crying when she told my aunt about it on the phone."

"What did my mom say?"

"She said she was honored that my mom trusted her enough to share the information. But she said as far as she was concerned, I was the same old Finn she had always known and loved, and it didn't change a thing about how she felt about me."

I smile. I can picture my mom saying that, and it encapsulates exactly how I felt when Finn told me in fourth grade. I mean, it helped explain some things but, in the end, what does a label matter? Finn has Asperger's, I have panic attacks—everyone has something they're dealing with that makes life challenging. We should all give each other a break for Christ's sake.

"What does any of this have to do with Molly?"

"I'm getting to that," Finn answers. "My mom did the same thing with Molly's mom. Remember how my mom used to switch off with Mrs. Bing, carpooling Molly and I to swim class every week? My mom figured she should probably tell her, too. But Mrs. Bing reacted differently. She was nice enough, but I guess she freaked out a little and was nervous about it, asking my mom if she should tell Molly.

"My mom tried to tell her that it was just an explanation for my quirkiness, but Mrs. Bing treated me differently after that—like I had a communicable disease or something. My mom told my aunt she regretted saying anything."

I nod in understanding and Finn continues, "Soon after that, Mrs. Bing told Molly that I have Asperger's and I guess she must have made it sound like a big deal because after that Molly started treating me differently, too. She looked at me like I was an alien and she stopped talking to me when we were riding to swim practice. I think she was afraid I was going to reach out and hit her or something."

I laugh out loud. The thought of Finn ever being violent is comical.

"My mom finally stopped the carpool because it was so awkward. Then, in fourth grade, Molly told you I was too weird to be friends with anymore, and that's why she hates you."

"What? Back up a minute, I'm not making the connection here."

He sighs loudly as if it's obvious. "When you told me the story, you said that Molly walked up to you and said you and I were both weird and she didn't want to be friends with us anymore. But I know that's not true. I was following a trail of ants behind that big oak tree in the corner of the playground and I overheard you two talking. Molly said that *I* was too weird and that she wouldn't hang out with you anymore if you stayed friends with me."

I'm embarrassed that Finn caught me in a white lie and I try to explain. "I'm sorry, Finn, I didn't want to hurt your feelings over some jerky thing Molly said."

"I don't care about that. You stuck up for me that day and that's what I remember. You told her I was the best friend you'd ever had and if she thought I was too weird then that was her problem and she should go work it out."

We both laugh as he recalls my words. I remember feeling indignant that she would say that about Finn.

"That's why she hates you," he continues, "because you didn't go along with it. And now every time she looks at you she's reminded of what a crummy human being she can be—and she knows you know it, too."

"You really think that's it?"

"I *know* that's it."

"But she was just a kid. She didn't know any better."

"Maybe … but you were a kid, too, and you knew better. And she knows better now."

I take a moment to contemplate his theory. "You know, you're not only genius smart, Finn, you're also pretty wise."

"I hope I have a decent grasp of human nature by now, after all those social skills classes my mom made me take. But I still get a lot of it wrong, I know. I could use your help with something that I'm clueless about. What should I get Liz for Valentine's Day?"

"How about a card with a twenty dollar bill in it?"

I laugh and he hits my arm.

"You're joking, right?" he asks, just to make sure.

"A card actually isn't a bad idea. Write something nice, from the heart, in it. If you put a twenty dollar bill in there, too, as a joke, I know she would think it was funny. And take her out to a nice dinner. Anything that shows you put some time and effort into it .... Oh, and don't give her the card until you're at the restaurant having dinner .... And be sure to pay for dinner. She likes the restaurant Butterfly downtown. You should make a reservation quick because they get booked up." I keep throwing out details because you never know with Finn what he might assume or not. He used to order for himself at Surf Pizza while I held our table and then expect me to go up and wait in line all over again to order for myself until I explained to him that he should order for both of us.

"Okay, but if she gets mad, I'm telling her it was all your idea."

"I promise she'll love whatever you do," I say reassuringly. I honestly don't blame him for feeling wary after what happened last year with Serena. If he had acted upset when she broke up with him, Liz and I never would have ribbed him so much, but he honestly didn't seem to care when she left. I don't think they were a good match. She never really understood him.

Valentine's Day is on my mind the rest of the afternoon. Alexander hasn't told me what he has planned. He made me agree we won't spend money on gifts because he knows I'm saving for college. He says it'll be more fun this way anyway because we have to be creative. Every day I toss out a guess and he always smiles and says, "Nope, not even close." I'm intrigued but also desperately wondering what it can be. I have something I've been working on for him, too, but I'm starting to worry that it won't compare to whatever he's doing.

On Saturday I rise early. When he first told me to be ready at six I assumed he meant for dinner but he made it clear he would be arriving bright and early and he said to wear clothes for outdoors—layers, because it will warm up later.

He picks me up and we drive on a winding road that leads up into the mountains and through impossibly tall redwood trees. It's still dark out and small tufts of misty fog reflect in the headlights intermittently. It feels a bit spooky, actually, like a scene from *The Legend of Sleepy Hollow*. They actually do a re-enactment of the Headless Horseman's ride during Halloween at Redwood Park, near where we're driving. I can see why. At a turn I almost don't see in the dark, Alexander pulls off onto a deserted one-lane road and drives on for some distance. We park in a small gravel lot and I realize by a small sign on the fence that we're in the back of Redwood Park. We must have entered through a ranger access road. I wonder how Alexander knows about this place.

We get out and Alexander grabs a large backpack from the trunk. "It's just through here," he says as he points toward an opening in the trees. "I have a torch." He pulls out a flashlight and we follow a small trail that winds through the redwoods and switchbacks up the side of the mountain. When we reach a plateau near the top, Alexander pulls a waterproof blanket out of his pack and spreads it on the ground to sit on. He has another blanket to put over the top of us to keep us warm. We nestle down side by side and he pulls me close under the covers and I rest my head on his shoulder. It's just before sunrise and the darkness is fading. We're facing the mountains to the east and behind us we have a clear view all the way to the ocean in the distance. "Now we wait," he says.

"For sunrise?" I assume that's what he means, but I can never be sure with Alexander.

"Sunrise and a surprise afterwards," he says with a smile. He knows I'm dying to know what he has planned.

We wait and slowly the sun appears, spectacularly, illuminating the sky and reflecting the wonder in my heart as I marvel that I'm sitting here on top of the world with an angel watching the sun come up over the San Mar Mountains.

Alexander reaches into his backpack and pulls out two Capri Suns and hands one to me. I laugh.

"What? You like these."

"I *love* them. And I love that you brought them. Sometimes I just find it hard to believe you're an angel."

"What do you mean?'

"I don't know. I guess you don't act very angel-y."

"Angel-y?" he repeats, teasingly. "How should angels act?"

"I have no idea. But somehow the idea of you shopping for Capri Suns makes me laugh. I don't know why. You're a perfect angel. And this day is perfect. And I love it."

Alexander smiles as we jab our straws into the shiny plastic pouches. He raises his for a toast. "To an eternity of sunrises together. There's no one I'd rather greet each day with than you," he says sincerely.

I smile as we touch our drinks together and take a sip. He pulls me closer and I rest my head on his shoulder again as we enjoy the view.

"Are you hungry?" he asks after a while. "I have muffins. The good ones—from Erin's." Erin's is our favorite bakery.

"Not yet. I just want to take in the view and enjoy this moment with you a little longer. I love your present. Thank you."

"If you really want to take in the view then now would be a good time to move on to the surprise."

"I thought this was the surprise?"

He shakes his head with a sly grin. "Not even close." He stands and puts out his hand to help me up. We walk to the end of the plateau and it's a breathtaking view, but I'm nervous about getting so close to the edge. "You're going to have to trust me on this one," he says with a smile as he nudges me closer. I look at him warily but he whispers "Trust me," again, softly in my ear. The heat of his breath calms me and as I lean into him, he pulls me closer into his arms. Just as I'm beginning to relax and feel safe, he leaps off the ledge, taking me with him.

Before I can scream we're transformed—into what, I'm not sure—but it's exhilarating and my whole being vibrates with a force more powerful than anything I've felt with Alexander before. We zoom over the hills and mountains at a breathtaking pace, swooping down to zigzag through the trees and then shooting straight up again as if we're going to touch the sky. We reach the ocean in minutes, flying over the cliffs and rushing straight down to the waves before pulling up at the last second and flying into the clouds again. The ocean spray is cold and vibrant and I've never felt so alive. We soar around the lighthouse on the edge of the cliffs, spinning around it in a spiral until we shoot up like a rocket at the top and fly back down to touch the waves again. Then we speed over the ocean's surface, inches from the water, and head out to sea, the world a blur around us. I should be terrified but I'm intoxicated with the electric rush. Alexander and I are one being, our connection so profound that it brings overwhelming tears of joy. We soar over the ocean and mountains for hours before alighting back on top of the hill where we started. As we touch ground I feel my body return to a solid state, re-forming from the soles of my feet on up. When the transformation is complete, we're standing face to face with our arms wrapped around one another. Alexander starts to step back, but I hold him close a moment longer. I want to preserve the feeling of being one entity, connected. It's pure bliss.

"Did you like it?" Alexander asks, grinning.

I nod, breathless, as we sit down. "I have ... no words."

"I've rendered Declan Jane speechless. That's one for the history books."

"You can *fly*?"

He nods, smiling.

"What *was* that? While we were flying I felt ... different."

"Energy state, babe. Pure energy," he answers, laughing.

"How come you never told me you could fly?"

He shrugs. "Never came up, I guess."

"Never came up?" I raise an eyebrow with mock indignation. "My uncle is in show business; My cousin lives in Tucson; I once owned a dog named Sparky—those are the types of things that might never come up. Being able to *fly*, on the other hand, is the type of thing you *bring* up because most people wouldn't think to ask."

"They might if they knew you were an angel."

I smile. He knows he's got me. "All right then, what other powers do you have?"

"You want me to list them?"

"Yes. But wait a minute, is that how you did the coffee cup thing?"

"What coffee cup thing?"

"In Mrs. King's class. You reached for her coffee cup before it started to tip. I thought I imagined it. Did you know it was going to happen?"

"You saw that? I was just moving faster than the spill. We don't always intervene—it's important to let mortals steer their own lives—but she was having such a bad day I wanted to restore her faith a little. People tend to focus on the bad and they forget all the times when things go right."

I nod. "So you can't see the future?"

"The future is a construct. Time isn't linear."

"Hmm. Okay … not exactly sure what that means."

"How about this: fate isn't set in stone. Free will can change anything."

"Better, I guess."

He nods.

"So what other powers do you have?"

"I think you know already." He starts ticking them off with his fingers. "I'm immortal."

"Knew that one. Go on."

"I can fly."

"Check."

"Guardians are much stronger and faster than mortals— even when we're not flying."

I nod. "I've seen that."

"We can heal our physical bodies."

"That one is amazing. If I hadn't seen it myself I wouldn't have believed you when you told me you were an angel."

"You wouldn't have believed me?"

I shake my head slowly as I form a smile. "I thought you were a little crazy, actually."

"Is that right? …so now the truth comes out," he replies, feigning offense. "But guess what? I already knew you thought I was nuts. I can read minds."

My face turns ashen. The idea of him knowing all the things I've thought about him since the first time we met is mortifying.

"The look on your face right now has me very intrigued to know what you've been thinking," he says with his lopsided grin. "Someday I hope you'll enlighten me … in the meantime I can't torture you any longer. I can't really read minds. I figured as long as you think I'm crazy, I may as well make things up."

I push his arm. "I can't believe you did that!" I let out a giant sigh of relief as he laughs. "God, I almost had a heart attack … all right, keep going then. What's your next power—a real one this time."

"You mean assuming I'm not delusional?"

"C'mon. This incredibly hot new guy comes to my school and tells me he's my guardian angel? It's not exactly the kind of thing you expect to hear."

"Fair point. Incredibly hot, huh?"

"Yes," I say with a smile, "as if you didn't know."

"I like hearing you say it." His deep green eyes lock with mine and suddenly I'm having a hard time remembering what we were even talking about.

"This is what I mean …" I say softly, "you don't seem very *angel-y* right now."

"I'm not feeling very angel-y right now."

His voice is low and I swallow nervously as he gives me that look that makes my knees go weak. "Any other powers?" I manage to squeak out faintly.

"I see auras. I'm looking at yours as we speak and it's beautiful, as ever, by the way."

I smile, besotted. "I wish I could see yours."

"You can feel it, which is even better. Take my hands."

Alexander floods me with energy that ripples languorously from the top of my head down through my toes over and over. I close my eyes to enjoy the peaceful feeling and when I open them again he's looking at me with that crooked smile of his. "Have I told you lately how much I love being around you?" he asks.

"Ditto," I sigh, and if I wasn't already, in this moment I am truly *gone*—hopelessly, irrevocably, positively lovestruck and there is no turning back.

"That was a demonstration of my last power, by the way. I can harness my energy to use as a force. To either fend off darkness, or—my favorite way—to impress girlfriends. Did it work?"

I smile. "I think you know the answer to that."

As I sit and bask in the feeling between us, I notice the sun has barely moved in the sky since we left on our flying adventure. "What time is it?" I ask.

Alexander checks his watch. "Seven thirty."

"How can that be? We were flying for hours."

"Time is experienced differently in an energy state. You can cover a lot of ground when you're moving as light."

"Why don't you travel that way all the time?"

"First of all, it might scare the heck out of people if I started popping up here and there in time. We're meant to blend in, not stand out and raise questions. But the biggest reason is because it requires energy to go in and out of that state and it takes time to regain full strength afterwards."

"Time travel … you forgot to add that to your list of superhero powers. You are very impressive, Mr. Ronin."

"You have no idea," he teases.

I smile. "I love your gift. It was unexpected. And it was stunning. Now I understand how you found this place tucked away in the park. It must be nice to be able to just fly off wherever you want."

"It's nice to be free of my mortal shell … no offense."

"None taken. If I could do that, I don't think I would ever switch back."

We sit on the picnic blanket and eat our muffins, enjoying the gorgeous morning and the tranquility of being on top of the world amongst the redwoods. As the sun rises higher in the sky, I tell him I'm ready to give him my present. He smiles eagerly like a young boy on Christmas morning. Oh God, I'm nervous. I hope this isn't disappointing.

"After watching the sunrise together and soaring over the ocean in a state of utter bliss, I don't know how impressive this is going to be," I say, trying to temper expectations, "but I worked a long time on it and it comes from my heart."

We sit with our legs crossed, facing one another on the blanket. I hold his hands, close my eyes, and relax, focusing on my energy center. Worry spills into my consciousness because although I've practiced hundreds of times, I've only been able to do this once successfully so far. I push the worry to the back of my mind each time it resurfaces and return my concentration to the task at hand. I focus on my feelings for Alexander and how much I want to give him this gift. I visualize the warm white light of my energy moving through my body and settling in my fingertips where it intensifies until I can feel its vibration, straining to be released. When I think I'm ready, I open my eyes and trace the image of a large heart in the air, where it holds, shimmering with white hot intensity. I quickly trace our initials within the heart, writing "D. J. loves A.R." and then add underneath "Always." The image is suspended in the air for a moment like fireworks in the sky, then slowly fades and disappears.

I search Alexander's face, hopeful that he liked it. His expression is a mixture of surprised wonder and what looks like alarm.

"It was stupid, I'm sorry," I say, embarrassed.

"Declan, no," he says softly, "it was perfect. More than perfect. I'm speechless not only because I love your gift but because I'm trying to understand how you did it. It was astonishing." He leans forward as if to kiss me and then stops, catching himself. He gazes into my eyes as he slowly kisses the tip of his index finger and touches it to my lips. He lets it linger there as our eyes lock until he slowly moves it down, parting my bottom lip and gently cresting my chin before he pulls it away.

"You bewilder me," he says.

"I wish I could make it last forever," I say softly.

He searches my eyes for a long moment before slowly rising to his feet. "I have an idea. Come with me." He takes my hand and helps me up.

We hike partly down the hill and follow a faint trail—or what looks as though it may have been a trail once—that winds deep into the redwoods until we arrive at last at a circle of towering trees around a clearing. I raise my head to try to see how far up they go.

"This is called a fairy ring," explains Alexander. "When the parent tree dies, sprouts form around the base to create a new generation. Some of the trees in this park are over a thousand years old. The parent to this ring was very large."

"It's beautiful," I say as I take in the trees arranged like quiet, stately sentries protecting us all the way to the sky. The sun is shining above and the clearing is lit up like a stage. It's hard to believe this was all made by nature. "It's so magical and private. I could stay here all day."

Alexander nods. "It's one of my favorite spots."

He takes my hand and walks with me to the center of the ring. There, he bends down and brushes aside needles and dirt to expose what appears to be the petrified remains of the parent redwood tree. A blinding white light emits from the tip of his finger as he forms first a heart and then our initials inside, "D.J. loves A.R." with the word "Always" underneath, just as I did. When he finishes, the image is seared into the surface, preserved for all time.

He stands up and smiles. "Now it will last."

I move into his embrace and smile. "I love it."

"And I love your gift … I'm still trying to figure out how you did it, though. You are the most amazing mortal I've ever come across."

"I had a very good teacher."

"Not *that* good," says Alexander with a somewhat quizzical expression.

I look up at the sky—it's so peaceful to be within this quiet ring of soaring trees. We stay for a long while and eventually hike back the way we came until we're back where we started on the plateau.

The sky is crisp and blue with billowy white clouds floating across, intermittently blocking out the sun. We lay down side by side on the blanket, hands entwined, and look up at the clouds.

"I see a monkey," Alexander says, pointing. "He's got his arm up over his head."

"That's a giraffe," I counter.

"Are you nuts? Anyone would tell you that's clearly a monkey. See the banana in his hand?"

For the next lazy hour we just lay there, enjoying each other's company and bantering back and forth about the images we see above us. After a while, our voices trail off and for several minutes we enjoy the movement of the clouds in silence. Then I have an idea.

"I just kissed your eyelids," I say.

Alexander is silent so I continue.

"Now I'm gently kissing the tip of your nose."

After a long pause Alexander decides it's his turn. "I'm holding your face in my hands."

I don't dare to look at him. We're still lying side by side, eyes closed, hands clasped. "I just kissed your chin and now I'm making my way down to the hollow of your neck."

"I like that," he murmurs huskily, "My hands are wrapped in your hair now."

"I glide my hand slowly down your chest until I slide it under your shirt and back up to feel your heartbeat and the heat of your skin," I breathe.

"Mmm," he groans softly, "I gently pull you up so I can kiss your face. I'm making my way to your lips, very, very slowly."

The air around us is crackling with intensity. I wonder if we should stop but I can't help myself. "I part your lips with mine and tug at your bottom lip, gently, with my teeth ..."

"Stop," Alexander says breathlessly before I can say anymore. He sits up and turns toward me, his eyes deep pools, hungry. "Declan, I'm sorry. I can't do this ... I want to, believe me ... but it's just ... I mean, I'm an angel but I'm also a man, and it's more than a guy can take." He covers his heart with his hand and flashes me a helpless look to try to lighten the mood.

"It's more than a girl can take, too," I say as I exhale. "I was honestly starting to wish I hadn't started it." I place my hand over my heart, too, and feel it thumping rapidly.

"A loophole," he says with mock determination as he squeezes my hand. "We need to find a loophole." Then he adds, more seriously, "I'm going to talk to Edwin about it again."

Chapter Twelve

I'm beginning to think of myself as a master at warding off negative energy. Whenever I feel that familiar panicky feeling start to rise in my chest and throat, I close my eyes and focus on my breathing as I imagine white light emanating from my core, creating an impervious shield around me. Molly's bursts of negativity don't send me spiraling anymore, and even calculus with Ms. Tamen no longer affects me.

I have never felt freer. I remember my therapist once asked me during a session, "Who would you be without your anxiety?" I didn't understand the question at the time and had answered flippantly, "Me. But without crippling panic attacks."

"But who would you *be*?" she asked again. "Think about it. Imagine a Declan free of anxiety. Who would she be?"

I wondered if she was trying to suggest that I was creating my anxiety as a crutch, to serve me in some way. In that case, I thought she was a charlatan because I knew that wasn't true. The attacks were debilitating and I would have done anything to be free of them. Why else would I have bothered schlepping to her office every week? I hated going because nothing seemed to help and I felt tremendous guilt because I knew the sessions weren't covered under my mom's insurance.

I didn't just blow off her question, though. I tried to go deeper and think about what she said but I couldn't conceive of a life without panic.

I was only half living. I see that now. Constantly being on the alert for the next panic attack cast a shadow over everything I did. I internalized an image of myself as broken— a freak—and I avoided any situation that might be a trigger. I was never able to go "all-in" or make plans without factoring in limitations created by my anxiety.

Meeting Alexander has affected my life in many ways, but teaching me how to control my energy and rid myself of panic attacks has opened the door to the most profound transformation. I'm still "me," only now I'm able to be *more* of me—Declan 2.0.

I'm lighter, more confident, and willing to put myself out there. Liz and my mom, and even Finn, can see the difference. I told them that Alexander taught me some breathing and bio-feedback techniques that are working for my anxiety and they're thrilled and, frankly, amazed. After all the years of agony, I'm finally *free*. Every time I think about it, my eyes well up. I feel like I can do anything now. Anything. My future is a blank page with a blinking cursor and I can fill it with any story I want.

It's Monday and I'm searching for Alexander after school. He's driving me to my shift at Jack's and I want to go home first quickly because I forgot my uniform. It's only a t-shirt, but Jack likes us to wear them. Liz forgets hers all the time and Jack jokes about it, but I know he gets exasperated when we don't remember. I can already hear Jack chastising us in my mind, "I'm trying to run a professional establishment here, ladies. If you don't have the shirt on, how will customers know who to blame when we get their orders wrong?"

I bump into Finn and he points me to the office. He saw Alexander and Molly there, talking with Ms. Preston, our principal, for their newspaper assignment. As I'm about to round the corner to the office building, I hear my name and instinctively stop to listen. I peek around the corner, shielded by the branches of a large lemon tree, and see Alexander and Molly in the middle of a conversation.

"All I'm saying is that every story should meet a certain standard and I don't think Declan's was as well written as it could have been," says Molly.

"I thought it turned out great," replies Alexander. "I saw a lot of positive comments online. She and Finn put a lot of work into it. If you had something different in mind you could have asked for changes before it was published. I'm sure she would have been open to your ideas."

"I don't know if you know this, but she has a lot of problems," Molly says in a hushed, conspiratorial tone. "I didn't want to upset her by asking for changes. I see her in the bathroom all the time looking like she's freaking out. It's kinda scary. Part of me wonders if she didn't *want* the story to be better, because I'm the editor. She's never liked me even though I've always been nice to her. I know you're new here and you haven't known her very long, but you should be careful. A lot of people say she's unstable."

A long stretch of silence follows and when Alexander replies I hear a simmering undertone in his voice. "Molly, you're a pretty girl, but what just came out of your mouth was ugly. None of what you said is true or kind, so don't repeat it." He takes a full breath in before continuing on a note of sincerity. "You have it in you to be better than that—deep down, Molly—I know that. You just have to open your heart. To what really matters."

There's another moment of silence (stunned silence, I assume, on Molly's part) and Alexander's tone shifts to neutral as he gets back to business. "I'll take these notes from our interview with Ms. Preston and write up the retrospective for you by next Friday. I'm in a hurry now to meet Declan. I have to go."

Molly is still standing with her mouth open, struck dumb. I pull back and lean against the wall where I can't be seen. I have to admit I'm a little speechless, too. I've just seen Molly get her comeuppance and I should be thrilled but mostly I just feel sorry for her. She's so unhappy.

Alexander rounds the corner and startles when he sees me. By the look on my face he can tell that I've been listening.

"How much did you hear?"

"Most of it, I think." I'm embarrassed to have been caught eavesdropping. "Thank you," I add.

"It needed to be said." He takes my hand and we walk to the car.

During the drive I tell him I need to stop at my house first so he heads in that direction. I can tell he doesn't want to talk about what happened with Molly. I don't want to waste any of our time together discussing her anyway.

"Edwin asked that you join us for dinner tomorrow night. Do you have to work?"

"No, I have tomorrow off. That'd be great."

He seems preoccupied, as he has been for weeks. I wonder if something is going on that he isn't telling me about. "Everything okay?"

He returns from wherever he was in his mind. "Yes. Of course. Why?"

"You just seemed far away, that's all." I do my best to sound upbeat but inside I can't shake a feeling of dread. "Is something going on with Avestan that I should be aware of?"

He shakes his head. "We have it under control. Good always wins out. Remember?"

I look over at him and he smiles at me but it doesn't reach his eyes and the worry in my stomach grows.

When we get to my house I run in and drop off my backpack and change into my Jack's t-shirt and a pair of jeans. When I emerge, there's a police squad car in Mrs. Binasco's driveway two doors down and she's talking with an officer. Mrs. Binasco has lived on our street since before I was born. Yesterday she shared pictures with me and my mom of an Alaskan cruise she went on with her four daughters. I wish I wasn't in such a hurry so I could go find out what's wrong.

"What's going on with Mrs. Binasco?" I ask as I get in the car.

"I spoke to her before you came out. Someone broke in while she was on vacation. She didn't notice anything was missing until today when she opened her jewelry box."

"Really? That's awful. I hope she's okay. I'm going to text my mom so she can check on her when she gets home from work." I fish my phone out of my purse.

"Are you making sure all your doors and windows are locked?" His voice is tense and it's making me nervous.

"Yes, we have an alarm. We're always careful," I assure him.

He's silent, contemplating. "What time do you need me to pick you up tonight?"

"Seven."

He nods. "I'll be there early."

Work is busy. In the middle of the dinner rush there's a shouting match between two inebriated customers that leads to a fistfight in the eating area outside. I nearly get caught in the middle as I'm clearing tables and Jack has to call the police to intercede. The whole episode is disturbing and scary, to be honest.

I ponder what Alexander said about how dark energy spreads. I don't mention the incident when he picks me up from work but the worry in the pit of my stomach feels like a rock. I yearn to feel carefree again, like I did on Valentine's Day.

"Can we fly again?" I ask, impulsively, as he's driving me home.

"Hmm?" He's distracted and only half listening.

"Can you take me flying again like you did before?"

"You mean right now?"

"If you want to … or some other time if you don't …."

"Sure, Declan. Whatever you say. We'll work something out … I'm a little worn out tonight though. You mind if I just take you home?"

"Oh. Okay. Of course I don't mind," I say, trying to mask my disappointment. *Something's wrong.* I can feel it.

He pulls into my driveway and walks me to the door, as usual, but there's a faraway look in his eyes as he hugs me goodbye. Later, as I get into bed, it takes a long time to push my worried thoughts to the side so I can fall into the sweet release of sleep.

"Do dogs and cats have auras?"

Alexander and I are in my room studying for our chemistry test. Books and papers are sprawled out around us on the floor. My cat, Willow, is sitting on my lap while I tickle her cheeks and rub under her chin the way she loves.

Alexander looks up, surprised at my non sequitur. We were in the middle of quizzing each other on atomic theory, which, in truth, he doesn't actually need to study—he's doing it for me. He explained once that when it comes to the science of the universe, our scientists have only grasped at the edges of understanding so far.

"Yes," he answers. "Some are more developed than others … usually with pets who have bonded with their caretakers over long periods."

I smile as I stare down at Willow and pet her. My dad and I rescued her from the shelter when I was in first grade. I remember it so clearly. There were endless cats to choose from and we were testing them out, putting them on our laps and seeing which one "chose us" my dad said. Some of the cats were skittish and scared and others were kind of pushy, nudging us with their heads to keep us petting them if we stopped for a second. Willow stood out. She was a gray tabby with tiger stripes, a little over one year old, and she was content to just be. She let me put her on my lap and she sat and purred. I said "Hi Willow" softly and she looked at me with knowing, intelligent eyes. I kept talking, telling her about myself and asking if she would like to come live with us and I swore she understood everything I said. My dad and I petted her for a long time and she clearly loved it but she was also fine to just sit and enjoy our company. I looked at my dad with hopeful eyes and he smiled and said it was obvious she'd chosen to be the newest member of the Jane family so we should take her home. I was over the moon.

My mom wasn't expecting us to bring home a pet—as I remember it, we'd just gone to get groceries and dad stopped at the shelter on a lark—but she took it in stride, like she always did. I drew a picture for Willow, to welcome her to our home, and my mom laminated it to preserve it. It's a giant rainbow with hearts all around and I wrote underneath, "The King of Love and Rainbows, who is a cat named Willow." I have no idea why I worded it that way. It's still tacked on the wall above her food and water bowls and it makes me smile whenever I refill them. My dad used to joke that Willow thought she was a dog because she always greeted us at the door, came when we called her, and she followed us everywhere in the house, just happy to be around people. After my dad died, Willow didn't go outside for months. She just kept going from room to room, looking for him and meowing. I understand how she felt.

"What does Willow's aura look like?" I ask. I know she must have a bright one.

He smiles and leans over and rubs her head the way he knows she likes. She purrs contentedly. "Why don't you guess? I'll tell you if you're right."

Willow stares up at me as if she knows what we're doing. If it's possible for a cat to smile, I swear that's the look on her sweet little tiny kitty face. I close my eyes to sense her energy and end up grinning immediately because it's so positive and loving. After a minute or two, when I have an image in my mind, I speak. "I see it as a bright, beautiful periwinkle."

I open my eyes to see Alexander laughing. "Did you have the giant box of Crayola crayons as a kid?"

"What? Why?"

"I love your color descriptions: cerulean, periwinkle, and what was that other one? Puce?"

I smile. "I *did* have the 64-count box with the very cool sharpener built into the side," I say as I toss a pillow at him. "But am I right? It's periwinkle?"

He reaches over and rubs Willow's chin, smiling, "Yes, you're right. I would have said blue but Willow agrees with you that periwinkle is more accurate."

Willow stands and stretches, stepping off my lap and sticking out her tongue in a big yawn. She must hear my mom pouring food into her bowl downstairs. Or maybe she's just tired of being the star of the show. She walks over to the door and turns her head to look at me, waiting patiently. I get up, open the door, and she rubs against my leg, emits two little meows that I interpret as "thank you" in cat speak, and trots downstairs.

I close the door and sit back down across from Alexander. "Can I ask a few more questions?"

"Of course, I'll always answer what I can."

"Is Edwin really your grandfather?"

He looks surprised. "Yes. Once. Sometimes people with a strong connection find each other again later."

"And your parents died?" It feels awkward to ask about this, but I'm wondering and want to understand.

"Yes. Many times. I've been both a parent and a child over many cycles."

"So you haven't always been Alexander Ronin?"

"I've always been me, with different labels."

"Why are you Alexander Ronin now?"

"I was in this physical form in my final mortal lifetime and I continue to use this shell when I need to. We choose our names when we become guardians and I chose one from my past. 'Alexander' means 'protector of man.'"

I smile at that. How apt. "Help me understand. In one of your lifetimes you looked like you do now, but you had a different name? And you died and became a guardian?"

He nods.

"How did you die?"

He instinctively touches the scar on his temple with his fingers. "That's something I'd rather not talk about, if you don't mind."

"Of course. God, I'm so sorry. I don't mean to pry." I kick myself inside for asking—who would want to talk about something like that?

We sit silent for a moment and I ponder what he told me. "If you looked like this in your last lifetime, aren't you worried someone will see you and recognize you? From who you used to be?"

He shakes his head. "It was many lifetimes ago."

"So that never happens?"

"Rarely. But have you ever heard of a doppelganger?"

"Wait, are you saying that when you see a person who looks like someone who died, you're actually seeing that person as a guardian?"

He shakes his head. "No. Most times, no, but it is possible. New guardians being careless, mostly. Or drawn to their past."

I run that over in my mind. "Who's in charge?"

"What do you mean?"

"Who tells you what to do?"

"We know what to do. If we need guidance, we can ask older souls."

"So there isn't *one* guy?"

"Or girl ..." he replies.

"Yes, of course. Man or woman. In fact, I'll bet it's a woman."

"If you're asking about pearly gates and all that, I'm sure you know that stories like that are created by mortals to fill gaps in human understanding. The same way ancient people explained thunder or an eclipse as the work of angry gods. The science is actually far more interesting and beautiful than any tales mortals have told."

"But *how* do you know what to do?"

"The same way cells know how to come together to form life. One cell begins to form the heart, another the brain, and still others continue to divide and grow and form every other part until you have a perfect organism with all elements working together. Each cell knows where to go and what to do to create and sustain the whole."

I absorb his answer. I could listen to Alexander forever and still have more questions. "Do you remember all your lifetimes?"

"Yes."

"And we've all had multiple lifetimes?"

"Some more than others. Have you ever met someone who seemed older than their years? Like an old soul?"

I nod. "But why don't we remember?"

"You do, but not consciously. Everyone's energy retains the knowledge learned in previous lifetimes. Sometimes children remember for a time—until the memories get crowded out as they grow older."

"You're immortal ..."

"Yes."

"Does that mean you're always going to look like this, stay like you are now?"

"Yes, when I'm in physical form."

"But I'm not." I pause because it's dawning on me what this means. "I'm going to keep growing older."

"Declan, shells mean nothing. Our energy will always be connected."

He searches my eyes and I know he sees the uncertainty. I don't want to continue talking about it ... for now at least. Each query only creates more and I don't like where the answers are leading. There is one question, however, that I've wanted to ask for a long time.

I look down at my hands, fidgeting nervously, and raise my eyes to meet Alexander's. "Can I ask one last question?"

He nods.

My voice quivers with hope and I strain to get the words out. "Have you seen my dad?"

There's a long pause and then Alexander leans over silently and pulls me in softly against his chest. With my head resting on his shoulder and his arms around me tightly, he answers. "Oh Declan, I'm so sorry, babe. It doesn't work that way."

He holds me for a long time.

Chapter Thirteen

Dinner is subdued. I don't know if I'm still carrying the weight of our earlier conversation or if there's an undercurrent of something going on between Alexander and Edwin. It's probably both.

Edwin greets me kindly, as always, and while he's preparing dinner he shares stories of close calls and misadventures he and Alexander encountered in Australia. A few times, as our meal is simmering on the stove, he walks over to the front window and looks up and down the street, scanning for something. It's discomforting.

"What is it?" I ask.

"Just looking to see if another storm is coming," Edwin says as he tugs the curtains closed tightly.

The weather has been dark and gloomy for weeks now. Powerful thunder and lightning storms—a downright rarity for San Mar—have been hitting with regularity. My mom was raised in upstate New York and although she loves California weather, she has always lamented the fact that we have very few thunderstorms here. "We used to have terrifically loud storms in the summer that would crack your eyeballs and light up the sky," she reminisced to me many times over the years. "Rain would pour down in buckets. Then the storm would be over in a flash and the clouds would part and the sun would come out with a bright sky and a rainbow. It was a gorgeous display of mother nature's power and beauty."

In San Mar, even when thunderstorms manage to roll in they're all weak cousins to the storms of my mom's youth. Lately however, the terrific rumbles and crashes of the storms in San Mar are so powerful and out of the ordinary that even my mom has admitted they rival New York storms. The last time we had one, the power went out and she jokingly looked up, raised her arms over her head, and cried out, "Uncle!" as a thunder clap shook the house. As we were searching in the dark for a flashlight, another ear-splitting crack sounded. "I give up!" she protested, "I've been asking for thunderstorms for years and now you're sending too many!"

"Dinner's ready. What can I get you to drink?" Edwin's voice brings me back to the present. He's holding a bottle of plain sparkling water in one hand and some flavored Pellegrino in the other.

"Pellegrino would be great, thanks. What can I do to help?"

"Why don't you and Alexander pour the drinks and I'll bring the food to the table. Then we'll be set."

The oddest thing about being around Edwin is we never talk about the fact that he and Alexander are angels. Our conversations are always pleasant but mundane—about the weather, or school, or his many stories of Australia, for instance. It's surreal and disconcerting. I have to keep reminding myself that he's the one who gave Alexander permission the night of the dance (which seems like a lifetime ago now) to tell me the truth. According to Alexander, Edwin is a powerful guardian, and has been for a very long time. There are questions I'd like to ask that perhaps only Edwin can answer. I don't understand his reasons for always directing our conversations to small talk but I'm wary of stepping outside the parameters he has us operating within.

On the surface, our dinner is congenial—we're making light conversation and having a nice meal—but simmering in the background is an atmosphere of thick tension between Edwin and Alexander, and it's building a deep sense of dread within me.

As we start clearing dishes, Edwin pauses mid-stride and snaps his fingers. "Oh shoot, I forgot to buy whipped cream. The pie won't be the same without it. Alexander, would you mind running to the store? By the time you get back, Declan and I will have everything cleaned up and we should be all ready for dessert."

"Sure," Alexander says with a shrug of his shoulders. "I'll be right back." He smiles at me as he grabs his keys and leaves.

As soon as the front door closes, Edwin's demeanor changes from jovial to coldly sober. He sets down the dish in his hand. "We need to talk," he says as he leads me over to the kitchen table and sits down across from me. His expression is so serious I'm terrified.

"Whatever's going on between you and Alexander can't continue." His words strike me like a blow to the chest. "You understand relationships between guardians and mortals are forbidden?"

My mind is racing. Why is he being so accusing? I was under the impression Edwin approved (albeit begrudgingly) of my relationship with Alexander. Moreover, I thought he genuinely *liked* me. It hurts to realize I've been all wrong … and the thought of not continuing to see Alexander is inconceivable.

"Yes, I know it's not ideal, but I love Alexander. Deeply. And I know he loves me." My voice quavers with fear.

Edwin softens, but only a little. "Declan, I know you love Alexander. And it's obvious to anyone with a pair of eyes that he's head over heels for you. But that's the problem. Truth be told, dear, I like you a great deal. If things were different …" his voice trails off as he rubs his eyes and lets out a frustrated sigh. "But they're not," he continues resolutely, "and there are things of far greater importance at stake here."

"Maybe I can help ..."

Edwin cuts me off. "You don't understand. Avestan has you in his sights now and you've become a difficult complication. You're the problem, not the solution." Seeing the devastation on my face at his words, he quickly adds, "As much as it pains me to say it."

There's a long stretch of silence and then Edwin strikes to the heart of his message. "The only way you can help is to make a very difficult decision. For Alexander's sake."

"For Alexander's sake?"

"Yes. He's been hiding it from you, but being with you is taking a toll on him. And it will only continue to get worse as long as you remain together."

"What do you mean? Taking a toll how?"

"Being around you weakens him."

My face flashes disbelief.

"It's true. And at the same time, Avestan's influence is building. Have you seen what's happening? Dark forces are gaining ground, expanding throughout the city. The crime, the storms—they're all signs. We can't lose the balance because once it's lost we may never be able to get it back."

"What are you saying?"

"Like attracts like. Dark energy feeds on itself and spreads, just as good energy does. If dark forces gain a majority, it will be nearly impossible to rein in as the evil multiplies."

"What does any of that have to do with Alexander and I being together?"

"Declan, I know this is hard to understand. Your aura is like no other mortal's I've seen. Ever. Destroying a power like yours could do untold damage. If dark forces gain a stronghold here and build momentum it could trigger a ripple effect." His expression is gravely serious.

"But how am I weakening Alexander?"

"There's a reason no Guardian has ever fallen for a mortal. Mortals typically hold no attraction—they're still evolving.

You, however, are somehow an exception and Alexander's feelings for you are forcing him to resist. Each day he spends resisting that earthly connection, his power diminishes. At the very least you're a distraction for him that I never should have sanctioned. I'm surprised he's been able to maintain his strength this long. Your aura has made you a target for Avestan. Alexander's love for you has only made it worse. And now, as Alexander is trying to protect you, dark forces will exploit his vulnerability and use his weakness against him. Eventually they'll destroy him. And you."

"Can't you protect him? I thought guardians were powerful."

"Even the greatest forces can be felled. One weak link threatens us all and Alexander's connection with you is making him vulnerable."

"I don't understand. What are you asking me to do?"

Edwin looks into my eyes. "You must convince Alexander that you no longer love him."

His words siphon the oxygen from my lungs and the room becomes small around us.

"I know it will be very difficult," he says gently, placing both his hands over mine, "but, Declan, I've thought this through and it's the only way he'll ever let you go. If you want to save Alexander, you need to take the love that you feel for him and figure out a way to convince him it was never there."

I'm having trouble breathing. I know Alexander will be back any moment. I can't face him. I feel manipulated and angry. Edwin must have planned the evening—to have me over for dinner and then send Alexander out so he could talk to me alone. How can he ask me to do this?

Beneath my roiling emotions, a rational corner of my brain realizes Edwin only wants to protect Alexander. I know I should feel grateful that he trusts me enough to tell me the truth. After all, Alexander has been keeping it from me. He's been at my side day in and day out and he never said a word that I was *harming* him. *How could he have done that?* My anger refocuses on Alexander. My mind is racing and my heart aches and I know I can't be here when he returns.

"Edwin, I'm feeling so many emotions right now I can't think straight. I love Alexander, and if I'm truly putting him in danger …." My voice breaks and Edwin gently squeezes my hands with compassion. "I would do anything to protect him … but I need time to think. I need to go home. I can't be here when Alexander gets back. I can't let him see my face or he'll know. Tell him I left feeling ill. Tell him dinner didn't agree with me—whatever you think he'll believe …. When do I have to do this?"

"The sooner the better," Edwin answers solemnly.

My heart breaks as I nod. "Tomorrow. I'll figure out a way to do what you asked by tomorrow."

His shoulders go slack with relief. "Thank you. I knew you would do the right thing." He glances at the clock on the wall next to us. "Let's go quickly. I'll walk you home."

The sound of our hurried steps on the pavement is lost to the wind as we walk in silence. Leaves are swirling in a mini cyclone near the streetlight on the corner. Edwin holds out his hand and somehow the wind stops whipping against my face, as if there's a shield around us. I'm too bereft and distracted to thank him or even care. He nods soberly to me when we reach my door. As I turn to go inside, he impulsively reaches out and hugs me tightly. "Thank you, Declan," he says quietly before he walks away.

The house is empty when I go inside. Thankfully, my mom is still out meeting with a client. I'm in no shape for small talk. Numbly, I go upstairs to my room and step out of my clothes as I walk into the bathroom. I drag my toothbrush across my teeth in a trance. As I get into bed and lay staring at the ceiling

I hear the ding of an incoming text from my phone on the nightstand.

It's from Alexander. "U ok? Call me."

"A little sick," I reply (that part isn't a lie). "Going to sleep. Thx 4 dinner."

"Thx 4 dinner that made u sick? R u nuts?"

"Ha. Going 2 bed. I'll b fine."

"K, call if you need me. Sweet dreams, babe, I love u."

I stare at the phone a long time, my heart breaking. I finally turn it off and set it on the nightstand without replying.

My mind is reeling with Edwin's request. How can I possibly convince Alexander I don't love him? *And how could I bear it if I did?* But what choice do I have? If what Edwin said is true, Alexander is getting weaker while Avestan and the other dark angels are growing stronger. All because of me.

What could I say that he would believe? I could pretend to be in love with someone else. No, he'd never believe it, and besides that, who? I've never been interested in anyone except for Alexander and he knows it.

I can tell him I'm tired of not being able to kiss—or anything else someday, for that matter. In truth, I would gladly spend an eternity with Alexander following those constraints if that's what it takes to be together, but at least this excuse has a ring of truth to it because resisting is so hard on both of us.

I can tell him his protectiveness is overbearing. He never lets me go anywhere alone and I'm starting to feel suffocated. This isn't true, but he doesn't know how I'm feeling, so it might work.

I have one final idea. It's the cruelest of them all. Combined with the others, I know it's the only thing that would cause Alexander to truly believe I never loved him. I don't think I can do it, but I know I have to. I consider running away rather than make up lies designed to hurt him. But what would I tell my mom and where would I go? Plus, I know Alexander would come for me and Edwin said the other guardians need him—he can't afford to be distracted any longer. I have to say something that will convince him he doesn't want to have anything to do with me anymore. The thought makes me sick. Literally. I run to the bathroom just in time for everything I've eaten to come up in waves as my stomach contracts over and over. When there's nothing left to expel, I dry heave until my stomach feels bruised from the inside out. I'm so exhausted I lay on the floor for a long time, staring at the cold, white tiles.

Eventually I drag myself to bed and let the tears flow onto my pillow. In the early morning hours I finally manage to escape into sleep.

Avestan is chasing me. I'm running as fast as I can but every time I turn around he's closer. It's misty with fog and it's getting dark. I'm running along the boardwalk, searching frantically for someone to help me but it's deserted. The wet cold soaks through to my bones and I'm desperate to find a hiding place. I hear Avestan getting closer and I know he's going to kill me.

As I run past the Haunted House I notice a door is ajar. I pull it open and go inside. It's pitch black and I move through the corridors by feeling with my hands, searching for a nook to hide in. The attraction is running and loud moans and screams are playing over and over, blasting through the speakers. At every corner something mechanical jumps out and I scream and back away, trying to find a safe spot to crawl into. I'm pressed against the wall, inching through the darkness when I feel long, cold fingers encircle my throat. "Did you think you could get away?" whispers Avestan, his mouth close to my ear. I scream as he squeezes tighter and tighter until I can no longer make a sound. He drags me through the exit door and throws me onto the pavement. I lay there, wheezing and pawing at my throat as I try to gulp in air.

Alexander appears and I run over, sobbing as I throw my arms around him. He steps back, pushing me away, and that's when I notice the tall, exquisite-looking blonde standing next to him. The same girl I saw waiting for him in the school parking lot. She laughs and says I was a fool to think Alexander ever loved me. Then she leans over and they kiss—a deep, long kiss. They walk away, laughing, their arms around each other. Avestan strides over, laces his fingers around my throat and starts to squeeze.

Waking brings a gasp of relief but also pain as the events of last night come rushing back. My alarm is going off but I'm not ready to let the cruel reality of what I have to do seep fully into my consciousness yet. I turn the alarm off and pull the covers over my head to try to go back to sleep. Another nightmare is preferable to what I have ahead of me.

Twenty minutes later my mom knocks softly and pokes her head around the door. "Declan, you okay? If you don't get up now, you'll be late for school."

"I'm not feeling so good, mom," I mumble with the covers over my head, "I think I'll go in late, if that's okay."

"Of course it's okay if you're not feeling well, sweetie." She sounds worried. "Let me take your temperature."

My mom and I never take sick days so I know how concerned she must be. "The Jane's have fierce immune systems," she always says. She leaves to get the thermometer and comes back to sit on the side of my bed. She tugs on the covers I'm holding and I slowly lower them down. I can feel how horribly puffy and red my eyes are.

"Declan, you've been crying! What's wrong?"

"It's nothing. Alexander and I just got into a fight," I lie. "I'll be okay in a little while. I just don't feel well now."

"Oh honey, I'm so sorry. What happened? Do you want to talk about it?"

I shake my head, looking miserable.

"You sure? I'm here to listen."

My eyes brim with tears as she strokes my forehead.

"You know," she says softly, "relationships can be hard sometimes. But you and Alexander seem very well matched … I'm sure it will all work out." I can tell she's trying to sound hopeful. "Let's take your temperature, though, just in case it's something more."

She places the digital thermometer under my tongue and I close my mouth to hold it in place. As we wait she continues to stroke my forehead gently. A tear escapes my eye and trails down the side of my face, pooling onto the pillow as I gaze back at her. If only my mom could make it all better like she used to when I was a kid.

The thermometer beeps and she pulls it out to read the result. "Ninety-eight point six on the dot. Well, at least you don't have a fever."

A raging fever would be preferable to how I'm feeling.

"Do you want me to stay home from work this morning? I could make you some breakfast and bring it up to you."

The last thing I want is food. "Thanks, mom, but I wouldn't be able to eat it. I'll be ready to go to school in a little while. I just need some extra time to pull myself together."

"Okay. If you're sure …" she sounds hesitant. "I'll let the school know you'll be in late. But call me any time today and I'll come home if you need me, okay? Everyone deserves a mental health day now and then."

"Okay," I smile weakly, "I love you, mom."

She leans over and hugs me tightly for a long time. "I love you too, sweetie. So much. I'm so sorry this happened."

After my mom leaves for work, I lay in bed going over and over in my mind what I have to do. My hope is that repeating it incessantly will anesthetize me to the pain when I actually have to speak the words to Alexander. I know I can't show my true feelings or he'll never be convinced. I'm not sure I can do it, but according to Edwin I have no choice: Alexander's life depends on it.

I turn on my phone and there are several voicemails and text messages waiting for me from Alexander, asking where I am and if I'm okay. He must have been worried when I didn't show up to homeroom.

I text him back, laying the foundation for my plan. "Still not 100%. Will b in latr. Talk after school?"

Our afternoon schedules are different so as long as I arrive after lunch I can avoid him if I take precautions between classes. But after school I won't be able to hide any longer. I'll have to do the one thing I never imagined I would do. Ever. And I have to make Alexander believe it.

After lying in bed for far too long, I drag myself to the shower and let ice cold water spray on my face to bring the swelling down. It's a miserable assault but it matches how I feel inside and I'm immune to the pain. I get dressed, pulling on jeans and the first shirt my hand touches in the closet. I put my hair in a ponytail and stare at my face in the mirror. Despair-filled eyes peer back. I can't avoid it any longer. I decide to ride my bike rather than drive Archie. It's misty wet and the cold air stings my face as I pedal into the wind but I don't care.

I arrive just in time for fifth period. Liz is already there and she waves to me as I walk in the door and sit down at the desk next to her.

"You okay?" she asks. "Alexander said you were sick last night and this morning. Food poisoning or something."

"I'm not feeling great."

"Yeah, you don't look so great. You look like you've been hit in the face with a million tiny hammers."

I feign a smile but it doesn't reach my eyes.

"Sorry, Dec. Just trying to make you laugh. You sure that's all it is? Food poisoning?"

"I'm just a little down, and not much in the mood for conversation. Mind if we talk later instead?"

"Sure," she says, sounding worried. "Whenever you feel like talking you know I'm always here." She reaches over and squeezes my hand.

I manage a small smile of thanks and we both turn to the front as class begins.

I don't recall a thing from any of my afternoon classes. My mind spins ceaselessly with what I have to do and how I have to do it. I think I'm going to be physically ill again when the final bell rings and it's time to meet up with Alexander. I remind myself over and over why Edwin said I must do this and I steel myself as I walk my bike to where he's waiting by his car.

He runs up to take the bike from me and gives me a hug. I keep my arms by my sides.

"How are you feeling? I was worried about you all day." He starts to lift my bike into his car and I stop him.

"Don't."

He looks puzzled. "What? Why?"

"Because we need to talk and I want to bike home."

A look of worry crosses his face. "Declan, what's going on?"

"You told me to tell you if I ever wanted out and, well, now I do. I don't want to be in this relationship anymore."

His look of shock and hurt pierces my heart. "What are you saying? How can you mean that?"

My resolve starts to crumble but I remind myself that Alexander's safety depends on him wanting to get as far away from me as possible. We can't just break up and remain friends. I have to be convincing and I have to be cruel.

"I can't be in a relationship with someone I can hardly touch. It's frustrating and ridiculous and, as you've said many times, there's no loophole, so there's no end to it. It's not a complete relationship and I deserve something more."

He looks at me with skepticism combined with hurt and complete confusion. I know it doesn't sound like me. I have to do better.

"And you're overbearing. Always needing to know my schedule, never letting me go anywhere alone—you're trying to control me and it's suffocating. I'm tired of having you around all the time. I need to be alone sometimes. I can take care of myself."

He looks as though I've struck him physically. He's frozen, incredulous. "But I'm protecting you. Don't you understand that? I love you and I could never let anything happen to you. I'll have someone else protect you if you want some space. All you had to do was ask. Declan, what's going on? What happened?" He pauses and then asks in a pained whisper, "Are you saying you don't love me anymore?"

The torment on his face is unbearable. I have to shut off my emotions completely or I know I'll fall apart. My heart bursts with anguish but it's time to play my last, cruel card.

"No, Alexander, the truth is, I never loved you." My mouth forms the words but it's as if they're coming from another person. I've disengaged from my body because it's the only way I can get through what I have to say next.

"I thought it was love but I realize now that it was a mistake. I suffered from panic attacks my whole life and I didn't think they would ever end. You released me from that pain and I never felt so free. It's only natural that I might confuse my feelings of gratitude for love. I'm a different person without anxiety. I'm in control. I misconstrued my feelings for you. Once I realized it, I felt obligated because you helped me so much, but I can't go on like this and I don't need your help any longer. I'm ready for a real relationship, with someone I truly love, and with someone who can act on their feelings. Not with a boy who can only talk."

The expressions that flash over Alexander's face change from hurt to disbelief and then to acceptance and even disgust. I can see in his eyes he's reevaluating what kind of person I am—what kind of person I must have always been but he didn't see it until now—and it cuts me to the core.

With hardness in his voice that slices like a steel blade, Alexander stares at me coldly and says, "I won't bother you again."

I mask the horror I feel inside as he gets into his car and drives away … out of my life.

I've done my duty successfully, Edwin will be glad to know. But I'm a broken human being and I'll never be the same again.

Chapter Fourteen

"Declan?" My mom calls out to me from the kitchen when I open the front door. She comes around the corner and when she sees my face she drops the dish towel in her hand and wraps her arms around me.

"Oh honey, what happened? Did you have another fight with Alexander?"

I erupt into heaving sobs at the mention of his name. "We broke up, mom. We broke up." That's all I can get out as I start shaking uncontrollably, my tears soaking her shoulder.

We stay like that for a long time: My mom rocking me side to side, hugging me tightly, and smoothing my hair. "It's okay, it's okay," she whispers, over and over like a meditation. Slowly my sobbing subsides and I pull away to look into her eyes and use both hands to wipe the tears from my face. It's a useless endeavor because more stream down to take their place, but I continue the effort, attempting to gain a measure of control.

"Why?" my mom asks, genuine pain in her voice. "What happened?"

I shake my head, still wiping tears. "It's for the best. I don't want to talk about it if that's okay. I just feel so sad."

"Did he hurt you, honey? Did he do something?" Her fierce mother bear protectiveness is kicking in.

"No. Nothing like that. I broke up with him. We're too different. It won't ever work."

"Really, sweetie? I never got that impression. Are you sure you don't want to talk about it?"

I shake my head slowly. "I think I just want you to hug me."

"Well *that* I can do," she says as she squeezes me tight and walks with me to the family room.

We sit on the couch and hug in silence for a while. I'm slouched down, resting my head on her shoulder with my feet curled to the side under a pillow. My mom smoothes my hair as she holds me and, eventually, my tears run dry. My eyes feel swollen and sore.

"Are you sure you don't want to talk about it, honey? I don't want to push you, but I might have some good advice."

"I don't even want to think about it," I croak, shaking my head.

"Okay, well how about if I run you a hot bath. You can soak awhile and then I'll make us some hot cocoa and we can sit on the couch and watch a movie. To take your mind off things. Maybe a funny one. We haven't watched a movie together in a while. I'll pull out some blankets and we can make it nice and cozy."

I nod, devoid of emotion. Maybe a movie would be good— anything but a romance. I turn to stare out the window. It's cold and gray outside and suddenly I shiver. I slide the dark brown chenille throw off the arm of the sofa and spread it over me. I can't help but think my aura is probably brown right now, too—a bitterly perfect mud brown to match how I feel inside.

My mom calls to me when the bath is ready. As I sink down into the hot, bubbly water, I just want to keep sinking. I slide down until my face is submerged, blocking out all sound, all thought. I don't want to surface. Eventually I come up for air and I lay in the tub, staring blankly at the wall, until my fingertips shrivel and the water cools. My mom has laid out flannel pajamas on my bed and when I come downstairs she hands me a steaming mug of hot cocoa.

We get settled on the couch and my mom flips through our Netflix and cable offerings, looking for a movie that will guarantee some laughs. I don't think any movie could possibly distract me from the pain I'm feeling but I'm willing to try. We settle on *Monty Python and the Holy Grail*, an old favorite. I hardly pay attention, but it feels good to be snuggled under blankets with my mom with something mindless in front of me. By the time Arthur battles the Black Knight (who keeps trash talking even after all his limbs are cut off) I even smile a little.

I go to bed early and sleep heavy, emotionally and physically drained. Somehow I make it through the next day in a fog. I expect Alexander to try to talk to me and I have plans to avoid him, but instead I find that he's the one doing the avoiding. The few times our eyes meet he stares at me blankly and turns away. I didn't think I could possibly feel any more pain than what I felt as he drove away yesterday but his disdain delivers me to another level of heartache.

As I round the corner into the quad at lunch, I see him talking to Liz and Finn so I stop and start to head in the other direction. Liz catches my eye and raises a finger as if to say, "Hold on a sec," so I wait close by, head down, kicking at the dirt with the tips of my Vans. A few minutes later Alexander hugs Liz and walks away. Finn and Liz come over to me immediately.

"You broke up with Alexander?" Liz asks, incredulous.

I nod.

"Why?" Liz and Finn ask in a chorus.

"What did he tell you?" I want to make sure my explanation squares with whatever he said.

"Something about the two of you not being right for each other after all," Liz says. "It doesn't really make sense to me."

Alexander's explanation sends a stab of pain directly to my heart. I swallow and steel myself to deliver the lie I prepared. "It was never going to work anyway. Eventually he'll go back to Australia and I'll be in college here. It's for the best, but it hurts and it's too hard to talk about, to be honest."

Liz searches my eyes, confused. "I still don't understand. But okay, I won't press you for now. There's no chance for reconciliation?"

I shake my head and she mirrors the sadness in my eyes as she hugs me tightly.

I'm desperately trying not to cry. I have to keep up the charade that I *want* this. It's the only way to make it believable.

"I'm really sorry, Declan. I liked Alexander," Finn says, sadly.

I nod. "Thanks, Finn." It feels good to be around his steadfast energy.

He reaches over and squeezes my hand gently. "It's going to be okay," he says, looking into my eyes.

I nod, but inside I know he's all wrong.

The next day passes in much the same way and then it's blessedly the weekend. I'm free to go to work at Jack's and come home without worrying about running into Alexander and seeing the blank disillusionment in his eyes. If I take the long way around, I don't even have to pass by his house. I can't shake the feeling I'm being observed while I'm biking to work, though, and I wonder if Edwin has someone else watching me for protection.

After closing, Jack stays inside to do some paperwork and I go outside to wait for my mom. I do my usual routine with Jimmy, giving him a bag of food and we exchange our typical chitchat. When I say goodbye I walk my bike to the front of the parking lot where I can see my mom when she pulls in. I don't want to ride home in the dark. Eric is the security guard on shift. He's fairly new and his routine is different from Antonio's. I don't see him walking the perimeter. He must be on the far side of the lot behind the falafel bar.

As I stand waiting, a figure steps out of the shadows and into my line of vision. I jump and emit a startled cry.

"I think you're being a little overly dramatic," says Avestan.

I look around for Eric but I still don't see him. Or anyone. I thought Edwin would have other guardians protecting me. Where are they? I grip my bike tightly and turn to head back toward the restaurant.

"There's no need to run away. I'm only here to give you some information. About your boyfriend."

"I don't have a boyfriend," I say as I start wheeling my bike away.

"Oh, right. I heard about the break up. Sad story. An interesting thing about that: you think you were putting one over on him, but he's the one who's been fooling you this whole time."

I stop walking.

"He told you I'm the bad guy, right? He's the righteous one? I'm sure he sounded convincing. But the line between good and evil doesn't exist. It depends on where you're standing at the time."

I don't say anything.

"Did you really think he loved you? I mean, an angel falling for a mortal is a stretch. And although I have to admit you hold a certain attraction, you're not exactly guardian material. Did that ever make sense to you, Declan?"

He's trying to make me doubt myself and it's working. I feel small and ugly. I know I need to picture the white ball of light inside me as a defense, but his words are distracting. He knows all the buttons to push.

"Here's the truth: Alexander was assigned to protect you. They always assign him to your type. He tells you he loves you blah, blah, blah, because it makes his job easier to keep you close. *All* the girls fall for it," he says with a bored sigh. "Did he tell you the "true love's kiss" story? It's so romantic none of you gullible mortals ever realize it's just his way to avoid you. He could kiss you if he wanted to. The fact is, he doesn't. You're just one of many, Declan. So let me ask you, who is the true bad guy here? Me—the one telling you the truth? Or him—the one who has been lying to you all along?"

It can't be true. He's just trying to get into my head. "Alexander would never do that."

"You don't want to believe it—I can understand that. But ask yourself, how can he love you when he's bound to another?"

I look up, surprised.

"He didn't tell you about Alenna? She's a guardian—far more suitable for him than a mortal." He pauses to let that sink in. "If you doubt it, ask him. You'll finally realize I'm the only one giving you the whole picture."

My expression is blank, confused.

"Declan, this is your last chance. Come with me and I'll tell you everything—including what Alexander doesn't want you to know. You owe it to yourself to learn the full truth. You *deserve* to know, don't you? Especially after the way he treated you."

"Declan? Everything alright?" Jimmy walks over to stand next to me. He must have come around from the back. It's a relief to see him.

"I'm okay. Thanks, Jimmy. Would you mind waiting with me until my ride gets here, though? Eric, the security guard, will be back around any moment, but I'd like the company."

I mention the security guard as a warning to Avestan. I don't want Jimmy to be in any danger by helping me.

"Sure, Declan," agrees Jimmy. Then he turns to Avestan with a hard stare. "Why don't you move along now."

Avestan pauses and then gives a small nod of assent. "Think about what I said, Declan. I'll be in touch," he says grimly as he turns and walks away, leaving me shaking.

"You sure you're okay?" Jimmy asks after Avestan is gone.

I start to nod and then let out a sigh of relief as my mom's car turns into the parking lot. "You want a ride to the shelter?" I ask, turning toward him.

"Nah, thanks. I think I'm gonna hang around here a bit," he says as he walks back to his favorite bench.

"Okay. Thanks again, Jimmy," I call after him. My mom pulls the lever to pop the trunk and I lift my bike in with trembling arms. I peer over in the direction Avestan was walking, but he disappeared.

My legs are still shaking as we drive away.

Chapter Fifteen

Alenna? Who is Alenna? I toss and turn all night, unable to sleep. Is she the beautiful blonde I saw him with that day at school? And at his house? And in my dream? Could anything Avestan said be true? Don't fall for it, Declan, I keep telling myself. Don't be an idiot. And yet … why didn't Alexander tell me about her?

And what about not being able to kiss? Alexander isn't the only one who brought that up—Edwin counseled me on the dangers of our relationship, too. After all, that was the reason he made me break up with Alexander in such a cruel way, so Alexander wouldn't have to resist all the time, weakening him, and …. *What if it was all made up?* Maybe Alexander grew tired of me so he and Edwin spun the tale together. That way, not only was the breakup my idea but I would conveniently avoid him afterwards, giving them just what they wanted.

Have I been a fool?

No, it can't be true. The look on Alexander's face when I broke up with him was real. And all those times he told me he loved me. You can't fake that. Or can you? I was surprised the day after I told him it was over that Alexander didn't even try to approach me. In retrospect, it seems that he accepted our breakup far too easily.

Twisted notions consume my thinking all night long and I start to doubt everything I ever believed. I detest Avestan for injecting these thoughts into my head. I can't bring myself to accept any of it as true, but one thing is painfully clear: he planted a seed of doubt.

I barely sleep. Sunday morning I don't have to work so I lay in bed all day, morose and confused. I have an English paper due Monday but I can't conceive of trying to focus on *The Sound and the Fury* so I put it off.

A big part of me wants to march over to Alexander's house and demand to know who Alenna is. But why am I letting it consume me? Nothing Avestan says can be trusted. I tell myself to just put it out of my mind. My plan to break up with Alexander succeeded. I should let it be, right? Mission accomplished.

And yet … I'm obsessed with the question of Alenna. If I ask and Alexander doesn't know what I'm talking about, I can rest easy that Avestan made it up. If I get a reaction, however …

In a moment of weakness, I pick up my phone to text Alexander. I changed his name in my contact list so that it shows up as "Don't do it!" to prevent myself someday from doing this very thing, but I ignore my own warning and type a message. It's short and to the point: "Why didn't you tell me about you and Alenna?"

Before I can stop myself I tap "send."

I drop the phone quickly onto my nightstand as if it's a burning coal and I chastise myself for my weakness—both for lending possible credence to anything Avestan told me, and also for communicating with Alexander. If what I know in my heart is true, I'm putting him in danger by contacting him. Oh, Declan, what have you done? Stupid, stupid girl.

A moment later I hear the familiar ding of an incoming text.

I pick up my phone, hand trembling, and read Alexander's reply: "Who told you?"

That's all he wrote but it's all I need to know. Alenna exists and he didn't want me to know about her. My heart dislodges and drifts like a paper doll to settle, torn, at my feet. I stare at the text for a long time, digesting it.

A flash of light outside and a loud crack of thunder startle me from my rumination. It was raining earlier, but now it's pounding on the roof so loudly it sounds like a freight train rushing past. According to Edwin the storms are a sign that Avestan's influence is growing. But maybe that's all a lie. It's raining because it's April, isn't that the more likely explanation?

Thunderstorms in San Mar *are* rare, though. "Ugh," I groan aloud, I could go back and forth like this for days. I have to stop the insanity and focus on something other than dark angels, bad weather, and exquisitely beautiful guardians named Alenna.

With a heavy sigh, I reach over and grab my laptop so I can finish my English paper. Anything to stop my mind from cycling endlessly, trying to parse truth from lies. Before I get started, in true procrastinator's form, I decide to access the San Mar Sentinel online. I want to see what the local paper has to say about the weather. As the website comes into view, the top headline grabs my attention: "Strange Lights Reported Again over San Mar." I click to read reports of mysterious flashes of light near the beach flats area. The same area where the surge in violence and crime started. No explanation has been found and the majority conclusion is that it's simply lightning, but eyewitnesses insist they've seen the flashes on clear days. A small, vocal group is claiming it's a U.F.O. presence. The article concludes with no answers and an open call for readers to submit photos. I'm not sure what to make of it. More proof of Edwin's claims? Or just lightning storms that Californians aren't used to?

I open up my essay and force myself to focus on my assignment. I realize as I'm typing that the truth about what Avestan told me doesn't matter. Whether it's because Alexander and I truly *can't* be together or because it's all been a cruel hoax and Alexander doesn't *want* to be with me, the result is the same: We'll never be together. What does it matter what the reason is?

My heart is broken either way.

Chapter Sixteen

Alexander isn't at school the next day, or any other day the entire week. I'm worried but at the same time I wonder if he's avoiding me so he won't have to explain Alenna. Or worse, maybe he's *with* Alenna. I never texted him back and, curiously, (and, in my opinion, damningly) he didn't text again.

It isn't easy but I keep trudging ahead and try to focus on normal things, like school and work, rather than dark angels and guardians and the world tipping toward evil. Liz, Finn, and I are in the quad having lunch and Liz is discussing her upcoming birthday. The afternoon is gorgeous with endless blue skies and nary a cloud to see. I toy with the idea that the weather is a good sign but honestly I don't know what to think anymore. Regardless, it's Friday and I hope it stays nice through the weekend. How I've missed the sun. I close my eyes and lean back on my arms to absorb the warmth of the rays on my face.

"Will you help me plan it?" asks Liz. "My mom wants to do it, but if I let her run with it unchecked who knows what we'll end up with—maybe another troupe of illustrated men in Speedos or that contortionist guy like last year. Remember that? Watching him cram his entire body into that tiny acetate box still gives me nightmares." We both laugh aloud at the memory. "We need to feed my mom normal ideas to keep her within the realm of the sane."

"I don't know—I actually love your mom's broad interpretation of entertainment. I'd like to see what she comes up with on her own," I threaten with a laugh.

Liz's father is a successful venture capitalist and her mom is an eccentric artist who loves to throw parties that are completely over the top. With money as no object, the events can get pretty out there. It embarrasses Liz to no end but I find the entertainment fascinating. Mrs. Warner always incorporates some bizarre performance art elements and, if nothing else, it makes for great stories. We usually end up laughing afterwards until our stomachs hurt.

"Do you work this Saturday?" she asks.

"Yes, but only until two." I welcome the distraction planning a party will provide.

"Great. Come over Saturday after work and we'll brainstorm," Liz says. "Finn, you're invited, too, of course."

"Right, because you know how much I love party planning," Finn replies dryly. Liz and I laugh. "I think you guys can handle it without me," he adds.

After school I work until closing and then I'm scheduled again Saturday morning. Keeping busy makes the weekend bearable. I line up a babysitting gig with the Bings all day Sunday, too. My mom is leaving for a week-long work training seminar on Sunday morning and I don't want to be alone all day with nothing to distract me. I'm looking forward to seeing Charlie and occupying myself with knight and dragon battles.

On Saturday, curiosity gets the better of me and I ride my bike past Alexander's house twice on my way to and from work, but no one appears to be home. I feel as if someone is watching me, though. Hopefully it's a guardian. What if it's one of Avestan's dark angels? I look around and everyone is a suspect. Maybe I'm just being paranoid. I can't help but wonder where Alexander and Edwin have gone and if their absence involves Avestan. Or Alenna.

I arrive at Liz's house at three on Saturday and her mom answers the door. "Hi, Fran, how are you?" I ask. It's been drilled into me never to call her "Mrs. Warner." She says it makes her feel old.

"I'm great, Declan, it's so nice to see you! Apologies for my appearance, I'm in the middle of a creative inspiration." She has a streak of paint on her cheek and she wipes her hands on the large pinstriped oxford dress shirt she's wearing, leaving smeared trails of orange and red paint down the front. "I'm sorry to say that Liz isn't here, dear."

"She isn't? I thought we had plans. Maybe I misunderstood."

"No, you're right. We were all going to discuss ideas for the party. But she got a call and she was out the door. I thought she went to your house—do you think you passed her on the way over?"

"Maybe," I say, puzzled. "I'll go back home and see if she's there. Thanks. It was nice seeing you."

"You too, dear, and tell Liz when you see her that I already have a few ideas I know she'll love," she replies cheerily.

As she closes the door, I hear Liz's dad call out in alarm in the background, "Fran, what in God's name is going on in the kitchen? And is that another one of my good shirts you're ruining?"

I laugh as I walk to my bike. Before I leave, I call Liz and she answers on the first ring.

"I see you in the driveway," she says, "I'll be right there. Sorry I'm late."

I look up to spot her driving towards me down the street. She pulls in and tells me she had to run some papers over to Finn's house for their next debate.

"I didn't think I'd be long but when I got there, he'd just gotten back from a long bike ride and he looked so cute and …" Liz explains, blushing.

"Enough said," I say, putting up my hand to stop her. "Glad you were able to resist him and make it back at all."

Liz hits my arm and we laugh as we go inside.

"Has Finn always been so smart?" We're through discussing party ideas and now we're having an early dinner by the pool at Liz's house. Mrs. Warner is asking me about Finn as a child.

"Yes. Always," I say. "I remember he was so bored the first day of kindergarten he raised his hand and said, 'Excuse me, I already know this information. I didn't sign up for this.' When our teacher, Mrs. Minka, told him his mom had signed him up he raised his hand again and asked what time it was. She told him and he said, 'I think I have somewhere else to be at this time.'"

Liz and Mrs. Warner laugh.

"They tested him and he was moved to an accelerated class the next day I think. His mom didn't want him to move too far ahead though because she wanted him to be around kids his age."

"Were you guys really friends with Molly as kids?" asks Liz.

"Yeah. Hard to believe, I know. She was okay in preschool and by the time we got to elementary school our parents had set up carpools and stuff that kept us together even when we didn't want to be. I remember one day Finn came over when he was about six or seven and told me that he never wanted to play with Molly again. He had been at her house after swim class and they decided to have roly poly races. They each found three roly polys and they put them on the ground and drew a finish line with chalk. Eventually one of the roly polys crossed the line and Finn was jumping up and down because it was one of his. You know how he likes to win."

Liz nods.

"Anyway, when he turned around, he saw Molly smushing the other roly polys with her thumb, one by one. He cried out, 'What are you doing?!' And she said, 'They're losers. They don't deserve to live.' Finn ran inside and told Molly's mom and she got in big trouble. Molly was mean to him for a long time after that. But don't ask Finn about it—he still gets upset that she killed those roly polys, to this day."

"Jesus, that girl is *diabolical*," says Liz.

"Her mom is nice—a little spacey, but well meaning. But her dad, Roger, was always an asshole," says Mrs. Warner. "What Molly said about losing sounds like it came straight from his mouth."

I'm shocked. I've never heard Mrs. Warner speak negatively about anyone. "Did you know the Bings well?" I ask. "When they were still together?"

She nods. "We moved here about a year before they divorced. We tolerated Roger at parties. I felt for Charlene, but I wasn't brokenhearted—or surprised—when they split. It was right before Charlie was born and I think Molly blames the divorce on that poor kid. It's no wonder Charlene pays you to babysit even when Molly's home. Roger and his new wife have two kids, I heard. He hardly sees Molly or Charlie anymore … it's sad. I'm saying too much, though. I shouldn't have had that last glass of wine. I hate to be a gossip." She stands abruptly. "Anyone want some more hummus before I take it inside?"

I shake my head. I'm still digesting Mrs. Warner's story—it explains a lot. "Thanks again for dinner," I say as I stand up alongside her. "I should probably get going. My mom's leaving tomorrow morning. Can I help clean up before I go?"

"Thanks, dear, but no need. I'm just putting it all in the dishwasher. Anna is coming in the morning." Anna is their housekeeper. "It was so nice to see you, Declan. Maybe you can convince Liz to go with that idea we talked about." She winks at me.

Over her mom's shoulder, I see Liz with her eyes open wide in mock alarm. She shakes her head slowly as she mouths the word "no." We laugh as she walks me through the kitchen into the foyer.

"What? You're not on board with the mime troupe? Or the living sculptures?" I ask Liz jokingly. "I actually liked the human bowling idea."

"Et tu Brute?" replies Liz as she shoves me out the door.

When I get home, my mom is busy packing. "I sent you an email with my itinerary so you have my flight numbers and hotel," she says.

"Do you want me to drive you to the airport tomorrow?"

"No, Julie's picking me up." Julie is her good friend and co-worker. "I'll have my cell phone with me so you can call if you need anything."

"I'll be fine, mom."

"No raging parties while I'm gone, by the way."

"Yeah, right. You foiled my secret plan."

"Are you really going to be okay, hon?" she asks, searching my eyes with concern. "I mean with Alexander and everything? I can cancel this trip if you don't want to be alone. No kidding—I know all this stuff and I'll take any excuse to avoid a week spent with Fred Fillner."

I smile. "That's ridiculous. I would never ask you to cancel your fantasy week with Fred."

She laughs. "It's so good to see you smiling. It makes me feel better about leaving."

"I'll be fine, mom. Really. I'm going to keep busy with school and work and go for a lot of long runs. It's only a week and I'll see you on Saturday."

She gives me a hug and I help her finish packing before we both go to bed early. I'm grateful to be babysitting the next day—anything to keep my mind off Alexander.

I arrive at the Bing's house at ten the next morning but Mrs. Bing's car isn't in the driveway. I knock but there's no answer. I ring the bell and knock again.

"Oh, it's you," Molly says with an impressive lack of enthusiasm as she swings open the door. "I didn't think you were coming until later."

"Your mom said to come at ten."

She doesn't move.

"Can I come in?" I ask.

"Charlie's not here."

"What? Where is he?"

"Relax. I'm sure my stupid mom will still pay you. My boyfriend took the little pest to the park."

"The park down the street?"

"I don't know. Probably."

"All right. Well how about I go and relieve him. Who's your boyfriend?" I didn't know Molly was going out with anyone. Her last boyfriend was the quarterback of the football team but he broke up with her when she cheated on him with his best friend.

"You wouldn't know him. He's in *college*. We met at a beach party."

"Oookay ... does he have a name?"

She sighs as if I'm burdening her with tedious questions. "He's tall and hot. You can't miss him. His name is Avestan."

The expression on my face startles Molly. For a split second I'm frozen. Then, in one fluid movement, I turn and run to my bike as waves of horror ripple down my spine. I can't let the shock overtake me.

"Jesus, what's your problem?" calls out Molly in irritation.

I'm gone before she closes the door. I tear down the street and continue over the sidewalk and onto the grass in the middle of the playground, where I stop to look around. I don't see them anywhere. Maybe Molly was wrong about which park they went to.

Then I see it.

On the edge of the bench where Avestan was sitting when I saw him here that day. The stark, gray snowglobe Avestan gave to Charlie and I threw out.

Before I can process what it means, my phone vibrates in my purse and I pull it out quickly to see a text message from an unfamiliar number. Three simple words stop me in my tracks:

"Looking for Charlie?"

Chapter Seventeen

My center falls through my body and my line of vision grows very small. Not Charlie. No.

The horror I feel is asphyxiating. "Why Charlie?" I type.

The reply drops me to my knees.

"Bait."

I caused this.

The world spins in slow motion and I feel the cool, wet grass seep through my jeans as all air collapses around me. My phone rings and I slowly raise it to my ear.

"Hello, Declan." Avestan's voice is deep and smooth.

"Why?" I whisper. "He's just a child. Bring him back. Let me talk to him."

Avestan's reply is slow to come, and chilling. "You know that's not going to happen."

"I don't believe he's with you. I need to talk to him," I plead.

"That isn't possible."

It's *not possible?* Has he hurt him? Panic beats like a hummingbird in my chest. "Why are you doing this?" I entreat. "He's an innocent child. Do whatever you want to me, but please let him go."

His reply drips acid. "*You* did this. I gave you the chance— several times—to come willingly. Now I've taken the choice out of your hands. In one hour at eleven you will meet me in front of the Big Dipper at the boardwalk. Come alone and tell no one. I'm watching. Deviate from these instructions in any way and I can assure you that no one will ever see Charlie again."

I beat back the panic rising in my chest using willpower I didn't know I had. "I'll be there," I say in a choked whisper. But there's no reply, only dead air.

I look at my watch: 10:10. I have less than an hour. I don't know what to do. Should I tell Alexander? Or maybe Edwin? I'm not even sure if I can trust anything they've told me so far. Moreover, Avestan's instructions were clear: Tell no one and come alone or he'll hurt Charlie. I can't risk it. An innocent little boy's life is at stake and it's all because of me. I have to fix this. Alone.

My mind is a jumble and I can't think in a straight line. I desperately want to talk to someone, *do* something. I pinch my eyes closed to hold back the tears. *Man up, Declan. There's no one who can help you. You have to help yourself.*

I take several deep breaths and enter a state of determined calm as I rise to my feet and resolve what I have to do.

When I reach the boardwalk, I lock my bike to one of the rusty metal racks at the entrance near the railroad tracks. I'm not sure why I bother. I doubt I'll ever be using my bike again. But somewhere inside I retain a measure of hope and I don't want to deny it, however remote. I hear the roar of the ocean on the other side of the boardwalk. The normally peaceful sound now feeds my anxiety. The sky is churning with dark gray clouds and large waves are pounding against the shore, building strength and speed—a storm is coming.

The boardwalk is deserted. I flash back to the nightmare I had when Avestan was strangling me and my stomach twists into a knot of dread. A few of the rides are usually open on the weekends year-round but not on days like today that portend a storm. I walk under the large painted archway that proclaims "Welcome to the San Mar Beach Boardwalk!" and turn left towards the Big Dipper. I walk slowly and scan my perimeter as I go, searching for Avestan. I'm twenty minutes early. I'm not sure what benefit an early arrival can bring but somehow the idea of being first makes me feel less helpless and out of control.

When I reach the Big Dipper, I look around nervously. The large blue sign on the entrance booth indicates that six tickets are required—the highest amount of any ride at the boardwalk. Tickets are a buck a piece. Or 25 cents on local's night. It's a wooden coaster, built in the 1920's without any of the loops or death-defying features of modern roller coasters, but it's rickety and there are no bulky restraints—just a nylon strap across your lap and a bar in front to hang onto—making it slightly terrifying before the ride even starts. It begins as a fast barrel through a dark tunnel and emerges into a slow climb with a deafening clank, clank, clank that builds anticipation until it pauses at the top—a long pause—and then you soar down, hair blowing back in the salty air. It turns thrillingly and then rises and plummets again, whipping around several times until three final, fast dips that lift you out of your seat, hovering weightlessly at the crest of each hill, creating the illusion (and one final, exhilarating fear) that you might hit your head—or your hands if you're brave enough to hold them up—on the wooden rafters above. It's my favorite ride at the boardwalk and I don't even know why I'm thinking of all this except for the fact that it's a distraction from my crippling worry about Charlie and I know I'll probably never ride it again. Or enjoy it in the same way, provided I survive what's to come.

I check my watch: 10:50. Directly across from me is a tarp-covered funnel cake stand with a large sign proclaiming, "Delicious Funnel Cakes!" and a list of toppings and prices. I stare at the sign in a daze, lost in my thoughts, when the sound of Avestan's voice behind me makes my heart seize in my chest.

"Planning your last meal?"

I spin around and the look in his eyes is chilling. I suspect I've erred gravely by coming alone.

"Where's Charlie?" I demand, channeling my fear. "I've done what you asked. Now let him go."

"I can take you to see him, but you have to come willingly."

Willingly. Alexander's warning rings in my head. But what choice do I have?

"Where is he?" I ask.

"Think of it as a sticking point. Between here and nowhere."

"You have to let me take Charlie home first. Unharmed."

"Do you really think you're in a position to be making demands? First you go with me. Willingly."

"I'm supposed to trust that you'll let Charlie go when we get there? I won't do it."

"A child's aura can be very valuable—it will be hard to let him go—but it's nothing like yours," he says, looking me over appraisingly. "I've told you what the terms are and you have my word.'"

"Your *word*? Your word means nothing to me. Less than nothing."

"You have no choice." His tone is icy and resolute.

"I rescind my willingness if you don't let Charlie go when we get there. Or if you've harmed Charlie in any way," I state defiantly.

"Ah, you mortals—always attempting to bargain and find loopholes. It doesn't work that way. Once you come with me of your own accord there will be no 'rescinding' of anything. Keep in mind as you stand here trying to haggle with me like a street vendor that the longer he's there, the worse it gets for him. I wouldn't waste any more time if I was you." He reaches out his hand.

The image of Charlie—trapped—in my mind causes me to slowly lift my arm and place my hand in Avestan's outstretched palm.

His skin is cold and all color slowly drains from our surroundings like wax dripping down the sides of a candle. We walk toward the beach and with each step I feel wretchedness consuming me. We're still at the boardwalk, but it's all a gray wasteland now and I know instinctively this is a different realm. It's a desperate, bleak place and my heart is slowly being crushed by the despair around me. I'm certain no one lasts long here, and that's probably a blessing. The thought of sweet little Charlie being here, for even a moment, engulfs me with a choking sob.

I feel Charlie before I see him. The sadness is unspeakable. He's curled up on the sand in the fetal position, rocking and moaning. I tear away from Avestan and run over to him but before I reach him I hit something hard and fall backwards. "Charlie!" I yell as I get up and pound on the invisible barrier between us. "Charlie!" I keep shouting and hitting the hard shell until my hands and arms are covered in bruises. He can't hear or see me. He's in a private hell and the anguish I feel from him is unbearable. I would do anything to make it stop.

"Let him go! He's a little boy! I did what you asked! Do it now!" I can't bear to see him suffering a moment longer.

Avestan slowly walks over and the barrier disappears with a shimmer. He bends down and picks Charlie up and with a swipe of his hand he steps out of the realm and they both disappear. They're gone a long while and then suddenly Avestan is at my side again, but Charlie is gone.

"There," he says, "it's done."

"What? How do I know he's home? And safe? And okay?" I demand. "And who's watching him?! *I'm* supposed to be there."

He lets out a heavy sigh and reaches up with his hand and grasps at the air with his fingers, tearing a hole in the gray realm we're in. He's opened a small window into the world I know. It's the foyer in Charlie's house and everything is in color as it should be. Charlie is smiling and telling Maria, the housekeeper, about all the fun he had at the park with Avestan.

"He doesn't remember anything," says Avestan, answering my unasked question. "He thinks he was playing on the swings at the park. When I took him home I told Molly you got sick and had to leave, so she asked the housekeeper to watch him."

My relief at seeing Charlie safe and happy nearly drops me to the ground. I feel as if I can reach through the portal and touch him as he's speaking. It's heartbreaking to be so close. I lift my hand to try to touch the colors but Avestan swipes the air quickly with his hand and closes the portal, disgusted.

"Now that we've disposed of the bait, we can proceed to the main event," he says with a gleam in his eyes.

Chapter Eighteen

"Do you realize what a find you are, Declan?" Avestan looks me over as if I'm a prized steer headed to slaughter. "I knew you were special almost from the moment I first saw you but I didn't realize how different you are."

"Identifying a mortal in the lifetime they're poised to be realized is rare and valuable. But finding a mortal who has an aura like yours ..." he trails off, "I didn't know such a thing existed. And to think that I may have missed it if it hadn't been for Alexander's lovesick attention."

The energy emanating from him as he rants is suffused with malevolence so acrid I can taste it. One part of me wants to keep Avestan talking so I can come up with a plan; another part of me wants to shut him up so that whatever he's going to do is over with quickly. For now, the side that hasn't succumbed to despair wins out. "Where are we?" I ask.

"A middle existence for tortured souls. You didn't arrive by the usual route, but now that you're here it doesn't matter. Nusquam would extinguish your soul eventually—I'm just going to hasten the process. Your power moves to my side of the balance sheet and Alexander loses. Win-win." His smile radiates evil.

"Why do you hate Alexander so much?" His venom is personal. He has to be motivated by more than just increasing dark energy.

"That's a long story for another time, Declan. I'm surprised Alexander hasn't told you about the rich history we share."

"What are you going to do to him?" I ask.

"Declan, if I was in your position, I would be far more worried about what I'm about to do to *you*."

He grasps my hand and pain jolts up my arm and explodes throughout my body. A guttural cry bursts from my mouth and then the agony sears my throat closed and no more sounds come. A million fiery needles run through every blood vessel and out through my hand in a steady stream of pain. My knees buckle and I drop to the sand but Avestan holds tighter, never releasing his grip. My heart and lungs are bursting and my chest is aflame. The pressure and tearing are unbearable. I feel my life force draining from me and at the same time inky despair is spilling into the empty space left behind. I know if I don't do something quickly the wretchedness will wholly consume me.

"Wait!" The sound emerges as a low, pitiful moan but it causes Avestan to pause for a split second. In that one moment of reprieve, I picture my white light—that beautiful, burning white light that I know Avestan is taking from me—and I concentrate everything I have on tearing off a tiny piece of it to hide, in reserve. I imagine tucking it behind my heart, undetected. The pain returns, fiercer than before, and when he finishes with me, I collapse, a depleted, desiccated shell, just as he intended.

When I come to, Avestan is standing over me. A deep black aura is beaming all around him with bright white light fighting for release at the tips. I can almost smell the rancid suffering and evil radiating out from his core.

"To draw power of this magnitude from a mortal is staggering." He flexes his fingers and marvels at the energy in his hands.

I'm crumpled at his feet, cloaked in pain and despondency beyond repair. He kicks my ribs with the toe of his boot. "Goodbye, Declan. I'll be sure to give Alexander your regards before I destroy the bastard."

As Avestan walks through the grayness of our realm and disappears back into the world, I pass out again, grateful for a respite from the pain.

Alexander and I are on the hill at Redwood Park, the sky is clear and blue and I'm wearing shorts and a tank top. The sun's warmth envelops me as I sit hugging my knees, enjoying the feeling. I close my eyes and tilt my face up to the sunlight to absorb it more fully.

"I wish we could stay here like this forever," Alexander says dreamily. He's lying on the blanket beside me wearing a t-shirt and board shorts. His long, tan legs sprawl out lazily and his dark hair curls slightly at the nape of his neck.

I lay back and turn to face him. "Me too. I can't think of anything that would make this day more perfect."

"I can think of *one* thing," Alexander replies, his voice low.

I blush as he smiles at me with those dark, mischievous eyes.

"We don't have to fight it anymore, Declan. That's why I brought you here today. To tell you. We can be together. In every way. We can kiss."

I shake my head, disbelieving.

"It's true. I found a loophole."

"We can kiss? Right now?"

Alexander laughs. "Yes, right now."

"And it won't kill you?"

"It won't kill either one of us … at least, not if we're doing it right." He smiles and I laugh. "But I want to wait. I want our first kiss to be at the right moment, in just the right place."

"When will it be then?"

"Patience, Miss Jane," he says with a laugh. "Anticipation makes things sweeter." He stands up and reaches down to grab my hand, pulling me up next to him. "Come with me, I want to show you something."

We walk hand in hand down the winding trail through the redwoods until we eventually reach a familiar clearing. He leads me to the center of the fairy ring and kneels down amidst the towering trees. "Do you remember this?" He brushes away the needles and dirt.

I nod, smiling wide as I gaze at our initials seared into the petrified remains of the tree. With the position of the sun in the sky and the way the rays are peeking through the trees that circle the clearing, the sun's spotlight is shining almost directly on it.

"Watch."

We stand together, arms encircling each other, staring at our secret declaration to the world. Minutes pass and I notice the sun's spotlight slowly inches over until it shines brightly on our initials like a beacon, the heart sparkling in the sun's rays.

He turns and gazes into my eyes. The charge of anticipation in the atmosphere around us is intoxicating and overwhelming.

"Now is the time and this is place," he says, his voice low, making my belly stir.

He pulls me close, and with his hands cradling my face, our lips meet for the first time.

I wake gasping and spitting out sand. I'm lying on the beach in front of the boardwalk. Everything around me is colorless, as before, but also silent. I can see the waves cresting and rolling in but I no longer hear the water crashing on shore or the seagulls off in the distance. I speak to make sure I haven't lost my hearing. "Hello?" I can hear my voice and my breathing but nothing else. It's gray and cold—so bleak it hurts—and I shiver to the core as I struggle to recall my own existence.

Slowly, it comes back to me: who I am, where I am, and how I came to be trapped in this hopeless abyss. The dream I had of Alexander is there and nearly gone in an instant. I don't want to let it go but I don't want to hang onto it either. The memory of something so perfect and beautiful doesn't belong in this heartless place.

I remember a flash of an idea I had before Avestan hollowed out my soul and I want to try it before the memory fades into the nothingness surrounding me. I watched carefully as Avestan opened and closed the portal and now I attempt it myself, swiping my hand across the air, as he did, and trying to grab a piece of the gray realm in front of me, to tear it open. I endeavor for hours trying different methods but it's hopeless. Nothing works. With tears of frustration running down my cheeks, I marshal all my focus and picture the tiny bit of white light I hid from Avestan. I find it there behind my heart, undetected—a trifling but oh-so-welcome bit of warmth in a cold, deserted body. I concentrate my imagination and it rolls out from its hiding place and makes its way across my chest and along my arm to my index finger where I form a mental image of it as a white hot laser, ready to fire at my command. I raise my hand and with a tiny bit of hope that somehow grows from nothing, I swipe once more, this time with my imagined weapon burning through to the outside world.

A flash of color shines for half a second and disappears. I got through! *I got through,* I whisper to myself with a sob of relief. Emboldened, I try over and over using different combinations of techniques until I figure out how to hold my hands and concentrate to keep the portal open. My watch stopped when we entered Nusquam so I don't know how long I've been able to keep the window open so far, but I estimate my best time at about 90 seconds. The problem is, I'm watching strangers. One portal opens onto two guys in their twenties eating in a McDonalds and having a mundane conversation about their weekend. Another window opens up on an empty bench at the bus station. I can hear people talking in the background amidst the sounds of busses arriving and departing but I don't see anyone. At least it's in the right town. I recognize the Metro station in downtown San Mar. As depressing as it is to finally open a portal and have it be devoid of anything meaningful, just seeing color and the prosaic goings-on of ordinary people gives me a connection to the world and plants seeds of hope within me.

How can I control what I see? I ponder what time it is. What day it is. Soon I'll be labeled a missing person and I shudder to think of my mom worried sick trying to find me. Losing me as well as my dad would be too much for her to take and I can't bear the thought. Thank God she's gone for a week. Finn and Liz will worry about me when I don't show for school on Monday. They'll try to reach me and eventually raise an alarm, but maybe I have a day or two.

The bleak despair pressing down from all sides makes me desperate to see my mom. I concentrate every molecule I have before attempting to open another portal. I vividly call to mind her face—her kind eyes especially—her voice, her laugh, and everything that makes her uniquely Judy Jane. I focus on how much I love her and I picture her aura, imagining her telling me it'll be okay and smoothing my hair the way she does when I'm upset.

Holding this image in my mind's eye, I swipe again and emit a gasping sob of relief and astonishment when it works. A window opens into a restaurant. My mom is sitting at a long table with her colleagues from work. Julie is next to her and they're laughing about something. Instinctively, with tears running down my face, I cry out, "Mom!" but she can't see or hear me. I try to reach my hand through the portal to touch her but my hand collides with a hard barrier. I may as well be trying to reach into a computer screen.

My mom is eating a salad as she and Julie chat. I notice a clock on the wall behind their table but I'm having a hard time making sense of what I'm seeing. It's only 11:00am—the same time I entered Nusquam. Or maybe it's 11:00pm? No. That can't be. Light is streaming in the restaurant windows from outside. I consider that maybe it's Monday already, but my mom has on the same clothes she wore to travel in that morning. Perhaps the clock is broken. Or maybe it's been more than a few days? No, there's no way my mom would be sitting there calmly laughing if she knew I was missing.

I lost track of time, to be sure, but under my most conservative estimates, I've been trapped in Nusquam at least a day. Does time move differently here? With minutes in the world at large passing as infinite time on my end? The window closes before I can wrap my head around it. Seeing my mom for those few moments has restored a part of me that was gone and now I crave more.

I want to view Alexander.

I know he can't help me, but I just want to look into his eyes again and see his smile.

I close my eyes and direct attention to my breathing, becoming centered. I concentrate on the peaceful calm I feel whenever I'm with Alexander. I picture his face and the way he looks at me with those green eyes of his—and the way it makes my heart flip and my stomach clench. I focus on letting all the love that I feel for him flow through me. I'm flooded with memories of the two of us watching the sun rise together, flying over the ocean blissfully connected, and staring into each other's eyes as the force of our attraction causes the air to smolder between us.

All the questions Avestan raised mean nothing to me now.
I don't care who Alenna is or if Alexander ever truly loved
me. I only know I love him on an elemental level and that's
enough. I swipe my hand and to my utter astonishment it
works.

Alexander and Edwin are sitting at their kitchen table
looking deadly serious. And they're discussing me.

"There has to be a way around it, Edwin," Alexander says,
"I've never felt this way—in any lifetime. It can't be all for
naught."

"Alexander, it's over. What you were doing was
unsustainable. We need everyone at full strength right now, as
you've seen the last few days," Edwin states grimly. "It's
better this way—trust me. It sounds like Declan made it clear
it was over between you two anyway, so you have no choice."

"That's what I don't understand. Out of nowhere she tells
me she doesn't love me anymore? It doesn't make sense,"
Alexander answers, heartache permeating every word.

"But you can't be together. That's the bottom line,
Alexander, and you have to accept it. Guardians can't be
distracted by earthly attractions. It compromises our mission
and our ability to protect. Not to mention the more permanent
ramifications if you gave into your impulses. There's no point
in going over this again. Nothing is going to change the facts."

"I just want to be around her."

Edwin presses his fingers to his forehead in exasperation.

"And how did she find out about Alenna?" Alexander asks.
"If you didn't tell her, there's only one person who could have.
And I can only imagine what he said."

"I don't know, Alexander. But it doesn't make a
difference," Edwin says, anger rising in his voice. "You can't
be with her, so what does it matter if she knows about Alenna?
Declan is the *problem*! Alenna is part of the solution."

"You've been watching her, haven't you? Has Avestan been around her? Where is she now?"

"Yes, of course we've been watching her. Alenna saw her arrive at the Bing's house. She's babysitting now," Edwin answers.

"No! That's wrong," I want to cry out, "I'm here. Trapped in this dead, wasted landscape." But I know it's useless. They can't see or hear me. I wouldn't want Alexander to put himself in danger by getting close to me again anyway. Edwin said it loud and clear—I'm the problem. And Alenna, apparently, is the solution. Edwin's words shredded my heart but I can't possibly add thoughts of Alenna to the despair I'm already drowning in. Alexander told me the night of the dance that I couldn't be saved if I came here willingly. There's no sanity in letting even a whisper of hope into my heart. I'm never getting out.

I swipe the portal closed, exhausted. At least another day, maybe more must have passed. There's no sunrise or sunset—nothing to gauge the passing of time. It's just endless gray for eternity. I close my eyes for the relief of sleep.

I continue in this manner—barely existing—for what feels like days, or weeks. I wake up and open a portal to see Alexander. He's always in the kitchen, always frustrating Edwin by not letting the subject of me drop. It's difficult to grasp, but only seconds or minutes have passed on their end since the last time I viewed. I know I'm violating their privacy by eavesdropping but the portal is the only thing that gives me a window—a small crack, but it's something—to peer out of my despair.

The next time I open the portal, desperate for contact, the conversation between Alexander and Edwin has shifted.

"Something has changed," says Alexander, "I feel it."

"We need to gather the other guardians and act now," says Edwin, his voice grave. "There's no more time for you to build your strength."

As I listen, my love for Alexander floods through me. I put him in danger, first by loving him, and now by walking into this hopeless realm, willingly, and allowing Avestan to take my soul. If the balance is shifting, *everyone* may be in danger. And I'm responsible. Avestan's last words were about destroying Alexander. If there's going to be a showdown, Alexander has been set up to lose before it even starts. And it's my fault.

The realization of all the suffering I may have unleashed is overwhelming. If Alexander gets hurt—or worse—I won't be able to bear it. A sob explodes from my throat and the depth of my despair joins with my love for Alexander and pours out of me. "No," I cry into my hands, "No."

Inexplicably, Alexander turns his head, startled, as if he heard me. A look of horrified recognition plays over his face for an instant as his eyes connect with mine, staring back at him in anguish.

As I stand there, speechless and frozen, the portal closes.

Chapter Nineteen

Frantically, I try time after time to reopen the window. Did Alexander truly see me? Hear me? I swipe madly to no avail. I'm in a frenzy of thought. I worry I have no reserves left to open that bridge to the outside world ever again.

I know I need to calm myself or it will be hopeless. I take a deep breath and focus on my breathing, trying to remember everything Alexander taught me. I concentrate on the small ball of white light I re-situated in my core. I focus on feeling its pinprick of warmth, trying to imagine it taking hold and multiplying. I immerse myself in the memory of my dream and the exquisite joy I felt, kissing Alexander for the first time. Holding that vision clear in my mind, I swipe my hand again and to my astounding surprise, it works.

To my greater astonishment, Alexander is staring directly out at me. "Declan?" he says, panic in his voice. "Are you okay? Can you hear me?"

I'm stunned. "Yes. You can hear me? And see me?"

"Yes, and yes." He lets out a resounding sigh of relief. "Where are you?"

"Avestan said it's called Nusquam. It's gray and cold. And silent."

The look on Alexander's face is sobering. He peers over his shoulder at Edwin in the background and I can see that Edwin is stricken by my words as well.

There's a long pause and then Alexander asks softly, "How did you get there?"

"I came with Avestan."

"I don't understand. Why would you do that, Declan?"

"He took Charlie. He brought him here first and said I had to come or he would kill him. It was the only way. I had no choice." My words tumble over one another as I try to explain.

"Why didn't you call me for help?" he asks, his words steeped in anguish.

"Avestan said I couldn't tell anyone or I would never see Charlie again. I had to go alone."

Alexander is silent.

"I *had* to," I plead. "And it worked. He let Charlie go. It was the only way."

Alexander turns to Edwin. "How could Alenna have missed this? Tell her to go now and make sure Charlie Bing is home safe," he says abruptly. Edwin pulls out his phone and makes a call. When Alexander turns back to me he lets out a long, slow sigh. "How did you manage to open this portal?"

"I made Avestan prove to me that Charlie was okay. He opened a portal and I watched how he did it. After he left I tried it myself."

"So he hasn't taken your energy yet?" His voice is filled with hope.

"No, he did. But I managed to tear off a small piece and hide it from him—at least that was what I imagined, and I think it worked. I focused on that little bit of energy after he left and I used it to locate you."

"How long have you been there?"

"I'm not sure. Since Sunday. Time passes differently here."

The sadness in my voice fills Alexander's eyes with pain and determination. "I'm coming for you," he says, his mouth set in a firm line.

"You can't. Don't say that. You told me once that guardians are forbidden to come here. And I know what happens when you're around me. You need your strength."

At my words Alexander turns to stare at Edwin—with surprise at first, and then with knowing disapproval and anger, as if his suspicions have been confirmed. Edwin stares back defiantly.

I ignore the tension between them and continue to press my case. "You told me the night of the dance that if I came here willingly with Avestan it was a place even you couldn't save me from. Whatever Avestan took from me, it made him more powerful than before. You and Edwin need all your strength to defend against him. You can't risk trying to save me," I plead. "I made my choice and I can live with it."

Alexander stares into my eyes. "Well I don't have to make that choice." He pauses and his demeanor softens. "Declan, you must know there is nothing you could ever say that would stop me from coming for you." His voice is husky with emotion.

My heart is touched and broken at the same time. We gaze into each other's eyes and sadness overwhelms me. I can't let him come.

"No," I whisper softly. And as he starts to protest I slowly slide the portal closed for good.

Chapter Twenty

Days pass and I chastise myself, wallowing in the wretchedness I'm slowly disappearing into. I should never have opened the portal to Alexander. My selfish desire for connection exposed him to danger again, distracting him at a time when he needs his strength the most. I alternate between worrying that my actions may have harmed him and despairing that I'm trapped, surrounded by endless gray, endless quiet, and crushing hopelessness.

"Declan." Alexander's voice awakens me. I'm lying on the cold sand, curled up in a ball in a never-ending attempt to get warm. "Declan!" I hear again. Maybe it's not a dream. I turn and am startled to see that Alexander has somehow opened a large portal and is standing in his kitchen, looking at me, calling out my name. I slowly stand and stare back. Is this really happening?

"Alexander, don't come," I say despondently.

"Declan, you have to trust me." I can tell by the look on his face that he's alarmed by my appearance. "Take my hand," he commands, and I think I must be dreaming again because his hand reaches through the portal into my realm. His forearm and hand are now colorless, beginning where his arm crosses over the threshold. But the rest of him is still in color, vivid, in his world. Can it be that simple? Can he just pull me out?

I reach my hand up to meet his, tentatively. I'm distrustful that any of this is real until I feel his warm flesh touch mine. When our hands clasp, I sob in relief. It isn't a dream. However, instead of pulling me out, he uses my willing hand as an opening to enter into my realm. At that moment, I hear Edwin cry out "No!" but it's too late. The portal closes. Alexander has crossed over and the toll it has taken on him is distressingly clear. He's bent over, hands on his knees, grimacing fiercely. He slowly drops to the ground, doing his best to hide what must be excruciating pain from the looks of him. "Well that was easier than expected," he grunts out with heavy sarcasm.

"Alexander!" I wrap my arms around him, tears streaming down my face. "Why?" I implore. "I thought you were going to pull me out. If I'd known you were going to come here, I would never have taken your hand!"

"That's why." His answers are short as he struggles to catch his breath. "It had to be like this. It's the only way."

I hug him tightly, breathing in his familiar scent like pure oxygen. "I'm so sorry I hurt you."

"None of that matters," he replies, hurriedly. "You have to go now."

"What?"

"I hold far greater power than you—it's more than a fair trade for Avestan."

"You expect me to leave without you?" My voice is incredulous.

"Declan, don't argue with me. There isn't time and this is the only way to free you from this place."

"Never. I would never leave you here. How could you even think I would? You shouldn't have come, Alexander. You're the one who needs to go back. Not me."

"Actually, neither one of you is leaving," says a familiar voice from behind us. We turn to see Avestan standing with his arms crossed smugly, staring at us both.

Chapter Twenty-One

"Let her go," demands Alexander, "You don't need her if I'm here. This is between you and me. It has nothing to do with Declan."

"It has to do with you both. I had no idea how in love you were, Alexander. It couldn't have worked out better if I'd planned it myself."

"Let him go!" I shout, "I'm the one who came here with you willingly. Alexander had nothing to do with it."

"You're both so lovesick you walked into this trap with eyes and arms wide open. And all for nothing—love between a mortal and guardian can never be. It's been great fun watching you suffer while you tried to resist though," he says with a laugh. "Now you can both languish endlessly. Or maybe I'll separate you. Which would be worse, Alexander: watching Declan in pain, or not being able to see her and *imagining* the pain she's in?"

Alexander flies at Avestan before I even see him move. A white hot ball of fury explodes around his fist as he lands a sickeningly loud right hook. Avestan's head snaps to the side at an unnatural angle and his jaw shatters at the impact.

He immediately retaliates by raising his hands and releasing a cannonball of energy that detonates on Alexander's chest, blowing him off his feet and smashing him into one of the support beams of the pier and splitting it open.

Alexander is up in an instant, rushing at Avestan again with murderous intent and nearly taking his head off with a powerful uppercut. He follows with a blindingly fast left cross that lands with a deafening crack. White light bursts from his fists at every contact.

As I watch in horror, I see Alexander using his fists, while Avestan has only to throw deadly charges from a distance. It's obvious Alexander is weaker. Yet he came through the portal anyway, against all reason, to save me. And he's fighting a losing battle in front of my eyes. Avestan is glowing—the blows Alexander delivers have little effect. Deadly power shimmers all around him as he emits another round that connects squarely with Alexander's chest. Alexander is thrown against the pier again like a rag doll. This time he lays there, unmoving, for a long beat before slowly rising, readying himself to attack again. My heart is in my throat.

"Stop!" I shout, "Avestan, you have me here, trapped for eternity. That was the deal. There's no reason to do this to Alexander."

"I can think of several reasons," Avestan replies slowly.

"But he's weak! And coming here made it worse! This isn't a fair fight and you know it. Let him go back," I cry plaintively.

"Guardians are forbidden here. He knew the consequences. Besides, this is between the two of us now," he replies coldly.

"Why?" I plead. "Why are you doing this?"

"Has he told you how he treated me when we were young? Always showing me up? Lording his perfection over me as if he was better? How our parents always favored him?"

Parents?

"You know that's not true, Avestan. We were close and I only ever tried to help you. You've been listening to dark lies for so long now you've forgotten what's real," protests Alexander.

"Of course—Alexander the perfect—the big brother who was only trying to help. Were you *helping* when you stole Alenna from me?"

My mind is reeling as I listen.

"She had no idea how you felt! No one did. If you'd said a word—*one word*.... You know that's true. If I'd known you were in love with her nothing would have happened."

"She was looking for *me*, but of course when she met my brother—Alexander the perfect—her attention shifted. You always had to turn on the charm, didn't you," Avestan chokes out in disgust.

"She might have loved you, you know. The way you behaved is what turned her away. Your resentment was poison and none of us knew why. You fed on twisted lies from dark forces and they changed you. I forgive what you did that day. It wasn't you. But you've been marinating in bitterness so long that you can't see the truth anymore. Is any part of the little brother I knew still in there?" The pain and frustration in Alexander's voice is palpable.

"You forgive me? *You* forgive *me*? Well, here's a headline for you: I don't forgive you. I'm not the only one with blood on my hands, Alexander. And the only twisted lies are the ones coming from your self-serving mouth." The hatred in Avestan's reply slices like a razor. "When I followed you that day to the lake—the happy couple—it wasn't lies that made me kill you both, it was betrayal. *Your* betrayal. Of your own brother. You bested me at everything my whole life and when I finally found something of my own, you took that away, too. You couldn't even let me have Alenna. If you hadn't wasted your last moments trying to be a hero, I might have lived that day. And yet even in death, you became a guardian—more powerful, you tell me, than the choice I made. You never stopped beating me. And now I see that you betrayed me for nothing. You don't even care for Alenna. You tossed her aside for a mere *mortal*. You make me sick. But now, finally, *I'm* the one with the power. And I can take away the one *you* love. I've waited for this. When I'm finished you can tell me how it feels."

I stand stock still, aghast, at Avestan's revelations as he directs his hand to me. I feel the charge he releases before I see it. It knocks me onto my side, a black orb of pain holding me down, in agony. Alexander looks on in horror. He rushes Avestan with such fury I'm surprised the force doesn't rend them in two. Avestan pulls the orb from me and trains it on Alexander, knocking him down and pinning him to the ground.

"How does it feel, *Alexander the perfect*? No one would choose you now, writhing at my feet like a pathetic little worm, would they?" As Avestan gloats his face morphs into a grotesque, demonic mask.

"You're killing him!" Despite my terror I run at Avestan in a blind panic but he releases a ball of energy that knocks me off my feet and pins me to the ground. My thoughts are a frenzied jumble. Alexander is in agony, dying on the sand in front of me and there's nothing I can do. The horror is unspeakable and none of it would be happening if he hadn't come here. For me. I want to close my eyes to shut out the pain and surrender, but I can't let him suffer alone.

"Alexander!" I cry. He's contorted in pain and avoiding my eyes. "Look at me, please," I beseech. Slowly, he meets my eyes and the look of torment on his face pierces my heart, but I don't look away. I hold his gaze and all the love I feel for him consumes me. It builds from the deepest part of my soul and radiates out with a force I didn't know I had left. I imagine the white ball of light in the center of my body burning brighter than ever before, and growing and multiplying infinitely. My whole being is thrumming with energy so powerful I can't contain it. I feel as if I'm levitating on beams of light. As we hold each other's eyes, I can feel that he's returning that love, a thousandfold, as he prepares to die.

"Don't go Alexander. Please!" My voice is so raw and deep I don't identify it as my own. I reach out and an enormous blast of light, containing every ounce of life left in my body, rockets from me with colossal force. Like a white hot star, it hits Avestan with fiery velocity and knocks him off his feet.

He stares at me, stunned, his face momentarily back to human form again, before he stands with steely determination and redirects the black orb away from Alexander and back to me, with greater force this time. I collapse on the sand with nothing left to put up resistance.

I know this is the end. With Avestan's blackness burning into me, I feel the small thread connecting me to life beginning to stretch and snap. I slowly start to let go and I imagine flying over the ocean with Alexander in pure bliss again. With great effort, I manage to open my eyes and search for Alexander for one last look before I surrender completely and enter the dark abyss. Perhaps if I last long enough I can provide the reprieve Alexander needs to save himself.

Alexander lies still on the ground, showing no signs of resistance. When his eyes meet mine, the love I feel is overwhelming. The delicate string of light that connects our hearts begins to glow and widen into a beam of pure energy pulsing between us. Alexander stand ups slowly and calls out to me in a voice too weak to understand. Energy builds and shimmers all around him as he gathers strength and speaks again, louder this time. "I'll always protect you, Declan."

He raises his hand and I can see the burning resolve in his eyes as he slowly trains his focus on Avestan's rippling, demonic visage. A fiery supernova of radiant, blinding light extends out all around Alexander in a white hot flash and then explodes with pinpoint accuracy on Avestan, holding him frozen. The light shimmers between them, vibrating, and I sense the strength, purity, and boundlessness of Alexander's life force. The light grows brighter and hotter, expanding all around us, until it consumes everything in its path, leaving no room for darkness. Avestan falls and lays stricken, motionless—empty.

Alexander stares at Avestan on the ground for a long moment with sadness in his eyes. He kneels to whisper something in his ear.

The last thing I remember is Alexander lifting me into his arms and tearing a passage through Nusquam. He steps out, holding me, into the world we left behind.

Chapter Twenty-Two

I awaken on the beach. Only now I can hear the waves and see welcome shades of blue in the sky. I look all around. The portal is gone and Avestan is nowhere to be seen.

Alexander lies beside me. I call to him but he isn't moving.

I lift his head onto my lap, calling out his name as I try to revive him. Panicked, I bend down low to his face and check for breathing. Long, desperate seconds pass until I detect a faint breath and a slight rise in his chest. "Alexander," I cry. "Please, Alexander. You did it. You saved me. Wake up," I repeat, whispering over and over as I cradle him in my arms and weep.

His eyelids slowly drift open and relief floods over me as he looks into my eyes. "You're okay," he says weakly, attempting a smile.

"You saved me."

"You knocked Avestan down. Mortals can't do that," he murmurs.

"All I cared about was saving you."

"About that …" he replies softly, leaving the rest unsaid.

"You're going to be all right," I insist, emotion ravaging my throat.

He doesn't answer.

"But you can heal yourself," I cry, "I've seen you."

"Not this time," he utters weakly, his voice barely a whisper.

"But you said energy never dies," I plead.

"Part of me will continue on, but not in this form," he admits solemnly. "Declan, I don't have much time and I need to say something." He pauses as he takes a breath. "I love you. I love you as I've never loved anyone before and I'll always love you—for endless time and eons beyond. You are light and beauty in the ways that matter and you always amaze, Miss Jane." He smiles. "Your heart is pure. I'm looking at your aura right now and it's breathtaking. It's your true and honest self, and *you're* breathtaking. Please know that. You're so hard on yourself, and I hear you put yourself down. I know you think I love you in spite of all the things you think are wrong. But what you don't understand is that I love you *because* of them. You have no idea how beautiful you are. How strong you are. And how much light you add to the world. I'll always take that with me."

"Please, Alexander," I implore with a sob. "Please don't go. I love you. I'll always love you. Please don't go … you can't go." My heart breaks within me. This can't be. It can't.

If he hears me, there's no sign.

His eyes close and I feel the light between us fade away as he takes his last breath and is gone.

Chapter Twenty-Three

Grief pours out of me in heaving sobs. I hold Alexander, cradling his head in my lap and rocking back and forth in a gulf of anguish I don't think I'll ever escape.

"No, no, no. Please, no," I plead, over and over.

I thought I knew the pain of losing someone I love, but this—this time it's because of me. It's *my* fault. The searing anguish in my heart drives me to beg that I be taken too. Instead. Please let it be me. Not him. Please, not him.

I rock until my tears run dry and then I keep rocking, the movement becoming smaller and smaller until eventually I hold still. Eyes inflamed, I stare at Alexander's face for a long time in heart-aching denial.

Slowly, I lean down to kiss him. For the first and last time. Lips slick with tears, my mouth meets his and the love I feel for Alexander envelops us both in warm, white light. I press my lips to his and hold still and the purity flowing from my heart spills over us in waves. In a dream, Alexander's lips part against mine, softly at first, returning my tenderness and yearning, and slowly building to heated passion. His hands rise up to embrace me, knotting his fingers in my hair, holding me to him as if he'll never let go. We're drowning in each other, the hunger between us raw and impossible to resist.

This can't be a dream. The intensity is too real.

I pull away and Alexander is gazing back at me, incredulous.

"Is this really happening?" I whisper.

"I think so," he says softly, equally mystified.

I touch his face, shoulders, arms—everywhere—with my hands and then pinch myself to make sure. "I thought you were gone," I sob, "I thought you were gone." I repeat it over and over as fresh tears of happiness pour over the salty remnants of grief.

Worry plays across Alexander's face.

"What's wrong?" I ask. I feel as though nothing can ever be wrong again. Alexander is alive.

"How did you bring me back?"

"I don't know," I say, still smiling. "You're here, Alexander! What does it matter?"

"It matters because there will be consequences. Restoring a guardian is beyond the power of mortals. And unless I dreamed it, we just kissed. That means I've broken my vow and your life is in danger." His face is grim and anxious.

"But I think the kiss is what brought you back. How can that be anything other than good? I'm still here," I say as I pat myself all over to show I'm still in one piece. "See? I'm okay. And from what I was feeling during that kiss, you're *more* than okay."

The corners of his mouth turn up a little, revealing a flash of the Alexander I'm used to, but his expression quickly reverts to apprehension.

"I don't know how I healed you," I say quickly, before he can protest again, "but I do know that it came from love, and how can that be bad?"

I search his eyes for a sign that he agrees with any part of what I've said but all I see is deeply troubled worry. "I love you, Alexander," I say softly, my eyes glistening with tears.

"I love you, too, Declan." He releases a heartfelt sigh. "That's the problem …what have we done?"

Chapter Twenty-Four

"You should never have gone to Nusquam," scolds Edwin as he paces back and forth across the floor.

Alexander, Edwin, and I are in their house discussing what happened. Edwin embraced us both mightily when we first got home and told him our story. Now, however, his relief has turned to alarm as he attempts to sort out what it means. Suffice it to say he isn't happy.

"I say that to both of you," Edwin admonishes us sternly. "How could you agree to go with Avestan? And Alexander, you know Guardians are forbidden to enter that realm. Going there was a grave mistake. Very grave."

I want to protest and tell Edwin that I had no choice, Avestan was holding Charlie, but we've already been over this many times and I know he's still working it through in his mind and I should just stay silent. Alexander, sitting beside me, is also quiet. He nods at me in approval and squeezes my hand.

"I understand about Charlie. That should never have happened and you can be sure nothing like it ever will again." The sternness in Edwin's voice is clear as he emphasizes each word. "But while you two were off in a place neither one of you should have entered, we've been here having the fight of our lives. We could have used you, Alexander."

Alexander nods solemnly.

"You're sure it was Declan that knocked Avestan over?" Edwin asks again. He keeps coming back to this question over and over.

"Yes. My strength was down before I entered and the crossover made it worse. Avestan's energy was far superior. I didn't have it in me."

I turn to look at Alexander. It's the first time he has admitted how weakened he was. My heart aches with the danger I placed him in.

"I remember looking into your eyes before I knocked him down," I say. "I felt your energy making me stronger. I think you had more to do with it than you realize."

Alexander shakes his head. "She did it, Edwin. I don't know how, but she sent out a burst that knocked him down. When our energy connected it revived me and when I saw Avestan killing her I released everything in a pure state. I managed to carry her out but I was drained. Completely."

"And you transitioned after you crossed over?" Edwin asks again.

"Yes," replies Alexander.

"You weren't just weakened?" Edwin persists.

"No," answers Alexander. "It was more than that. I was gone."

"And that's when you kissed?" Edwin directs the question at me.

I nod. "I thought he was dead. I just wanted to kiss him— just once." My voice holds a mixture of yearning and apology and Alexander squeezes my hand and looks at me tenderly.

"You kissed him? He didn't kiss you?" Edwin asks.

"Yes," I answer.

"Well, it started that way," Alexander cuts in, "but that's not how it ended." His tone is serious but he can't resist flashing me a sidelong glance that makes me blush.

Edwin is not amused. His brow furrows as he stops pacing and stands silent for several minutes. He starts to pace again and then stops and emits a small sound. Before anything intelligible can emerge he snaps his mouth shut and resumes pacing. After a few more minutes he stops, mutters to himself, and then, finally, he speaks.

"There's only one explanation."

I stare at Edwin anxiously.

He pauses, clearly hesitant to give voice to his thoughts. At last, he relents.

"Declan, you're not a mortal."

Chapter Twenty-Five

My eyes flick from Edwin to Alexander and back again, stupefied. "What?"

"No mortal can do what you've done," says Edwin, "but you're no guardian, either. You haven't been realized and there's no other way to become a guardian. *That*, I know." He states the last part as if he's reassuring himself that the universe hasn't turned completely upside down.

I wait for him to answer the obvious question that hangs like an anvil in the air around us but instead of speaking he takes one green apple and one red apple from the bowl on the table and places them a few inches apart on the counter. *He's going to eat at a time like this?*

"Watch," he says as he regards me shrewdly.

He grabs both apples, lightning fast.

"Which apple did I grab first?" he asks.

I look at Alexander with confusion. It's obvious he grabbed the red one first. Is this some weird Jedi mind game or a trick question? "The red one," I answer.

Edwin nods his head. "To a mortal it would have looked simultaneous."

"Give me your hand," orders Edwin before I can respond.

I hold out my hand and he pulls a knife from the kitchen drawer beside him.

"Whoa, whoa, whoa," I say, yanking my hand back with alarm. "What are you doing?"

"I need your blood. As a final test."

My facial expression is more than a little wary.

"I need some of yours, too," he says, nodding his head to Alexander. "Why don't you go first."

Alexander looks at me and shrugs. He takes the knife and slices his finger, dripping blood onto the plate Edwin holds out for this purpose. Immediately, his finger heals as if the wound was never there.

"Your turn," says Alexander, shifting to face me. "I promise I'll make it as painless as possible."

I hold out my hand and wince as he slices the tip of my index finger and drips blood onto the other side of the plate. When he's finished he holds my finger between his hands and as he draws them away I'm amazed to see that the cut on my finger has vanished. "All better," he says with a smile as he hands the plate back to Edwin.

As we watch, Edwin tilts the plate, causing Alexander's blood to run into mine. When the two pools combine, I gasp. The mixture turns iridescent and glows with a brilliance that takes my breath away.

Edwin regards me with renewed certainty. "It's been staring me in the face since the day Alexander told me about your aura. The purity of your spirit, your empathic qualities, your ability to harness energy … and the power you displayed today. It can only be one thing."

I swallow nervously as I wait for him to spit it out.

"You're a sprite."

I turn to look at Alexander, but he's as speechless as I am.

"I heard ancient guardians speak of sprites but I thought they were only a myth," continues Edwin. "I've never come across one in all my lifetimes. I had to do the test to be sure."

"What, *exactly*, is a sprite?" I ask hesitantly.

"A being in between mortal and guardian—an angel's apprentice, if you will. It's a good thing, Declan," he says as he puts a reassuring hand on my shoulder, "A very good thing, indeed. In fact, it changes everything."

"How?" Alexander asks.

"You aren't a fallen guardian, for one," Edwin says, clearly relieved. "Your weakness came from resisting, not from being drawn to a mortal. That explains why it took so long to be affected. You didn't break your vow."

It takes a full minute for the implications of what Edwin just said to sink in.

"Are you saying Declan and I can be together?" asks Alexander, confirming.

Edwin nods with a smile.

Alexander and I both turn to each other at the same time and whisper, "Loophole," in unison, making us laugh.

"I should have known you'd find one," Alexander says. "You couldn't resist me much longer."

"I think it's the other way around," I say as he pulls me onto his lap and wraps his arms around me. As I gaze into his eyes all I can think about is how much I want to kiss him, *right now*, until I remember we're not alone.

I turn to see that Edwin is clearly happy for us but looking uncomfortable. "Do you want me to go on?"

"Is the rest good?" I ask, warily.

He shakes his head. "But you need to hear it. Alexander should never have gone to Nusquam." His lips are set in a firm line as he eyes Alexander. "However, considering the fact that he was saving a sprite and almost lost his life, I believe the high guardians will go easy on him. But as far as you bringing him back, Declan, until we figure this out, the story is only that he was weakened and your powers as a sprite revived him. Nothing more."

We nod in agreement but inside I'm still confused by all the secrecy.

"While you were gone, the resistance the other guardians and I encountered was stronger than we can defend for long. Avestan and the others will be back. And he'll be pursuing you with a vengeance. We need to regroup. We can't let down our guard."

He pauses for a long moment and then adds softly with great emotion, "I'm grateful to you, Declan. I felt Alexander's essence leave and I thought he was gone forever."

"Me, too," I reply, my voice cracking.

My eyes meet Edwin's and I see the love in them as I squeeze Alexander's hand, emotions overwhelming me.

Chapter Twenty-Six

"I think I know where we're going," I say as Alexander holds his car door open. It's Monday afternoon, only twenty-four hours since Alexander rescued me from Nusquam, but the whole ordeal has already faded to nearly a dream. I can't reconcile the bleakness I was in with the brilliant sun above me now, no clouds in sight. Alexander drove me home after school and told me to change into something dressy but to also bring runners (his parlance for sneakers) in a bag. It's all very curious.

"You'll find out soon enough," he smiles. He looks me over admiringly as I slide my legs in. I'm wearing a navy cocktail dress with a halter neckline and nipped waist. "Beautiful inside and out, as always," he says with a smile of sincerity as he closes the door.

Alexander has on the slate gray suit and crisp, white shirt he wore the night of the dance. His dark hair curls slightly at the nape of his neck and his green eyes gaze at me appraisingly. My eyes trail from his impossibly handsome face down to the open neck of his shirt and I turn slightly pink as if he can tell where my thoughts are leading. I have to force myself not to stare as we weave through the streets of San Mar, making our way to the highway.

"Excited?" Alexander asks.

I nod with a smile. "I've been excited ever since Edwin told us we can be together."

"The fact that he found us a loophole almost makes up for the fact that he forced you to break up with me. *Almost.*"

Alexander was furious when Edwin confessed everything but I convinced him that it was all done out of love. He's almost come around to forgiving Edwin. Almost, but not quite.

For my part, I was upset about some of the revelations, too. Why Alexander never told me Avestan was his brother, for one. He explained it was many lifetimes ago, but I still don't understand. Apparently they were very close until Avestan's obsession with Alenna caused him to view Alexander through a dark, twisted lens. His resentment spiraled until that final, fateful day at the lake. With his last breath, Alexander fought to save Alenna and he mortally wounded Avestan in the process. The result was death for all three, but they fell to different fates. Alexander and Alenna became realized as guardians and Avestan chose to trade his soul to the darkness. Alexander told me he kept the scar on his temple as a reminder of the power of evil and its ability to turn brother against brother.

Not surprisingly, I found out that most of what Avestan told me was lies, but the part about Alenna is still a little murky.

"Can I ask you about Alenna?" I ask as we're driving.

"You can ask me anything."

"Is she the blonde that met you in the parking lot at school once?"

"Yes."

"Tall, immaculate blonde" is what a small, insecure part of me is thinking—of course she would have to be exquisitely beautiful … *"Cut the crap, Jane. He's with you,"* says my inner drill sergeant, rolling her eyes and making me smile a little.

"You and Alenna were a couple then? As mortals?"

"Yes."

"And as guardians?"

He glances at me. "After we were realized, we were bound to each other for a time. Partly because of the way we crossed over."

"So you loved her?"

He nods. "I still do. But I came to realize I love her as a friend."

"What about her love for you?"

"I suspect her feelings are the same as mine."

"Did she say that?"

"Declan, when I met you, everything changed. My universe shifted. My connection with you is like nothing I've ever felt. When Alenna meets her soul mate one day she'll feel it, too, and she'll realize what she and I have is different."

"She must hate me."

"She's a guardian, above all, and she wants me to be happy, as I do her. She helped protect you. She's a good person."

"Why didn't you ever tell me about her?"

He shrugs. "I didn't think it mattered. Have you told me about all your old boyfriends?"

He has a point. But the difference is I don't *have* any old boyfriends.

"Why does Avestan think you stole her from him?"

He sighs and shakes his head. "It was such a long time ago and it all seems so banal now," he says, almost with disgust. "He met her through friends and fell for her but never told her. He never told anyone. She came by looking for him one day and I was home. After that I kept running into her at various places and it progressed from there. The most frustrating part of the story is that Alenna *was* initially interested in him. If only he had said something ..." Alexander's voice trails off.

I feel the weight of Alexander's words. The idea that their fates were set in motion over something that could just as easily have gone the other way ... as if a flip of a coin changed their lives forever. I wonder if all of life is like that—just the sum of a billion random coin flips that determine our destinies.

"Please tell Alenna I'm grateful to her for protecting me."

Alexander nods. "She dropped the ball with Charlie but she kept you safe at times when I couldn't."

"So she was the one?"

"One what?"

"The one protecting me after you and I broke up?"

"She was one of many."

"Then how come Avestan was able to get close to me? He came to Jack's and told me you never loved me."

"Guardians aren't meant to shield mortals from life. People have to make their own choices and face the consequences. Our purpose is to guide mortals down a positive path and remind them what matters. We do what we can to protect them from danger but we can't always step in."

"So Alenna was there watching? Letting me talk to Avestan?"

"No. Jimmy was."

The look on my face shows I'm beyond surprised.

"You didn't suspect? Sorry, I thought you worked that out. You've always been able to see into his soul."

I feel clueless. *Jimmy is an angel and I didn't know?* "Why didn't he tell me?" I ask.

"First of all, remember, you're not supposed to know we exist. But he wouldn't be inclined to tell you anyway. You know he has his own style. He likes to stay under the radar, play a role, and see how people treat the least among us."

I think about Jimmy as an angel. After the initial shock, I realize it makes sense. I've always felt Jimmy's goodness. Solid goodness. At his core. And he was always there, protecting me, late at night, after work. I smile. *Thanks, Jimmy.* I stare out the car window and can't help but laugh a little as I continue to digest this information. As we wind our way through the redwood trees, my eyes follow the curves in the highway and after a while I feel certain of where we're going. I dreamed of this.

As the car bumps and bounces down the rural access road we turned onto, Alexander looks over at me and grins. "Pleased?"

"Very."

"I still have some surprises for you, though," he promises with a mischievous glint in his eye.

"I think I dreamed about this day, you know."

"So you already know my surprise? What happens?"

"I don't want to ruin it by telling you, in case I'm right," I hedge.

"Did you like it?"

"It was perfect. But I woke up before it ended and I didn't want it to end."

"We'll see what we can do about that." He smiles and his voice is low and filled with promise.

He parks off the dirt road and opens the door for me. I bend over to undo the ankle straps on my heels so I can change into sneakers.

"Wait. On second thought, I have a better idea," he says as he reaches down and lifts me into his arms. "You look far too good in those to have to take them off." He starts carrying me down the trail.

"You can't walk with me the whole way like this," I protest.

He cocks his head to the side with a dubiously raised eyebrow. "First of all, you know how strong I am. Second of all, it's like lifting Tinkerbelle. And third of all, you don't even know how far we're …" he stops. "Wait. Maybe you do know. Let me ask you this: did I carry you in the dream?"

"No. But, we weren't dressed like this."

"Well, you're not walking in those heels. And I like this better anyway."

"Okay, but just put me down for a second. It's beautiful here. Let's kiss for a moment." I smile at him invitingly.

He tilts his head. "You have no idea how tempting that is. But we've held off this long and we're going to remember our first kiss for eons, so I want it to be perfect. There's a time and a place for kissing. And *this*," he looks around as if he's surveying our surroundings, "unfortunately, is neither."

"But we've already kissed."

"Our first *conscious* kiss, I should have said."

"You felt very conscious during that kiss."

He smiles. "But this time we know we can kiss. And we're both expecting it. The anticipation makes it sweeter."

The *anticipation*. That's what he said in my dream. I smile and we continue on the trail, deep into the towering trees.

"Alexander?" I ask after several minutes.

"Yes."

"What if being with a mortal … or near mortal … doesn't turn out to be everything you hoped?" My voice is quiet.

He stops walking and sets me down, facing him.

"Declan, do you have any idea how many times I've imagined kissing you? The way I feel when I'm with you? I know it's going to be beyond anything we could ever hope for. My only worry is that I'll get carried away. I have to be careful and remember my strength."

"You would never hurt me," I assure him.

"You have no idea what being around you does to me. We need to take things slow while I learn my limits."

"Okay. But remember, I'm not a mortal. I'm a *sprite*."

"And we're still learning what sprites like you can do, aren't we?" he teases as picks me up and throws me over his shoulder. "I should have known you were a sprite. I thought you looked like a beautiful little pixie fairy the first day we met."

"Put me down," I say, laughing. "Why are you carrying me like a sack of potatoes?"

"Because I don't want you to look when we get to our destination. I have a surprise waiting there. At least I hope it's a surprise … and I hope it's still there … wasn't any of this in your dream?"

"No," I say, still laughing. "I promise I'll cover my eyes! Just hold me like you were before. My dress is bunching up and we're risking indecency here."

"All right, all right," he says with a smile. "If this is about you not wanting to show off your knickers, I have to respect that." He swings me around and holds me in his arms, making sure I cover my eyes until we reach the clearing. He's right that I know where we're going, but I'm unsure about the surprise.

"Okay, we're here," he says as he sets me down slowly, facing him. "Don't turn around yet."

He rolls his shoulders and yanks down his shirt cuffs with his fingers, straightening his suit like James Bond after a skirmish with a villain. I have to laugh. He looks as fresh and gorgeous as he did before we started walking into the forest. I attempt to adjust my dress and run my fingers through my hair. I hope I'm halfway as presentable.

"You look beautiful," he says, reading my mind. He grins with anticipation. "Now you can turn around."

I spin around and see a large white blanket spread out in the clearing with a cooler on it and Alexander's iPod plugged into a speaker dock. There's a small table next to the blanket, draped in a white tablecloth with two white chairs. Strings of bright blue and white lights are wound around all the trees surrounding the clearing and a garland of silver hearts surrounds our carved initials in the middle.

I'm completely awed as I take it all in. "Alexander, it's beautiful."

"It was inspired by your aura."

"How did you even do this?

"Being able to fly has its perks," he says with a smile. "Wait until the sun goes down and they all light up. They're solar powered."

"And the rangers? You do realize this is a state park? With no special dispensation for angels?" I tease.

"The park closes at dusk and they've already done their rounds. We're deep enough into the interior that no one will come here, trust me. And I can clean it all up in seconds when we're ready to go later … *much* later." The look in his eyes as he says those words makes my knees go weak.

"This wasn't in my dream, you know."

"I'm glad to hear you don't always know what I'm up to."

"You're very unpredictable, Mr. Ronin. I like that." I put my arms around his neck.

"As are you, Miss Jane—and I wouldn't have it any other way. But if you're daring me to kiss you right now, I regret to inform you that it's still not the time, although it *is* the place," he says teasingly, looking at his watch.

He takes my hand and leads me to the blanket. As we sit down, he slides me onto his lap, puts his arms around me, and says, "Watch."

Just as in my dream, a beam of sunlight shines through the trees surrounding the clearing and the spotlight slowly moves until it alights on our carved initials. The garland of tiny, mirrored hearts surrounding the words sparkles brilliantly, reflecting the sun's rays all around us.

"One more thing," Alexander whispers huskily in my ear as he leans over to his iPod and presses play. Etta James' soulful voice begins crooning "*At last*" and I melt against him.

He slowly stands, smoothly pulling me up with him, and holds out his hand. "Shall we dance?"

I nod and he takes my hand, draws me in close, and wraps his arms around me.

We sway together to the music, slowly, our bodies in gentle contact as we gaze into each other's eyes.

"Now is the time and this is the place," says Alexander as he bends down and presses his lips to mine.

The End

Reader's Note

Thank you for reading! If you'd like to find out what's next for Declan and Alexander, please turn the page for an excerpt from *Fallen*, available now.

And thank you in advance for supporting authors and helping other readers by considering leaving an online review on amazon, goodreads, and/or your favorite blog/website forum for romance readers.

I read all my reviews and they are all sincerely appreciated.

A.J. Messenger

Visit ajmessenger.com and subscribe to A. J.'s newsletter to be the first to know about upcoming releases.

 ajmessenger.com

 facebook.com/ajmessengerauthor

 @aj_messenger

The Guardian Series

Guardian
(Book One)

Fallen
(Book Two)

Revelation
(Book Three)

More titles by A.J. Messenger coming soon.

Excerpt from Fallen
(Book two in the Guardian Series)

Preface

I'm melting into the sea.

I'm folding into a warm, welcoming blanket that I want to immerse myself in fully so I can stop this endless effort, endless struggle, getting nowhere.

Why fight the inevitable?

This is how it ends. No more pain. No more worry. Wherever Alexander is, he won't have to put himself in danger for me anymore.

Gradually I cease swaying my arms and legs in the waves and let my body flow beneath the sea, drifting downward, ever deeper … quietly and peacefully … into the abyss.

Avestan has finally won.

A. J. Messenger

Fallen: Chapter One

"What if I jump off a cliff?"

"What?" Alexander squints at me strangely, shielding his eyes from the sun with his hand.

We're sitting on our surfboards out in the ocean during a lull between wave sets. I've never been great at surfing but I love the combination of peaceful, meditative swaying punctuated by thrilling, adrenaline-pumping exhilaration. And it's a great workout—I'm always exhausted afterwards. I get why Alexander likes it so much.

I smooth away the lock of hair that has dipped in front of my right eye and tuck it behind my ear for the hundredth time. *Note to self: never cut your own bangs. No matter how good they look on Liz.* "You're going to stay as you are now," I say, "as an angel, forever. And I'm going to keep growing older. But what if I jump off a cliff? Or get eaten by a shark? Right now? Then I'd stay this age always."

His eyes meet mine for a long, slow stare. I can't quite pinpoint his expression but from the slight turn at the corner of his mouth I think he's going to humor me. "Okay, for the sake of convoluted arguments, let's say you *did* jump off a cliff—"

"Or got eaten by a shark."

"She says nonchalantly as we sit in the middle of the ocean on surfboards the size and shape of seals." His delivery is dry and his eyes flash bewilderment, or perhaps amusement.

"As if saying it will make it happen?"

"What you focus on ..."

I squint at him. "Is that really true?"

"Not always directly. But what you choose to give your attention to—or not—can shift the energy around you."

I consider his answer. "Well it's not as if you'd let anything happen to me."

"No," he says with a smile as he leans over and gently tucks my errant hair in place again, "but I'm enjoying the peace out here in the water with you and I don't particularly feel like fighting off a shark today."

I laugh. "Okay. I jump off a cliff then."

"You're forgetting the fact that you would die."

"You said energy never dies."

"Okay," he smiles, "you'd transform."

"Right … I'd transform into a guardian and then you and I would be together as guardians forever. You said my aura showed I was about to be realized."

He shakes his head. "You can't become a guardian that way. *Intent* matters. And there are no guarantees about anything, including becoming a guardian."

"So there's no way around it."

"Even if it was possible," he says, "you know you could never do that to your mom. Or Finn and Liz. And I wouldn't let you."

"I know," I concede. He's right. I would never leave them that way. "I doubt I'm going to become a guardian anyway," I add.

"Why?"

"Wouldn't I know it if I was? Wouldn't I feel especially wise … or *ready* in some way? My whole life I've felt like I don't know what the heck I'm doing from one moment to the next. How could I go from that to being a guardian?"

A smile reaches Alexander's deep green eyes. "Declan, it's the people who think they know it all that have the most to learn."

"Well," I say, considering his words, "that may be, but I haven't done anything particularly important."

"What's important? You see people for who they are and you understand the connection we all share—that's a rare quality." He pauses before continuing. "But I understand how you feel. When I look back, most of what I did throughout most of my lives doesn't seem spectacularly grand."

"What do you mean?"

"I wonder sometimes how I came to be a guardian."

"You do? But you were good."

"Yes," he nods, "and you're good, too, day after day, in big ways and small that ripple out with consequences you'll never realize."

"And that's enough?"

"Apparently," he says with a smile as he spreads his arms wide, "since I'm sitting here now as your guardian."

I smile, shading my eyes from the sun. "I hope you're right."

His expression turns thoughtful. "It's about doing the right thing, when it's not easy. And it's about cycles and learning more each time. But I've wondered if my being realized was more about the way my life ended."

"You mean because you tried to save Alenna from Avestan?"

"More like something to do with lives being taken so abruptly—with fear ... and violence. I don't know," he says, his voice drifting off, "I used to wonder if becoming a guardian was a way to bring peace and maybe I wasn't truly worthy. I took my brother's life, after all."

"You were trying to save a life."

Alexander looks down at his surfboard, not saying anything.

"I understand," I say softly.

He looks back up and meets my eyes.

"I can imagine how that must hurt," I say, "with the way things ended."

Alexander holds my gaze for a long beat and in my mind I try to imagine the shock and horror of being murdered by your own brother and being forced to stab him back as you try to save someone you love. The rage Avestan must have been consumed with—to kill Alexander and Alenna with a knife, up close and personal. I look at the jagged scar Alexander keeps on his left temple as a reminder and my heart hurts for the memories he must hold of his last mortal life.

"I've never actually voiced these thoughts aloud," he says.

I meet his eyes. "You saved me from Avestan ... against every odd and obstacle. If that doesn't prove you were meant to be a guardian I don't know what would."

"We saved each other," he says quietly. "But you're right—when I'm with you I feel as if I'm where I'm supposed to be. And Edwin always says certainty is for idiots."

"That sounds pretty informal for Edwin."

He smiles. "Okay, what he actually says is 'To pursue truth we must doubt all things as much as possible.' In other words, only those fooling themselves are cocksure."

My eyebrow rises. "Is that an Australian thing?"

"What?"

"Cocksure."

"What do you mean?"

"I want to know if I should add it to my list of favorite words you use, like jaffle or tosser."

He chuckles. "It's just a word. It means arrogantly confident."

"I know what it means, silly. It's just not heard much in everyday conversation."

"To society's detriment," he says with a wry smile.

I laugh and I find myself surveying his kind eyes and warm smile and marveling at this angel before me. How I love the way Alexander sounds, from the timbre of his voice to his accent to the odd words he sometimes tosses out. He's so different and I love that. Even if he wasn't an angel he'd still seem otherworldly to me.

"Well," I say, forcing myself to focus back on our conversation, "I think it's a mark of your intelligence and worthiness that you're not cocksure. The very fact that you've questioned if you were meant to be a guardian means you were meant to be one."

He smiles.

"And any lingering doubts keep you striving that much harder to do good," I add.

His smile reaches his eyes and they crinkle handsomely. "Have I told you how much I love sprites?" he says. "Especially smart sprites that embrace doubt and mock my vocabulary?"

I laugh. "Well I have a long, sordid history of doubting myself. So if doubt can serve a good purpose for once, I'm all for embracing it."

He holds my gaze for a long beat and then his eyes trace a path around my face. "Your aura is beautiful right now," he says softly. "It's shimmering brilliantly with vivid whites and rich blues ... it's hard to tell where you end and the ocean and the sky begins. I never get tired of looking at you."

Our eyes meet and the air around us is charged with electric energy. Combined with the quiet sounds of the water lapping and the soft undulation of the swells, I feel as if there's no place in the world I belong other than right here, right now, in this moment with Alexander. I take a deep breath and surrender into the sensation as he holds my gaze.

"Do you feel this right now?" he asks. "Between us? How our auras blend? You don't have to come up with crazy ideas like jumping off cliffs. This feeling we have when we're together makes age meaningless."

I nod. "I know you're right," I say, looking down. "I guess I just like the idea of growing old together ..."

"Like that couple we always see holding hands as they walk on the beach," he says. "I understand."

I meet his eyes, surprised. "Yes ... I don't know why it matters so much. Maybe it's because my mom and dad didn't get to ... I look at pictures of us with my dad sometimes ... it's been almost ten years now ... my mom and I keep getting older but my dad is frozen in time. Like we're leaving him behind."

Alexander leans over and takes my hand. "You haven't left him. He's still around. Somewhere. Everywhere."

"Why don't I feel him then?" I ask.

"Would it make you feel better to know that someday you could all be together again?"

"You said there are no guarantees. For any of us."

"There aren't, but there are some things I *know*. Things that are right with the universe. And you and I are one. I know, in every thrumming part of my being, that we were meant to find each other. The way our energy connects … it's a kind of harmony I've never felt before."

I close my eyes for a moment to focus on the feeling. "It's like we're on the same frequency," I say softly before I open my eyes again.

"Yes," he says with a smile. "Some energies belong together, and from everything you've told me your mum and dad had a deep love between them. When you have a powerful soul connection like that you tend to find each other over and over across lifetimes."

I nod. The idea of them together again, in a future life, does make me feel better. And it feels right. Maybe I could find them, too. The thought makes me smile.

Alexander leans over and kisses me softly. "I love you," he says.

"I love you, too," I say and my heart swells with the truth of it.

"Should we head back?" he asks as he looks around. "I think the waves are all rubbish now."

I nod. "I can't feel my feet anyway."

"Told you you should have worn booties."

"I like the way the board feels under my feet," I say as I swing my legs out of the water and lie on my chest so I can start paddling.

"Aye, but if you can't feel your feet, you can't feel the board."

I splash water in his direction. "Don't spoil my argument with logic."

He laughs. "Give me your foot." He eases his board alongside mine and places his hands around my foot. Immediately it feels enveloped in soothing heat.

"*Ohhh,* that feels so good," I groan. "Where were you an hour ago?"

He smiles. "You do the other one."

"How?"

"Imagine your light sending warmth to your foot."

"I can do that?"

"Only one way to find out," he says with a shrug. "Didn't you say you felt warm when you used your energy before?"

He's right. It's worth a try. I close my eyes and conjure a ball of white light in my core. I imagine it growing brighter and spreading out to my limbs and then rolling over to my right foot. Very slowly, as I focus and concentrate, I feel my foot thawing from within, getting warmer as the white light unfurls from my heel to my toes. It's not as hot and as fast as when Alexander warmed my other foot but *I'm doing it myself.* "It's working," I say with amazement as I open my eyes and look at Alexander.

"One more sprite power you can add to the list," he says.

"Ability to warm feet while surfing. Check," I say. "That'll scare the pants off the dark angels."

Alexander bursts out laughing. "I think you're far more powerful than you realize," he says as I bask in the warmth of my newly-toasty feet and we paddle happily towards shore.

We strip off our wetsuits when we reach the sand and sit back on our elbows on our towels to soak up the warm summer rays. I'm wearing a bright yellow bikini and

Alexander has on a pair of blue and yellow Billabong board shorts that hang low on his hips. His ab muscles ripple as he rolls himself up to unzip his backpack and extract two Capri Suns.

"Do you remember the first time we had these together?" he asks as he sits back and hands one to me.

"Up on the mountain when you took me flying for the first time," I say with a grin. "On Valentine's Day."

He nods and meets my eyes. "I wanted to kiss you that day."

"Is that right?"

He nods again. "Very badly." His voice is low and husky.

I smile, besotted, and my eyes trail to his kissable lips as that familiar electric charge hangs in the air between us.

"If only I'd known I could have come close like this," he says as he leans over until we're a breath away. "And I could have kissed you, like this," he says as he grazes my lips, softly at first, and then harder as the kiss deepens.

We lie back on the towel and I melt into the sensation, my arms around his muscled frame as his lips part mine, our tongues teasing and exploring. He groans, deep within his throat, as our bodies entwine and I sigh softly, but before long Alexander pulls back and lies down on the towel beside me. He closes his eyes and rakes his fingers through his dark, tousled hair, letting out a long, slow breath as he faces up to the sky. "We should probably get going soon," he says finally.

I steady my own breath and peer around at the emptiness in all directions. "Why?"

He turns on his side to face me and I do the same.

"Because everything else falls away when I'm with you," he says with an intensity in his eyes that makes my breath hitch in my throat.

"And?"

"And," he smiles, "I'm still getting used to the idea that we can do this." He leans over and kisses me again softly.

"You're getting used to it?" I say.

He nods, slowly. "Yes … I'm getting used to the fact that I can kiss you here …" he says as he kisses one eyelid softly. "And right here …" he says as he kisses the other eyelid. "And over here …" he murmurs as he trails kisses along my cheek and over to my ear where I feel his breath hot on my skin. "But especially here …" he says as he makes his way back to my mouth and kisses me with an ardor that makes me sigh.

"I love it when you sigh like that," he groans.

I smile against his lips as I kiss him back.

The invisible string between us glows and embraces my heart with a warm, white light that crowds out the worries in the back of my mind—about how Alexander and I can be together long term, or when Avestan will be back and how he'll seek his vengeance against us.

When we finally sit up to watch the sun set with our arms wrapped around one another, I rest my head on Alexander's shoulder.

He holds me close and kisses the top of my head softly before he asks a question I've been avoiding for far too long.

"Declan, do you want to talk about what happened to your dad?"

End of Chapter One

Read Fallen (Book Two in the Guardian Series)
and
Revelation (Book three in the Guardian Series)

Made in the USA
Las Vegas, NV
14 November 2021